More Praise for Jonathan Wilson's

The Red Balcony

"*The Red Balcony* pleases on several levels: as an adventure tale, a star-crossed romance, and a detailed period piece. Wilson's novel is also strong as a legal thriller."

—The Wall Street Journal

"One of the most satisfying literary portrayals of the pre-state Yishuv ever written . . . Between its near-painterly descriptions of the verdant Palestinian landscape and its lively portrayals of Tel Aviv cafés and Jerusalem neighborhoods, Wilson's prose is brimming with historical verisimilitude, intriguing revelations, and immersive detail."

—Jewish Book Council

"If you want to understand the current Arab-Jewish conflict as well as the ideological division tearing apart Israeli society . . . *The Red Balcony* is [one] place to start."

—Los Angeles Times

"Atmospheric . . . Morality and passion collide in a sophisticated legal thriller." *—Kirkus Reviews* (starred review)

"Wilson illuminates life in Palestine under the British Mandate in this engrossing legal drama . . . Vivid atmosphere animates Wilson's story of expatriates . . . Historical fiction fans are in for a treat." *—Publishers Weekly*

The Red Balcony

The Red Balcony

JONATHAN WILSON

SCHOCKEN BOOKS, NEW YORK

All rights reserved. Published in the United States by Schocken Books, a division of Penguin Random House LLC, New York, and distributed in Canada by Penguin Random House Canada Limited, Toronto. Originally published in hardcover by Schocken Books, a division of Penguin Random House LLC, New York, in 2023.

Schocken Books and colophon are registered trademarks of Penguin Random House LLC.

Library of Congress Cataloging-in-Publication Data
Names: Wilson, Jonathan, [date] author.
Title: The red balcony : a novel / Jonathan Wilson.
Description: First edition. | New York : Schocken Books, 2023
Identifiers: LCCN 2022015022 (print) | LCCN 2022015023 (ebook) |
ISBN 9780805212860 (paperback) | ISBN 9780805243703 (ebook)
Subjects: LCGFT: Legal fiction (Literature) | Thrillers (Fiction) | Novels
Classification: LCC PR6073.I4679 R43 2023 (print) | LCC PR6073.I4679 (ebook) |
DDC 823/.914—dc23/eng/20220429
LC record available at https://lccn.loc.gov/2022015022
LC ebook record available at https://lccn.loc.gov/2022015023

www.schocken.com

Cover images: *Roofs,* woodcut on paper by Jacob Pins © The Estate of Jacob Pins. Ben Uri Collection / Bridgeman Images
Cover design by Madeline Partner

Printed in the United States of America
First Paperback Edition 2024
2 4 6 8 9 7 5 3 1

For Sharon,
and to the memory of my brother Geoffrey

To understand historical reality,
it is sometimes necessary not to know the outcome.

—PIERRE VIDAL-NAQUET

The Red Balcony

Jerusalem
MARCH 1933

~~~

Kohler, the receptionist, eyed the large brown paper package stamped, postmarked, and tied up with string that sat on the front desk between his silver bell and a diminished pile of the local German-language newspaper, the *Mitteilungsblatt*. He shifted it to the side in order to make room for two additional sets of newspapers, popular items for guests on their way in to breakfast even though the news they carried was always a week old. He had no interest in the bland front page of the London *Times,* but a photograph of a thin-faced figure with his hair swept back and its accompanying headline in the *Frankfurter Zeitung* briefly caught his attention: Josef Goebbels had been appointed minister of information and propaganda in Hitler's new government.

He switched on the overhead fan and a wisp of smoke fell from the gears. Early morning light filtered through shade and touched the brown and mahogany furniture in the lobby, spinning dust motes off its armchairs. Kohler opened the blinds, returned to his desk, caught the sleeve of his jacket in his hand,

and ran it across the polished wood to accomplish an extra shine. The newly admitted light spilled through the front windows and cut sharp white diagonals onto the wall behind him.

Kohler banged his hand on the bell and the two Arab boys, Ahmed and Ibrahim, who acted as weekday porters, clattered upstairs from the basement and appeared in the lobby. They looked around in vain for guests to assist and luggage to transport.

"Here," Kohler said, handing over the package, "take it up." He muttered some instructions to the boys and then they were gone. Easter was a month away; the great rush of pilgrims, mostly German, some British, was yet to arrive. Soon they would swell the congregation in the Church of the Redeemer, crowd the Via Dolorosa, and fill the Hotel Fast to capacity. Kohler, as Ellrich the manager had requested, was doing what he could to ensure that these tourists of the Holy Spirit received a rousing and congenial welcome upon their arrival.

The boys stood behind a balustrade that topped the ornate stone parapet on the second floor. Together they lowered the banner attached to the flagpole, removed the old flag, and replaced it with the new. A stiff breeze blew in from the desert to the south; the sky, shot through now with blue morning light, shimmered over the walls of the Old City. From their vantage point the boys could take in the distant bustle of activity around both the Damascus and Jaffa Gates. They winched the flagpole back into place.

Kohler stepped out of the hotel and crossed the cobblestone street, shooing a mongrel dog from his path. There was the Union Jack, and now hanging alongside it was the new German flag with its striking black swastika snapping in the March wind high above a broad swath of the streets of Jerusalem. Kohler observed it with pride. Perhaps, he thought, it might even be visible from his own home where it sat tucked in among a row of stone houses that his grandfather Stefan, a dutifully committed Templar from Ludwigsburg, had helped to build on the Street of Ghosts.

Two British soldiers in steel helmets, rifles in hand, approached on Kohler's side of the street. He had an impulse to stop them and point out the new flag, but he held back, and they passed by without looking up.

JUNE

Arlosoroff came out of the Jewish Agency building on King George Street, slumped into the back of the car, and laid his briefcase on the seat next to him. He was exhausted. He brushed a thin layer of dust from the sleeves of his suit jacket, imagining that the grime of Europe was still on him, staining his shirt cuffs.

After Berlin, after the train south and the nauseating boat trip from Italy to Egypt, he'd had only one day of rest in which to recover his equilibrium. Then, it was back on the train, this time from Cairo to Tel Aviv, and finally, home to the pure joy of embracing Sima and hugging his baby son. He had one warm, fragrant June night in his own bed, the sea lapping into his dreams, and the following morning he was on the last leg of his journey, up to Jerusalem to present the fruits of his labor, the putative terms of the transfer agreement he had negotiated with Hitler's new government—the economic equations, his own dismal science at its most dismal.

He tried to view the situation in its essence, simplified. What the Nazis wanted: an end to the international boycott of German goods precipitated by their brutal treatment of Jews, which was visible to anyone who walked the streets of German cities—the beatings, arrests, exclusions, disbarments, dismissals. What Jewish Palestine wanted: exit visas for those persecuted German Jews, and if the Nazis wouldn't let them take their money out, which they wouldn't, then Arlosoroff wanted, at the very least, a deal to allow fifty thousand Jewish migrants to use their funds to purchase German goods for export to Palestine.

He saw two side effects. One that could only be whispered was the invigoration of the Jewish economy in Palestine with German instruments and equipment in the factories, German machines on the farms. And one that couldn't be spoken of at all: a boost for the German economy, with all that implied in a country committed to a vast military buildup. It was an ugly, unsavory deal, but how else could the Jews purchase their freedom to leave?

And, of course, the British, rulers and governors of this thin strip of land, they too must be brought on board, appeased and paid, a thousand-pound entry fee for every Jew coming in. Where, he wondered, would that money come from? A detail yet to be worked out.

In Jerusalem he outlined everything to the other members of the agency's executive committee, plumbed the depths of the moral quandary of dealing with the German government at all, threw darts of clarity through the blue smoke of cheap cigarettes, traced the degree of progress and possibility that he had discussed in Germany. In the end he took a sip of water, looked around the table, noted the concern etched in every face, and offered the soft landing of his conclusion: news of a village in Pal-

estine that would become a major center for transferred German
Jewish youth once the agreement was complete. This, he proudly
affirmed, had been the positive content of his lunchtime discussion with Sir Douglas Wharton, the British high commissioner.

He briefly closed his eyes, opened them to find the driver
staring at him in the mirror. Was it a hostile look? Maybe. An
hour and a half and he would be back once more in Tel Aviv. He'd
told Sima that he'd meet her at five-fifteen p.m. A walk and then
an early Sabbath dinner at the Kaete Dan boardinghouse. The
driver turned the key in the ignition, Arlosoroff rolled down one
of the rear windows, and before long the car began its serpentine descent out of Jerusalem, past terraces of gnarled olive trees
clamoring upward from the sunbaked earth.

He took out a clean white handkerchief, removed his glasses
to clean the lenses. In Berlin on the Kurfürstendamm he had
walked past overflowing flower stalls, and a woman with bright
red cheeks had offered him a huge bunch of fragrant blue violets.
When he had shaken his head no, she had proffered instead a
bunch of honey-colored daffodils. If Sima had been with him he
would have bought it for her. But, of course, she couldn't be, and
a good thing too.

Prague, Warsaw, London, Berlin, meeting after meeting.
The untethered urgency of it all. In Germany Hitler's Brown-
shirts beat up Jews on the street with impunity, made arrests
for no reason, filled detention camps; in the city squares, there
were funeral pyres for books, and behind shuttered windows
thousands of Jewish lawyers and doctors forced from their
professions. Even the kosher slaughterers had been banned—
henceforth the only meat available to Jews was cuts that they
could not eat. Click of his childhood tongue, the murmur of
memory; he'd been happy there once, immersed in his studies,
or rather not unhappy, the same way that he'd always felt about

German culture—he admired it, but it didn't touch his heart. No aromatic flowers could hide the stench of what was happening now.

For a while he simply lay back and absorbed the heat while the air thickened and circled him. Stripping off his jacket had made no difference; his powder-blue shirt was stained with sweat.

A British army vehicle labored up the hill on the other side of the road. Arlosoroff followed its path, then opened his briefcase and removed a newspaper. His own angular, bespectacled face was on the front page accompanied by an article. That day he was probably one of the most hated men in Palestine: for fanatical Revisionist Jews, he was the traitorous envoy sent to Europe in order to set up and validate a deal with the devil; for the local Arabs, he was the Jew trying to force wide the gates of admission for an influx of European refugees.

He read the first few lines: "There will be no forgiveness for those who have for greed sold out the honor of their people to madmen and anti-Semites. . . . The Jewish people have always known how to size up the betrayers of the nation and their followers, and it will know today how to react to this crime." He cast the paper aside and stared out of the window. Only yesterday, before he had set off for Jerusalem, Shaul had reached out his tiny fingers and played his favorite game, pulling off his father's ring and then replacing it, only this time he had tried to slide it back on his mother's finger, and Arlosoroff, his voice rising from some chill winter as if he were a guest from the future, had cried out, "Not yet!"

3

Tel Aviv

The hotel waiter presented the bill. As he moved away Sima almost imperceptibly lifted her head in his direction. "Haim," she whispered, "did you see how he looked at you?" Arlosoroff told her she was imagining it. His reassurances were chivalric. "No Jew would kill *me,*" he'd told her in March after first hearing the rumor that he had been targeted; then, as if to confirm the strength of his conviction, he'd left his pistol with a friend before setting off for Germany. He had yet to retrieve it.

Outside, they felt the warm air of a balmy summer night, heard the soft lapping of the surf. Haim breathed deep, an invisible weight slipping off his shoulders. Sima, in her white summer dress, held his arm. If she was nervous, she didn't show it, and if anyone recognized him, he wasn't aware of it. On their short walk before dinner two men had passed them, but otherwise the beach had been deserted.

Far out to sea the red running lights of freighters; stopping for a moment to follow the slow hulks, Haim and Sima might have been any young couple out for a late evening stroll on a June night, caressed by the Mediterranean breeze, the humidity of the day gone, the moon hiding its light behind a bank of clouds. In this moment of tranquility Haim thought they could be forgiven for imagining that vituperative anger directed toward him by his political enemies was nothing more than a mild admonishment from a group of disputatious friends who, when it came down to it, wished him no ill.

They walked north toward an area where the dunes were higher. Were they being followed? Sima turned to see two young men a short distance away, one tall and one short who seemed to waddle as he walked. She squeezed Haim's hand. When the men overtook them Sima released her grip.

The men were a short way ahead now. But they stopped abruptly. One of them was pissing in the sand. Sima froze and pulled on Haim's arm, turning him around to show him the carcass of a donkey washed up on the shore. They heard the deep, distant blast of a freighter's horn.

Suddenly the men were there, positioned on either side of the couple. One of them shone a torch in Haim's face.

"What's the time?"

There was a shot, the blood poured from Haim's chest, and then she was on him, wrapped into his bloodied shape as he crawled forward. The men ran into the dunes, and then came a rush of bystanders responding to the gunshot and Sima's screams as she knelt over Haim, pressed her face into his neck and shoulders, begged him not to die.

In the hospital, almost an hour later, he whispered, "Look what they have done to me."

4

Tel Aviv

AUGUST

Ivor Castle emerged from the Esther cinema into the yellow slant of early evening sunlight and the unremitting late summer heat he had tried to escape inside. He had been in Palestine for three weeks—settling in, taking steps to arrange the official residency that would allow him to take part in the Arlosoroff murder trial. It was Ivor's father who had secured him the position of assistant to Mr. Phineas Baron, the distinguished king's counsel who was leading the defense of the two Russian Jews accused of the crime. Edwin Castle, who had prudently changed the family name from Schloss two years before the outbreak of the Great War, was himself an eminent barrister, and Ivor had followed in his father's footsteps, graduating from Balliol College, Oxford, with his BA in jurisprudence a year ago. So here he was in steamy Tel Aviv, and this was the first working day that he had allowed himself some free time.

For two weeks the Esther had advertised only "Austrian-language" films: a trick, or so he'd been told, to get around the local Jewish boycott of German films, or any that featured a known Nazi actor. There were simply too many eager German-speaking paying customers in the city. Now, mercifully, management had succumbed to the box-office bonanza promised by *King Kong*. Beauty had killed the beast, but who wouldn't want to hold Fay Wray in the palm of his hand? Beauty was responsible for all kinds of problems, including Ivor's own. At Oxford he hadn't been able to resist with Annabelle Benton, and she had married someone else, and the same with Andrea Loewenstein and Clara Halsted, each of them stunning in their own way and each committed, inexorably it seemed, to both reeling him in and casting him out.

His evening was open; he wasn't due in Jerusalem until the following afternoon. Once there, he would conduct a preliminary examination of a potential witness, Tsiona Kerem, a woman whom the police had somehow overlooked, or rather noted and dismissed. She had, according to police notes, sat for a lengthy period in the Jerusalem café where a waiter believed he might have spotted Stavsky and Rosenblatt, the two men accused of Arlosoroff's murder, in the hours before they set out for Tel Aviv on the night of the killing. And if it *was* Baron's clients in the Hasharon, and if the hour was late, then how could the accused have managed the ninety-minute drive to Tel Aviv in time to murder Arlosoroff on the beach?

Baron had spotted Tsiona's name in the Jaffa records, where the police, whom he regarded as singularly incompetent, had simply noted that she had been concentrating on something else and remained unaware of the café's other patrons. They had left it at that. The waiter who had oh so tentatively identified the two men had ended his shift and left the Hasharon before they did. The other denizens of the café had also come and gone, the place was crowded, and no one could remember seeing either Stavsky or Rosenblatt. But Tsiona had lingered. For Baron she represented the strong hope of a firm alibi for the accused men, and it was Ivor's job to draw her out.

Baron had delegated the vital task of interviewing Tsiona to Ivor because it would have been both irregular and unseemly for him to have done it himself. While Ivor talked to the witness, Baron would spend his Tuesday afternoon taking tea in Jerusalem with Myles Elliott, the solicitor general, and then the following day he'd lunch with the high commissioner, Sir Douglas Wharton. Ivor had learned that Miss Kerem would be traveling the rest of the week, north to Safed; hence the urgent need for him to assess her capacity to become a linchpin for the defense.

Ivor walked now in the direction of the sea and the cooling breeze that he craved, but it was a forlorn hope; experience had already taught him that it was better to succumb, to accept the sweat that drizzled down his back and the permanent presence in his pocket of a handkerchief to wipe his brow, the clammy sensation of his shirt and shorts stuck to his skin. "You have dark hair and an olive-skinned complexion, you won't burn," his mother had told him shortly before he boarded ship in Southampton, but the hottest place she had ever visited was Provence, and she had taken that holiday with his father in balmy May. Ivor felt his eyebrows singe almost as soon as they docked in Haifa. The tip of his nose was still red, painful to the touch; likewise the back of his neck. In a few minutes the brown hues of the setting sun would envelop the city, but there would be no relief; the night would bring its own version of life in a cauldron.

He had already visited the site of the murder; there wasn't much to see. Earlier that day, the police had shown him plaster casts of footprints washed away weeks ago. Ivor had earnestly stared at the sand anyway, reviewing the escape routes taken by the killers at least up to the entrance of an orchard, where the trackers had lost them.

Now he walked in the opposite direction, toward the Casino café, where the presumptive killers, his clients, had supposedly passed and repassed their victim and his wife in the forty-five minutes or so before their deadly assault. It was close to the Casino that one of the men, according to Mrs. Arlosoroff, had stopped to urinate into the sea, or was he simply using the occasion to expose himself to her, a threat and a warning of what was to come?

Ivor arrived at the café as the lights came up on all three stories. The place was beginning to fill up, men in long trousers and sports jackets, women in dresses—it seemed to be one of the few recreational spots in the city where formality was regarded as a virtue. At his own hotel, the Bella Vista, an orchestra played six nights a week on the patio or in the garden, but neither those who listened nor those who danced followed a dress code. Ivor liked that immediately about Tel Aviv. He had hated wearing his gown at Oxford, or perhaps he had just hated being a Jew there, something that the leveling conformity of the black robe had distinctly failed to hide.

The Casino was elevated on concrete pillars lapped by the incoming waves; balconies projected from all sides that quickly filled with customers eager to take in the starlit expanse unfolding across the darkening sky. The entire oddly baroque edifice looked as if at any moment it might slip its concrete moorings and float into the Mediterranean. Ivor took the stairs up to the entrance and pushed the door open. Inside, the décor was unapologetically Viennese, or at least that was how Ivor imagined it: tall dark wood cabinets; a long, polished mahogany bar with white-coated barmen sporting black bow ties; heavy burgundy drapes; gleaming silver ice buckets; small round tables, each with three chairs and an ashtray large enough to accommodate the residue of a thousand cigarettes, while their smokers joked, argued, flattered, and cajoled into the early morning hours.

Ivor stood at the bar nursing a bottle of Tennent's Pilsner: Scottish beer with Hebrew writing that he couldn't decipher on the label. He wasn't sure what he thought about this little outpost of the empire. He was a Jew, so he supposed he should have felt somewhat at home, but he didn't, not so far anyway. On the other hand, his sympathies didn't really lie with the British Mandatory power either. Phineas Baron seemed to dislike more or less everyone who populated this perplexing place: Jews, Arabs, the local government, the military—all were found wanting in one way or another. But the case. Well, the case intrigued him no end.

Farther down the bar a young man in a khaki suit, well built, with tousled sandy hair, hunched over his own beer. As soon as he lifted his head, Ivor saw his freckled face and instantly recognized him. It was Charles Gross, one of the few Jews he had been with at Oxford—one who had chosen to take the brazen rather than the self-effacing route through their university years.

A year ahead of Ivor, Gross had been reading history at Corpus Christi. He'd lived in the college annex on Magpie Lane and Ivor had visited him there on several occasions. Gross's room was heated with a coal fire; there was no running water. Every morning a college servant woke him up bearing a ewer of hot water for washing and shaving. The toilets were a cold run across the quad. Ivor's own Balliol hadn't been much better.

There were two other Jewish students whom they knew at Oxford: the Stone twins, Jeremy and Paul, mathematicians at Trinity. The four of them sometimes drank together in the Turf. Other students referred to the group, amiably enough it seemed, as "the kosher quartet." Behind their backs, people probably got a little more inventive. The Stone twins both exhibited the req-

uisite thick glasses, substantial noses, and crinkly black hair that
were irresistible fodder to the knee-jerk anti-Semite.

Ivor walked the length of the bar and tapped Charles on his
shoulder. When Charles turned, Ivor had the sense, although he
couldn't be sure, that Charles had spotted him already and chosen to look the other way.

"Good Lord, Castle, what on earth are you doing here?"

"I might ask you the same."

"Anglo-Palestine Company, been working for them for about
a year," Charles offered.

"I never saw you as a banker."

"Someone has to help fund the citrus plantations."

"Ah," Ivor said, "you're a man with a cause."

"Yes, I'm the first, and maybe also the last, of the British-born
Zionists."

Ivor laughed. At Oxford Charles had been an eloquent advocate for the Yishuv, the Jewish state-in-waiting, provoking arguments and picking fights with anybody who he thought might be
a worthy antagonist. He admired Weizmann to a degree, for his
tenacity; his willingness to say unpopular things; his innocent,
if democratic, nationalism; and his unwavering belief, from the
very start of his political life, that the homeland for the Jews
must and could only be in Palestine. A position no one would
argue with now. In contrast, Charles had only contempt for Ben-
Gurion and the Labour socialists who, open to both diplomatic
and territorial compromise, formed the Jewish majority in Palestine. Beneath contempt were the cultural Zionists, men and
women uninterested in the formation of a Jewish state, happy to
live in peace with the Arabs on the ancestral lands in some weak-
kneed binational entity, and convinced that the way forward
for Jews was the way back, a return to the autonomous Hebrew
culture, language, and literature abandoned in the course of

European assimilation. No, Charles's hero was the charismatic leader of the Revisionist Party, Vladimir Jabotinsky. A true militant leader, a territorial maximalist whose idea of a homeland for the Jews covered the entire landmass of Palestine and stretched into Transjordan. No truncated corner of Palestine would do for him, and to heck with the Arabs. For Charles, Jabotinsky was the necessary scourge of "pretentious proles" and enthrallingly an advocate of universal Jewish military training and discipline. Charles saw the need to transform diffident Jews into active, daring warriors. And why should they not start by standing up for themselves at Oxford? It was no accident that *Judge and Fool,* Jabotinsky's novel about the biblical hero Samson, sat prominently on his college desk. Like both its author and its subject, Charles wanted to bring the house down.

Ivor hadn't paid much attention to Charles's interminable alcohol-fueled paeans to Jabotinsky, delivered in his stentorian voice (an inheritance, probably, from his father, who headed a firm of London auctioneers), but neither could he entirely avoid them. At Oxford there simply weren't enough Jewish friends to go around.

In any case, for the two years that they overlapped, Ivor's extracurricular attention had been entirely elsewhere, focused on girls, and one in particular at St. Hilda's, Mary Buss, who, aside from an unforgettable May night after champagne and strawberries following a trip to the Trout Inn to view the peacocks (she had read Havelock Ellis and decided that she was, after all, eager to experiment), hadn't been all that focused on him. In fact, it was only late in their largely chaste romance that he had run into her on Broad Street with a copy of *The Well of Loneliness* in one hand and Jane Peters, the prettiest girl from Lady Margaret Hall, holding the other.

"And you?" Charles asked. "Here to help drain the swamps?"

"Hardly. I'm working on the Arlosoroff case. I'm Baron's assistant. He's leading the defense."

"And what tasks does the great Mr. Baron have you performing? Have you met with the accused?"

"Only once. Neither of them speaks English. Not much to report I'm afraid."

Ivor had sat opposite Stavsky and Rosenblatt in a cramped, stuffy, windowless interview room in the Jaffa prison while an interpreter translated their Russian and apparently mangled Hebrew into mongrel English. It had not been a productive encounter. The two men, not much older than himself, hot and irascible, didn't consider him worthy of their time and wanted to talk only to Baron. Stavsky, spindly with an abbreviated set of teeth as if he had gnawed to no effect on resistant material, seemed to develop a particular animus toward Ivor, although perhaps it was simply an anxiety about his apparent youth and inexperience; Stavsky was, after all, on trial for murder. Rosenblatt, shorter and stouter than his companion, sported a thick mustache; his sweat-stained shirt was open at the neck and hair sprouted from his chest like stuffing from a mattress. Taken together, Ivor thought, the two men resembled Don Quixote and Sancho Panza; all that was missing was the lance, the horse, and the donkey. After the meeting Baron had let Ivor know that he wouldn't be seeing much of Messrs. Stavsky and Rosenblatt. The research projects that he had in mind for him lay elsewhere.

"Arlosoroff deserved everything he got." Charles almost spat the words out.

One of the barmen pressed a switch and two small electric fans mounted high on the wall whirred into action. Ivor was grateful for the cool air on his skin, but it failed to lower Charles's temperature; his face had begun to redden.

"He cut a deal with the Nazis. It's despicable. I'm glad

he's dead. It wasn't us, but I wouldn't have been unhappy if it had been. Still, it was Arabs murdered Arlosoroff, everyone knows that, especially the people leading the prosecution. It's a frame-up."

"'Us'?"

"The Revisionists. Did you think I'd changed my spots? We want this country flooded with Jews, and fast, but the economic boycott of Germany has to stay. No compromise with Hitler, that shouldn't be difficult to understand. And when it happens, a state committed to free enterprise, not some ersatz Russian Revolution, all hands to the scythe and the shovel."

Ivor indicated to the barman that he should bring two more bottles of beer. Now, in contrast to their years at Oxford, he was interested to hear what Charles had to say about Palestine, and the Arlosoroff case in particular.

"You're certain our clients are innocent. Well, that's good to hear. So, let me ask you something: Do you have any information that could help us?"

"I believe I might," Charles said, "but if I give it out, you'd better make damn sure that you get them off because otherwise there will be all kinds of trouble."

"Tell me."

"Not now. I have to be somewhere. So, you're at the Bella Vista with all the other pale-skinned new arrivals from the old country?"

"I am, but not for much longer, it's a bit pricey. Moving out tomorrow as it happens. But you knew I was here?"

"Only found out recently, was busy, planned to get in touch as soon as I could."

Charles slid a few coins toward the barman and gestured that he was paying for two. He left abruptly before Ivor could protest.

Ivor drank his second beer, and then the one he had ordered for Charles.

By the time he left the Casino the building was bathed in bright summer moonlight. On his way down the stairs Ivor reached out to grip the iron railing. He felt bleary-eyed, but three beers alone couldn't have done that. He walked close to the sea, observing his own footprints on the dark fringe of the beach, as if to see how quickly they might fade or be distorted before a plaster cast could be made.

As he stared out over the white foam, the sudden unfolding of a wave caught him by surprise. Ivor looked down to see his plimsolls soaked through and his feet tangled in seaweed. He extricated himself, took off his shoes and socks, and turned and walked barefoot across the sand in the direction of Allenby Street, avoiding as best he could the detritus that was scattered in his path—discarded sardine cans, chocolate wrappers, cigarette stubs, the occasional empty beer bottle, and countless shells of cracked pistachio nuts, as if the beach had been seeded with them.

5

Jerusalem

At the entrance to the Hotel Fast, above the top floor's louvered shutters and half-open windows, the Union Jack and the Nazi swastika flew side by side from flagpoles tethered to the wrought iron railings. All guests welcome, Ivor thought.

The city appeared to be in a midday stupor, offering half-deserted streets and not the stifling heat of Tel Aviv but encroaching desert dryness with no sea breeze to provide even the illusion of relief.

Ivor made his way down Jaffa Road, past shuttered shops and dusty parked cars. By the time he reached the neighborhood of Machane Yehuda with its Jewish market, the city had woken up from its siesta. In a broad cobblestone courtyard water delivery was in progress; a hundred empty petrol cans, scrubbed out and functioning now as jugs, were stacked in twos on the ground. A long, unruly line of older women all similarly attired in colorful cotton dresses, aprons, and white kerchiefs pressed forward to stake their claims while clusters of small children played nearby.

Ivor made his way through the crowd and was soon lost in

a maze of narrow streets that emptied into small squares. All around him, sheets billowed on washing lines stretched above tin-roofed shacks, and behind them narrow red-roofed stone dwellings leaned into one another like conspirators. He left Machane Yehuda and crossed toward Bezalel Street. By the time he located Tsiona Kerem's flat, on the second floor of a stone house, set back inside an overgrown walled garden, his throat was parched, but that wasn't the reason that he was rendered momentarily speechless when she opened her door.

"Are you going to speak?"

"Miss Kerem? I . . . I'm sorry I'm late. I got lost."

She had a kind of instantly arresting beauty, unconventional perhaps, but no less compelling for it, that up until this point he had only read about: Beatrice when Dante first saw her, perhaps, if Beatrice had been in her twenties and not a nine-year-old, or something like that, Beatrice in her crimson dress. *"D'allora innanzi dico che Amore segnoreggiò la mia anima,"* Mr. Dalrymple, his teacher at St. Paul's, had passionately declared as he moved his restless students through the preparatory Oxbridge scholarship texts. "From that time forward love fully ruled my soul." But Tsiona's dress was more of a cinnamon color and complemented her short-cropped burgundy hair (henna had clearly been applied). The dress itself had short sleeves that showed her slender arms and a deep V-neck revealing a white embroidered camisole that Ivor found at once alluring and modest. He knew he should stop staring, but he couldn't, not yet. Tsiona's dark eyes, one slightly wandering so it appeared she could not quite look at him directly, nonetheless held him fast.

"Are you going to come in?"

They sat at her kitchen table, which was covered with an oilcloth and ornamented by a small vase that spilled yellow blooms over its lip. Ivor took his notebook and fountain pen from his briefcase and set them down. His impulse was to charm her, compliment her English (if warranted), to talk about anything except the subject defined by his mission. Yet he had to collect himself; his clients faced murder charges that, if they held up, could warrant the death penalty.

"Perhaps we might begin with some background?"

"You'll have tea?"

"Tea would be lovely."

He looked around. The flat was on two levels; the lower, where he assumed there must be a bed, was partially curtained off. In the visible area stood an easel presently supporting a large canvas, next to which scattered paint tubes and brushes in glass jars rested on an upturned wooden crate. Numerous other canvases leaned against the walls, some face out, and there were sketchbooks piled on the floor alongside broken sticks of charcoal, bottles of turpentine, rags, and crumpled newspaper. Through open windows that ran the length of the room Ivor saw a plum tree, heavy with fruit, dipping its head over the walls of Tsiona's balcony and sturdy thick-stemmed geraniums that emerged from earthenware pots and window boxes in a tangle of summer reds and pinks.

But Tsiona had not been painting the view: The work in progress on her easel showed the top half of a young man with swept-back bright orange hair and orange eyebrows. The sitter, whoever he was, had been heightened beyond reality, transformed by color and form: His face was too thin, his neck too long; only his prominent nose seemed proportionate. The figure sat in a neat gray shirt and tie gazing forward out of brownish-gray eyes while behind him a blue disk hung against a bruised sky. In the foreground on the left side of the painting Ivor recognized the ochre folds of the curtain that apparently hid the bed. Tsiona's model (was he only her model?) must have sat with his back to the window deep into the night while she stood before him and painted. Absurdly, irrepressibly, Ivor felt jealous.

She moved briskly in the studio-cum-kitchen, opening a biscuit tin, removing a donut-shaped pot from a two-ring gas hob and replacing it with a kettle. "Only one ring works," she said, then washed a pair of glass tumblers out in a small sink. Ivor observed her movement as if he were watching the riveting first moments of a great actress's appearance in a new play. The bubbling kettle, the blue flare of gas and clink of the teapot, the pause for the tea to steep, the way she pushed a strand of hair away from her eyes: He had a front-row seat.

Tsiona handed him his cup and sat down across the table. He wanted to ask for milk but felt that to do so might magnify his Englishness and lead her to identify him with the much-maligned Mandate authorities, so instead, like her, he took a slice of lemon from the small saucer she had placed in front of him and added it to his drink with a spoonful of sugar.

"Yes," she said. " 'My Life So Far' by Tsiona Kerem, or 'Unholy Thoughts in the Holy Land.' "

A beam of light fell across the table and one side of Tsiona's face, dramatizing her striking appearance. Ivor, trying again not to stare at her misaligned left eye, wondered if her vision was in some way impaired, though her beauty, he thought, was unhindered, even enhanced.

"I was born in Jaffa on the same night that a fire broke out in a home near our local police station. My father rushed out of the house and filled buckets to help douse the flames. One of his Bulgarian cousins was trapped in the house. He didn't make it out. When my father came home and the midwife handed me to him, he stood weeping, covered in soot, ashes in his hair."

Ivor, who had taken out his notebook and begun to write, now lifted his head and gazed at Tsiona, searching for the least hint that this dramatic overture was some kind of put-on. But she returned his stare with a look of full seriousness, then raised her eyebrows as if to say, "Shall I continue?" Ivor nodded his assent.

"When I was five my parents moved to Tel Aviv, early settlers of the new town. Our home on Rothschild Boulevard (no doubt you've walked there) had two stories, the first of its kind. We looked down on everyone else."

Ivor stopped writing and smiled at her.

"And you?" she said. "Background?"

"Our house was rather grand, I'm afraid. London, St. John's Wood, Upper Hamilton Terrace. My father is an enviably successful barrister."

"So, you also looked down from your upper terrace."

"You would think so, wouldn't you? But our neighbors tended to look down on us."

It was Tsiona's turn to smile. "I know about that," she said. "I lived in London. I was two years at the Slade, followed by eighteen months in Paris, at the Academy of André Lhote. I much preferred that."

"No bright orange hair in London," Ivor said, gesturing toward the portrait on the easel.

"Precisely."

"And now?"

"I used to teach at the art school next door, but it ran out of money and closed down. Now I give private lessons and do my work. From time to time, I show it, and I meet with my friends, who are mostly painters and poets. We are the first and maybe also the last Bohemians in Palestine. We drink cheap cognac, and they get drunk and tell stories of the countries in which they were born. I am the only one who is not from somewhere else. They all, every one of them, even the most ardent Zionists among them, suffer from *nostalgie de la boue*. It's an infectious disease, and it leads to a lot of singing, mostly in Russian. And in case you were wondering, as you see I have no husband, there is no fiancé, and I will never marry."

Ivor, who had been scribbling as fast as he could, lifted his pen from the page. "Why not?" he said.

"Because I want to be free."

She was playing with him.

"If you don't mind, I need to ask you about June sixteenth. The police report asserts that you were in the Hasharon Café on the Jaffa Road that evening."

"I am there most evenings."

"And you were there on June sixteenth?"

"I was." She leaned forward and rested her head in her hand. Her gold bracelets glinted in the room's filtered sunlight.

"Can you tell me—and it would be most important if you could answer me accurately—what time you arrived and when you left?"

"It was almost dark when I got there, I stayed for an hour, maybe two."

"And the times?"

"I really don't remember. Seven, when I got there, eight or nine when I left."

"I'm sorry to pressure you, but if you think hard, could you be more specific?"

"I wasn't paying attention to the time; I was busy concentrating."

"On what?"

"I was drawing. That's where I draw at night, in Café Hasharon."

"What did you draw that night?"

"It wouldn't interest you."

Ivor reached into his briefcase and produced two photographs. He placed them on the table before Tsiona.

"Did you see either or both of these men that night?"

"The police already showed me these. In fact, they left two of their prints with me. They were hoping to jog my memory."

"And?"

"And I don't remember. It's possible."

"Only possible?"

She shrugged. "I sit in a corner. I draw. People come and go. I concentrate on my tea and on the paper before me. Look, here."

She rose from her chair, picked up one of the sketchbooks from the floor, and handed it to Ivor. He turned the pages. They were filled with elaborate abstractions, black lines, crosshatchings, serpentine designs, shaded arabesque edges, thick pencil marks that looked like tree branches or railway maps.

"I . . . I thought you . . . well, portraiture."

"That too," she said. "I told you. I don't like to be confined. . . . Listen, I have to leave now, I have a lot to do today, but you've arrived on an auspicious occasion. It's my birthday. I'm having a party here tonight. Why don't you come?"

"I . . . I have to . . . that's so very kind of you but I must get back to Tel Aviv." His heart was pounding. "Unless . . . I suppose. And I do have more questions for you, if you have time early tomorrow. I could leave tomorrow. Yes, why not? Yes, thank you. I will come."

"We start late."

"How late?"

"Ten. And now you have the rest of the day before you."

He should not, under any circumstances, attend the party of a prospective witness. That much was clear.

.   .   .

Phineas Baron had warned him about the Hotel Fast: "Worst service in Palestine, and that's saying something." Nevertheless, that was where Ivor had decided to check in. From his room he could see the crenellated walls of the Old City and before them a line of tawny camels led by an Arab boy moving purposefully in the direction of the Jaffa Gate. When he opened the window of his small room the cries of the muezzin filled the blue air.

After leaving Tsiona he had walked aimlessly as if he could not quite recover his bearings. It was only when he found himself on a burning unpaved street that offered no shade at all that he turned more deliberately in the direction of the hotel. On Jaffa Road children played on slides and swings on the grounds of the Alliance Israélite Universelle; he heard the mingled Arabic and Hebrew of their shouts and cries and stopped to watch them for a while.

In the lobby of the hotel an animated group of German tourists led by a priest, undoubtedly on their way to visit the holy sites, had bustled past him and into the street. Ivor wondered what they thought of their country's new flag, presently hanging motionless in the windless afternoon. Were they proud? Ashamed?

Now Ivor lay fully clothed on his bed and gazed at the ceiling while the fan above him turned lazily. He closed his eyes: the sun-baked walls of the buildings he'd passed on his way to her house, the scent of oleander and late summer roses, stones that wanted to burst his heart. He knew he would go to see her tonight.

Tsiona's flat was crowded, and even though its windows and the door to the balcony were flung wide open the mixed odor of linseed oil and turpentine permeated the rooms, mingling with cigarette smoke and the scent of jasmine and honeysuckle carried in the warm night air.

Tsiona more or less left Ivor to introduce himself, and in the course of an hour he stood on the periphery of numerous conversations. Very few were conducted in English, but all of them appeared to involve raised voices, laughter, and impassioned arguments. In the bits he could understand, one tall, elegant man with an American accent argued that Picasso was more womanizer than artist, that lust was stronger in him than talent, and a heavyset individual with a boxer's broken nose and the oversized hands of a construction worker, callused and seamed, expounded on the fate of Berlin under and after the Nazis, how the damage they did now would kill it for the future and prevent the city for all time from recovering as a cultural mecca.

Tsiona's kitchen table was covered with plates of salted herring, black bread, goat cheese, tomatoes, olives, aubergines, yogurt, grapes, and a bowl of oranges, while bottles of vodka, arak, and brandy stood guard over the food. All that Ivor wanted to do was be near her, but she remained elusive, dancing from group to group as he tracked her movements, trying to remain inconspicuous. Among the guests there were not only the painters and poets that she had promised but also architects, sculptors, writers, actors, composers, photographers, and filmmakers—information he quickly gleaned, because it seemed these creative types could hardly stop talking about either themselves or their "work."

Considering the diversity of their views and attitudes, so volubly on display, the men were surprisingly uniform in appearance, almost all choosing the pioneer-coded outfit of khaki shorts, blue shirt, and sandals, but here and there Ivor spotted the odd incongruous figure, one in particular in a suit and tie with thin-rimmed spectacles on his nose who seemed to embody the austere thought and intellectual discipline of old Europe. There were far fewer women than men circulating in the room.

Ivor saw them all, quite simply, as "not her." Here was a woman in a colorful geometric fabric V-neck dress that reached just below her knees, held at the waist with a black sash; there was another in purple with an open neckline; a third, pretty as you could want, in a red and white print with a black tie around her waist; in his imagination they were all kissed and dismissed.

Then suddenly, when he had almost given up hope of maneuvering himself into Tsiona's path, she appeared by his side. She had changed from earlier in the day into a white dress embroidered at the neck and on the cuffs of its short sleeves. She touched his arm, and he felt the shock of it as if someone had opened a gate to let him glimpse an Edenic future in the walled garden outside her home, star filled, intoxicating.

"And this, my dear friends, is Mr. Ivor Castle, who has arrived in our cultural backwater to help Mr. Phineas Baron prepare for the Arlosoroff trial."

Almost immediately Ivor found himself surrounded and peppered with questions. His abrupt transformation from wallflower to sunflower caught him unprepared, and for a few moments he turned his face from one eager questioner to another as if looking for an escape route. He was not without poise, the years of back-and-forth at Oxford on the finer points of the law had at least bequeathed that, and soon he was able to assert himself, establish his defenses, and ward off his interrogators. No, he couldn't talk about the case; no, he could not at all relay his own thoughts on the, in this room anyway, widely presumed guilt of his clients. And what did he think of Palestinian justice? Trial without jury? "How could we have a jury?" someone said. "They would argue for years, even if it was all Jews." Everyone laughed. The questioning was aggressive at first, but without animus, and when that strategy failed, backslapping bonhomie took its place; Ivor was everyone's new best friend.

The man in the gray suit and tie took him by the elbow, tried to direct him away from the encircling group, and whispered, "Let's talk one-on-one, man-to-man."

Ivor continued to stonewall. He wished Tsiona had kept quiet, as even his saying nothing was saying something. If word of his presence at this party reached Baron, he would be in a mass of trouble. But then, Tsiona as possible witness aside, why shouldn't Ivor have been there? Baron went to parties; he'd heard him (at length) discourse on social life in Palestine and Jerusalem in particular—its general dullness, the magnification given to otherwise undistinguished individuals by the smallness of the place ("The smaller the pond, the bigger the fish"), the tedious official receptions, the "at homes." He'd heard about the innumerable cliques: the English official clique, the English church clique, the American clique, the Greek clique, the American-Jewish clique, the German-Jewish clique, the Palestinian-Jewish clique, the Muslim-Arab clique, the Christian-Arab clique, and so on. Only one hostess seemed to meet Baron's approval, a Miss Annie Landau, principal of the Evelina de Rothschild School. "Try to get yourself invited to one of her shindigs," he'd advised Ivor.

Eventually interest in Ivor subsided, but not before he had received a lecture from one of the poets, punctuated by interpolations from the others in his coterie, on the iniquity of the Revisionists and their absolute failure to understand the significance of Arlosoroff's mission to Germany. "The liquidation of the Jewish property in Germany through the export of German goods to Palestine is essential to build the economy here. And why are the Nazis interested? Because it greases the wheels of their own industry. And they are afraid of the boycott movement. The deal is not perfect, but it's better than what we have now. No one should care how Jewish Palestinians get help, even if it comes from Nazis, and no one should be murdered on account of it."

It was almost two a.m. when the last guests began to depart. Ivor had lingered on the balcony, smoking cigarette after cigarette as the air cooled. He knew he should leave (should have left, as many had, after Tsiona had blown out the candles on her birthday cake), but he couldn't bring himself to do so. And then she appeared in the open doorway.

"Would you like to sleep out here?" she asked.

"I imagine that would be beautiful," Ivor said. He looked down at the narrow, overgrown garden path that led to the door in the wall through which hours earlier he had entered, passing the moss-green trunk of a lemon tree, whose fruit hung now like yellow lanterns in the moonlight.

"We could drag the mattress out," she said.

The room was silent behind her; all the guests had departed. Before he could reply there was a knock on the front door. Tsiona turned inside and went to open it. Ivor followed her into the flat, and as she descended the stairs to the door Ivor stood looking down. Tsiona blocked the path of entry to her visitor but Ivor could see him, and he recognized the face immediately. His hair and eyebrows weren't bright orange, they were jet-black, but the features were identical to those in the portrait on the easel. They spoke in low voices, and in Hebrew; if he was remonstrating with her it had no effect, for after a few minutes' conversation he stepped back and Tsiona closed the door. As she ascended the stairs, she appeared to be smiling to herself.

"Now," she said to Ivor, "help me with the bed."

She slipped off her shoes and raised her arms, and Ivor lifted off her dress. He bent to kiss her and felt the slight trembling of her body. The moon, bone-white, slid across the sky. Ivor kissed her breasts.

"Let me lie down," she said.

The mattress was obscured by the cement walls of the balcony with its geranium-filled window boxes. The plum tree dipped its head over the lovers as both concealment and blessing.

"Kiss my back," she said, and turned on her front with her face in the pillow.

Ivor kissed all down her spine and then, inspired, began to kiss the freckles on her back, which he connected in a geometry of kisses. She opened her legs a little and his mouth traveled the inside of her thigh, then down one leg before coming back up the other. Now it was his body that trembled. He stood, a little awkwardly, and took his shirt off and removed his shorts. As he did so she turned on her back and for a moment he saw her face garlanded by tiny pink cyclamen that sprouted in crevices in the wall behind her. And then he was in her, propped on his arms, lowering himself on top of her, his lips pressed to her neck. He came almost immediately. "I'm sorry," he said. Tsiona laughed. He lay beside her and she stroked his face. "Here," she said, "put your hand over mine." His finger moved on hers between her thighs as she brought herself to a climax.

The night folded around them. Her eyes were closed but he knew she wasn't asleep. She must have sensed him looking at her, known too, somehow, that she was everything he desired. She opened her eyes wide for a moment and caught his gaze.

"You will never get what you want from me," she said, and turned away from him onto her side.

Ivor woke to the screech of stray cats in the street below. He had barely slept, and now he sat up and watched the dawn light unfurl in pink strips behind the walls and tower of the abandoned art school on the corner of the road. Tsiona lay sleeping under the sheet that he had pulled over their naked bodies as the night turned chill. He wanted to forget what she had said to him, but he couldn't. It would always be there now.

He rose, pulled on his shorts, and headed indoors to the bathroom. On his way back he bent to pick up one of the sketchbooks that lay scattered in the corner of her painting area. There were pages of ornate designs, lines and markings similar to those she had already shown him. He returned the sketchbook to its place and picked up another one. This was different; each leaf in the folio showed a different face, some distorted in the Cubist manner, others more realistic charcoal and pencil portraits. Ivor lingered over each sketch. He knew he was looking for evidence of the man she had given the orange hair who had come to the door last night. He didn't find him, but instead, he came across an impression of two figures, and felt a jolt go through him, for, while he could not be 100 percent certain, it appeared that Tsiona's thin pencil lines had delineated in a few deft strokes the sinewy body and lean face of Stavsky and the portly appearance of Rosenblatt. Surely it was the two of them, seated opposite each other at a café table, an ashtray and a packet of Astra cigarettes on the tessellated surface between them, a mirror behind them, and in the mirror, the barely visible outline of a woman sketching. Hurriedly he turned the next few pages; several appeared to have been torn out, leaving ragged edges where she had flattened the spine, and then, as if floating unmoored on the page, two faces appeared, and this time there could be no mistake, thick unambiguous pencil marks, reproduced likenesses that could barely be differentiated from the faces in the photographs that Ivor had shown her.

Naked again under the sheet, he made love to her one more

time; she was drowsy, pliable, as if half-drunk on the fragrances that lifted from the garden. When he came, she put her hand over his mouth to stifle his cries. Ivor lay on his back; the sky was swept in blue, pale rose–colored at the edges; the windows of the flat reflected the sun's rays. He would have to ask her now about the sketches, but he closed his eyes against the encroaching sunlight and when he awoke, she was gone.

She had left on the table the herring, bread, olives, and yogurt from the night before and added a bowl of jam. Everything else had been put away, the half-empty bottles shelved, the flat tidied. He imagined she would return soon; probably she had made a trip to the corner grocery and any minute he would hear her ascend the stairs. But an hour passed, and he was still alone. Beyond the walled garden the city had woken in a cascade of noise—honking horns, scraping tires interspersed with the slow clops of a dray horse, and the hard slaps of women beating rugs on their balconies. Ivor brought the crucial sketchbook to the table, Exhibit A. Your Honor, pages from the sketchbook of Miss Tsiona Kerem. You will note the resemblance of the figures to the defendants. Yes, Your Honor, Miss Kerem will testify that she executed the drawings between the hours of seven and eight p.m. on the night of June sixteenth, thus rendering it impossible for either Mr. Stavsky or Mr. Rosenblatt to have reached Tel Aviv in time to accost and murder Mr. Arlosoroff on the beach. Yes, thank you, Your Honor, the defense rests.

But Miss Kerem had disappeared. Ivor waited as long as he could, covered and stored the exposed food, dragged the mattress back inside, reviewed the contents of Tsiona's bookshelves, flipped through the pages of her sketchbooks, took paintings from their stacks and set them individually against the wall. It was only while gazing at one of her landscapes—hills bleached by the sun, muted blue and green watercolor blots for trees, and in the foreground a lone yellow flat-roofed house—that he remembered her saying she was traveling to Safed today. No note on the kitchen table, no whispered goodbye as he lay sleeping, no kiss: "You will never get what you want from me."

6

"So, Castle, undated sketches, you say."

Baron, disclosing through his raspberry face and ineffectively concealed slur the aftereffects of a long champagne lunch
with High Commissioner Wharton, sat across from Ivor at a
small table in the white-walled dining room. It was late in the
afternoon and the YMCA was more or less deserted. The building had opened only three months ago, and Baron had insisted
that Ivor take a quick tour. They had passed beneath its elegant
arches and stood silent before the domed buildings, one on either
side of the high central tower with its rounded minaret-like head.
The design, purposed to accommodate a place of serenity where,
as the engraving on the stone entrance asserted, "political and
religious jealousies could be forgotten," looked, irrepressibly, as
if Sigmund Freud had been its chosen architect.

"I know," Baron said, gesturing toward the pink stone tower,
"cock and balls. Everyone's saying it, when the women are not
around. And the women are probably giggling about it too. Mind

you, once you get past the laughs, excellent addition to the Holy City."

Through the room's long windows Ivor watched three cars pull up and park, their occupants spilling out toward the limestone walls of the King David on the other side of the street; the bar of the hotel, Ivor had heard, was the favorite watering hole for the clutch of officials who manned this challenging ersatz outpost of the British Empire. Baron had wisely chosen its new across-the-street neighbor for their meeting, a far less populous venue doubtless on account of its commitment to conference, study, education, and sports rather than boozing.

The street fell silent. At a nearby table a woman opened the window closest to her and Ivor saw dust motes spinning in the sunlight. He thought of Tsiona, the beauty in the odd set of her eyes, the touch of her hand on his face, and felt her sudden, unexplained, and baffling departure as a darkness he couldn't penetrate. His yearning was already too much to bear.

A waiter in a white jacket approached with an offer to provide more hot water for the teapot, but Baron waved him away. Baron removed his round tortoiseshell glasses, patted his puffy face with a napkin, stared at Ivor as if to bring him into focus, then settled his glasses back, pushing the frame down on the bridge of his nose. There was a plate of Froumine biscuits on the table; Baron reached for one and bit into it.

"Glad they broke the strike," Baron said. "Would have lost one of the tastier items available in this disaster of a place."

"The strike?"

"Oh, last year, before you arrived. At the Froumine factory, Labour flexed its muscles, wanted to unionize the workers. The bosses brought in scabs. One of them was a young woman, sterling member of Betar, the Revisionist youth corps, or so they said. Naturally, the grown-up Revisionists got behind her; any fight with Labour is their fight. The management won."

"They fought about biscuits?"

"They fight about everything, and good job too, keeps us busy."

Baron pushed his cup and saucer a little to the side.

"If she'd dated the pages it would represent the beginnings of an advantage. Although even if she had, it is not my understanding that artists generally record the hour of their work."

"She doesn't even know I've looked at them."

"No," Baron said. "And when exactly did your poking around occur?"

Ivor had tried to prepare himself for this inevitable question; he wanted at all costs to suppress the blush that he knew would rise to his cheeks, but now, the moment upon him, he wasn't sure that he had succeeded.

"She went out to buy mint leaves for tea before the market closed. I had a half an hour or so."

"You didn't go with her? No touristic fascination?"

"No, she told me to stay. 'You can look at the paintings,' that's what she said."

"And you also opened and looked at her sketchbooks."

"I did."

"So, first you must confess that you are a snoop, and once you have surmounted that obstacle you must ask her to confirm date and time of execution. One wonders what her level of accuracy might be in that regard. We can only hope for the best. A concrete piece of evidence to corroborate memory would be a bright feather in our caps."

"Should I go after her?" Ivor wondered immediately if he had sounded a little too eager.

"To Safed? Well, this is not a case that will hang about too long on the cause list. I think we can anticipate a speedy move to trial, and a packed court of spectators all agog for a display of lurid fireworks and an exchange of heavy broadsides."

"So then, yes. I should travel north?"

"I had a case there a few years ago, a stunningly naïve instance of perjury. An old man, Druse, had charged one of his neighbors with stealing two goats. The prisoner, convicted by the civil magistrate, appealed to me as president of the court of first instance. I cross-examined the plaintiff. In the course of the cross-examination, he admitted that only one goat had been stolen. 'Then why did you say that he had stolen two?' I asked. 'Perhaps I was angry,' he replied."

Baron took a sip of his tea, then stared at Ivor as if waiting to see if he would press his case to locate Tsiona Kerem. Ivor held his tongue and reached for a biscuit.

"She shouldn't be too hard to locate," Baron continued. "Small town, vast majority Arab, how many Jewish plein air artists of the female persuasion would you imagine set their easels there? And, Mr. Castle, word of advice, try not to get smitten."

The Egged bus, showpiece of a brand-new company, bumped and occasionally coughed its way through a landscape of green undulations, fields of oats and corn that bent into waves. Through an open window next to his seat, the breeze in his face, Ivor tracked a line of high blue thistles and acanthus leaves. In the distance a microscopic red and white spot resolved as the minutes passed into a farmyard full of agricultural machinery, stacked around a reservoir pumped by an Aermotor.

An hour from Safed, the heat of the day enveloped the bus in a harsh obliterating light, and Ivor was glad when the road began to climb between little white houses with small fresh gardens, where the green foliage of the grenadines was studded with coral roses.

He wasn't just "smitten," although he had to admit that Baron, even while a bit sloshed, had exhibited sharp powers of perception. No, he was far beyond smitten, still kissing Tsiona's back, touching his lips from one tiny birthmark and freckle to another, breathing in the scent of her skin.

The bus was half-full—two women in black kerchiefs, one with a crying child in her arms; an old Jew with kaftan and fur bonnet; two young teachers supervising a small band of girls on a summer outing, blue veils around their caps, each student with a satchel on her lap. The bus continued its climb through fields of grasses and past the odd patch of fading red flax or pale yellow crucifers, flowers in the twilight of their season.

Through the driver's window, very high in front of him, Ivor could see a white point slowly expand to become the city of Safed. For the first time in an hour or so, proximity to his goal brought temporary release from thinking about the object of his obsession and allowed him to concentrate his mind elsewhere, away from Tsiona qua Tsiona, the fragrance that lifted from her hair, for example, which was presently quite overwhelming the exhaust fumes belching out from the bus, and back to the pressing demands of his vocational task, in which she played only a small if possibly vital role.

He began to go over troubling aspects of the case that lodged in his mind: In the immediate aftermath of the attack, when Sima Arlosoroff's memory was fresh, three times, on each occasion to a different witness—once in a phone call to the police station in Jaffa, once in a motorcar on the way to Hadassah hospital, and finally when shown photographs of the possible assassins—she had described the assailants as being Arabs in a way that suggested she was quite incapable of any mistake or misapprehension, going so far, on the last occasion, as, allegedly, to state and demand, "These are Jews; show me photographs of Arabs." It was only later, according to her first formal statement given to the police, that she began to insist that the murderers were Jews, and indeed that she had cried out, "Help! Help, Jews have shot him!" as her husband lay bleeding on the beach. All this should have been, and indeed was, good news for the defense. And yet, the relative darkness, the panic, the vehemence of her reversal, her written statements, her ability to identify the men from their photographs, and the indistinctness of some of the reports in which she supposedly accused Arabs all mitigated in the direction of doubt.

But then there was Charles Gross's hint at the Casino that he held important information, which, given his political leanings, could surely only reinforce the innocence of Stavsky and Rosenblatt. If nothing proved enough there was, of course, Tsiona, but once she had reasserted herself in his mind all thoughts of trial and error were gone, and in their place was the inescapable sense that even as he had held her tightly in his arms, she was a fugitive.

In Oxford once, on a wild wet night, fat raindrops hammering on the windows of the Junior Common Room, coda without warning to a day that had begun with the sky pewter and the wind chilly and insistent, Ivor had engaged in a conversation about love with several members of his college's small Freudian subculture—two scientists, two philosophers, and a lone aspiring literary critic. The most ardent of Freud's admirers, Julian Moore-Filbert, a devotee who slept with a copy of Brill's translation of *The Interpretation of Dreams* on his bedside table, had offered a definition of the true love object as "she for whom there can be no substitute," and Ivor, reflecting on the substance of his various dalliances with Annabelle, Andrea, and Carla (and even open-minded Mary Buss, whom he had every reason to feel grateful toward), found himself agreeing that thus far in, no such being had materialized. Until now, that is, after one day and one night with Tsiona Kerem that he would have dragged back if he could: the beads of sweat dropping between his thin chest and her full breasts, and the way the cool breeze rising in whispers through the night had licked them dry.

When Ivor dismounted from the bus, he walked into a wall of hot air that took his breath away. The bus station, at this hour almost deserted, was a place of languid stupor. A Hindu soldier manning an English armored car sat half-asleep at the wheel. Four years ago, the city had been a place of terrible riots and a brutal massacre, eighteen Jews slaughtered, many wounded, the main Jewish shopping street looted and burned. At home in London for the summer, Ivor had read about it in his father's copy of *The Times,* but the news hadn't really touched him. At Oxford he had resisted Gross's enthusiasm for Palestine; as far as Ivor was concerned, the ancient homeland of the Jewish people might just as well have been the Outer Hebrides. But Baron had felt it necessary to fill Ivor in on some of the gorier details of August 29, 1929, before they parted company at the YMCA: a woman tied to the grille of a window, then burned; a schoolteacher and his wife hacked to pieces; children murdered in an orphanage, heads smashed, hands severed. For his own part Baron had been involved in some of the trials about the looting and arson.

Ivor had observed that Baron, while Jewish himself, liked to adopt a "pox on both your houses" attitude to Jews and Arabs in Palestine and, whenever possible, to retreat into his pristine Englishness, if only additionally, and from that fortress vantage point, to revile the local British authorities, but even his almost impregnable misanthropy could not quite resist a hint of fellow feeling in the story that he had to tell.

As Ivor left the bus station in the direction of a nearby hostelry, shaded by a few desultory pines and eucalyptus trees, he passed two dilapidated stone buildings and wondered if their broken walls and rubble-strewn floors were unreconstructed markers of the city's violent past.

He didn't really know where he was headed. He peered in through the open door of the hostelry to a clean, fresh, chalk-whitened room, its middle table covered by a blue-checked tablecloth and porcelain plates. In one corner an Arab in a white turban and kaftan sipped a tiny cup of coffee; in the other a Jewish laborer wearing the inevitable khaki shorts, blue shirt, and work boots was biting into a pickled cucumber. A woman in an apron bustled into the room from the kitchen, accompanied by a young girl with Gretchen braids down her back.

The proprietress, or perhaps she was the cook, said something in Hebrew and beckoned Ivor to come in, and the girl began quickly to lay cutlery on the table. Ivor held up his hand to stop her but continued to survey the room. It was as if he'd imagined Tsiona would be right there waiting for him, and the fact that she wasn't left him rooted to the spot and unsure what to do. To ask for her was clearly absurd, but on the other hand if he had learned something in his brief sojourn in Palestine it was that everyone seemed to be in everyone else's business. At home in England, it was quite the opposite. He had once witnessed a man have an epileptic fit in the middle of *The Sign of Four* at his local Gaumont, and the audience had ignored the man for the longest time, as if his seizure were entirely a private affair that they had no right to intrude upon. In the end it was only irritation that led a couple in his row to go to the poor man's aid, but by that time the ushers, waving their torches, had arrived on the scene.

The woman moved toward Ivor and, switching to English, beckoned and said, "Come, come." Ivor remained frozen. The two men in the room lifted their heads to look at him.

"I'm sorry," Ivor said. "I was looking for someone."

He walked on, finding his way to the Jewish quarter of the city and down the cobblestone streets of a market, shuttered for the hours of midafternoon heat. Only one stall remained open, its sacks of rice, bulgur, lentils, and beans stacked under a tin awning with a low canopy of dark linen stretched beneath it. Ivor, his throat parched, stepped into the interior. A teenage boy in a black skullcap stood behind the counter.

"What do you have to drink?" Ivor asked.

The boy gestured toward a wooden crate half-filled with brown glass bottles.

"That's all?" Ivor said. "No water? No pop?"

"Pep," the boy said, and handed a bottle to Ivor.

It was beer but Ivor hadn't seen this brand before. He examined the bottle, which featured a bizarre figure, a knight on horseback with a flag streaming behind him, but on his head, where you would expect to find a medieval visor, there was the familiar British colonial pith helmet. A few words in Hebrew were raised in relief on the glass along with the name at the root of the boy's confusion, Pep.

"Well, if that's all you have, I suppose I don't have a choice."

Ivor stood beneath the canopy and drank the beer. Farther down the street a woman in a long skirt and what looked like a man's checked shirt with an embroidered jacket over it had appeared with a broad paintbrush in one hand and a bucket in the other. She wore a red kerchief on her head. Ivor watched her climb the steps of a short ladder and begin to slather wide swathes of paint onto the wall of her home. It seemed an unwise enterprise for this time of day, but she worked hard, covering the stone in broad strokes, indifferent, it seemed, to the burning sun.

While he was observing her and draining the last of his beer there was a small flurry of activity at the end of the street. A motorcycle turned in from a side road, came to a sharp halt, and, with its engine revving, deposited a passenger who jumped off the back seat and waved as the rider took off. The passenger turned and Ivor recognized him immediately. It was the visitor who had come to Tsiona's door in Jerusalem on the night that he had slept with her. If he noticed Ivor, he paid him no attention but set off at a quick pace in the opposite direction from the little store. Without hesitation Ivor followed, keeping at a distance of twenty to thirty yards. They rose through narrow winding alleys, some shadowed by high stone walls, and now Ivor saw quite clearly the damage that had accrued four years earlier and was yet awaiting repair: a home sheared off on the diagonal, with living rooms exposed; a roofless synagogue still blackened by kerosene fire.

At a high point the walker in front and his lagging shadow emerged from the alley to a clear space, and here the path diverged, one route leading to a boxlike stucco dwelling and the second to a flat patch of ground near a rocky outcrop where Tsiona had set up her easel and box of paints. She stood to the side of her work, in a wide-brimmed hat and a white short-sleeved kaftan belted around the waist, brush in hand, contemplating whatever she had just accomplished.

The walker called out to her, and without turning around, she lifted her arm and waved. He shouted something in Hebrew and then continued on the path toward the hut. Ivor stopped in his tracks. The lingering effects of the beer combined with the oppressive heat had given him a pounding headache. Or perhaps it was the presence of the other man that had set off the crashing sensation in his skull.

Ivor waited until the walker had entered the hut, and then he began to make his way down the path toward Tsiona. Her canvas was awash in blues and purples. From a few yards away Ivor could see not what she saw, only what she had transformed, a house with a high crenellated wall, a donkey with a bright yellow saddlebag, a tiny female figure next to it, and in the background, the hills of Safed merging with the sky. Stopped short for a moment, Ivor felt as if the surrounding blue of the natural sky had enveloped the painting and become a part of it.

"Tsiona."

She turned, and the expression on her face could not have been angrier. "What are you doing here?"

"I'm sorry. I'm so very sorry to disturb. Mr. Baron sent me, I'm afraid we have some questions that couldn't wait."

"I don't believe you."

Ivor stood in the harsh light, his white linen shirt stuck to his body, his trousers clammy on his legs. Tsiona had a canteen of water on the ground near her easel but he was afraid to ask for a drink.

"What do you think?" she said. "I come here to be alone and to paint."

"But you're not alone."

Her eyes widened.

"My God," she said, "that is none of your business. Do you think you have a claim on me?"

His response was abject, a downward glance, an uncomfortable silence. But he had to rouse himself; no one wanted a lover who was a weakling.

"I saw some drawings in your sketchbook. They look like our clients to me. Of course, you couldn't know it was them.

In either case we need to know when they were done. It's absolutely exigent."

He was damning himself further with each word that he uttered, but at least he wasn't backing down.

"You looked through my sketchbooks? Did you also go through my drawers?"

"Of course not."

"Well maybe you should have. You might have found the murder weapon. I understand the gun has yet to be retrieved."

She laughed, then bent to pick up the canteen and proffered it to Ivor.

"Here," she said, "and you should wear a hat."

She had softened toward him, perhaps only for a moment, but even so Ivor luxuriated in the change. There was hope, even if another man was waiting for her less than two hundred yards away.

"Did you sketch them that day, when you were in the café, on the night of the murder?"

"I have no idea. I told you, I go there all the time."

The sun beat down as if it had nothing better to do than cause Ivor the maximum discomfort possible. Sweat from his brow trickled in rivulets down his face and the back of his neck; his shirt collar was soaked. This entire journey had been a complete waste of time, and worse. Now he was going to have to imagine her in the white hut, cooled by the night air, in the arms of someone else. No greater proof of love than the jealousy it engenders.

"I have to get to work," she said. "If you stay, I'll get irritated."

Ivor wiped his hand across his forehead.

"Come to Jerusalem," she said. "I'll be back in a week."

She turned once more to the canvas, dipped her brush in a tin of powdery blue, and began to make a series of quick marks.

"Please try to think," Ivor said, "is there anything at all you can remember? The likenesses are so strong. Perhaps if I showed you—"

Tsiona wheeled around in anger. "You stole my sketchbook?"

"No, no. I removed nothing. I meant, on your return, if you could take a second look. The figures have a pack of cigarettes on the table between them." His persistence, he knew, was exasperating her.

"What brand?"

"Astra."

"Oh, of course, now it's all coming back to me. It was evening, they were smoking, I overheard them planning to murder Arlosoroff, it must have been at precisely seven-eighteen p.m. The fat one said, 'Let's shoot him on the beach at night so no one will see.'"

Ivor's shoulders drooped.

"For the last time," Tsiona said, "I'm asking you to leave me alone."

Ivor retraced his steps. When he arrived at the branch in the path he glanced to his left and saw Tsiona's companion standing in the doorway of the hut watching him. The man, whose black hair Ivor had first encountered in a riot of orange paint, maintained a neutral expression, but then, as Ivor was on the point of turning away, he offered a brief wave, which, rightly or wrongly, Ivor experienced as a dismissal.

On the bus back to Tel Aviv he was lucky enough to get two seats to himself. Ivor sat with his back to the window and stretched out his legs. The sky was drained of the somnolent afternoon and refilled with evening darkness. Prohibited from sleep by endless bumps in the road, Ivor reviewed the debacle of his visit. He couldn't wish away the man she had with her, and yet he wanted to believe that she would not rush directly from his own arms into somebody else's. At the thought of how he had been waved away his face reddened. He had merely succeeded in aggravating Tsiona and in return had received a humiliation to depress the heart. As for the murder case, he had learned nothing at all.

The bus came to a brief halt; Ivor listened to the loud rasp of cicadas high in the trees. A few new passengers boarded, and the bus lurched forward. Before long the sound of waves kissing the shore indicated proximity to the journey's end. A screech of brakes and a sudden jolt startled Ivor from his near slumber; a featureless world pressed its darkness to the windows. Ivor sat up, and his tongue felt heavy in his mouth; nevertheless, it curled around three words she had spoken to him and he murmured to himself, "The fat one."

7

Tel Aviv

~

The streets were crowded and noisy—radios; megaphones; peddlers; newspaper and shoeshine boys; vendors of ice cream, hot dogs, and corn on the cob—and the swirl of sound followed him all the way from the central bus station. It was a relief to Ivor to step inside the new lodgings he had found in a rooming house on HaYarkon Street and to close the door behind him. A week! He had plenty to occupy himself with, of course, a fuller acquaintance with all the details of the case for a start, but his aching and urgent thought was a simple one: He had to see her again.

Ivor poured water from jug to bowl, splashed it on his face, and toweled himself off, then removed his boots before collapsing onto the narrow bed, which barely accommodated his long frame. Outside, the noise that Ivor had endeavoured to block out gathered strength, and the window of his room—which, unless he was to suffocate, he had no choice but to leave half-open—was no match for the polyphonic din outside.

He lived now only a short walk from the Casino. Perhaps a drink or two (or more!) would help him bring on the necessary oblivion, the kind that he had known at Oxford after a long night in the public bar at the Turf or the King's Arms.

He couldn't get her out of his mind. He unbuttoned his shorts, released his cock, relived spooning into her, his hands reaching around to cup her breasts. And he had said, "You're so beautiful," then whispered it again as he came, then as now.

A light knock on his door roused him from both sleep and his bed. He opened the door with full expectancy that his magical thinking had worked and Tsiona, conjured, had flown to his side. If so, she had chosen to present herself in the body and with the face of Charles Gross.

Charles's cheeks were bright red. He was dressed in a loose white shirt and white trousers held up by a black belt, his studied informality offset by the official-looking leather briefcase held in his hand. He stared at disheveled Ivor, whom sleep had overtaken before he could remove his own shirt and shorts.

"How did you find me?" Ivor asked.

"Does it matter? You're not in hiding, are you?"

Charles entered the room and sat down at Ivor's small desk. There was nowhere for Ivor to plump himself down except on the end of the bed. His mouth was sandpaper dry and he realized that his fly remained undone and gaping like a mouth, his underpants sticking out like a white tongue.

"Give me a minute," Ivor said. He walked down the narrow corridor toward the boardinghouse's communal bathroom. Luckily no one was in there. Ivor cupped his hands under the tap, brought the water to his face; he brushed his teeth and made the necessary adjustment to his shorts. He looked in the mirror and for moment couldn't discern if the black spots that he saw there belonged to the glass or his face. He ran his hands through

his uneven short crop of dark hair, the results of a misspent fifteen minutes at a sheepshearer/barber on Allenby Street.

"You look like shit," Charles said when Ivor reentered the
room.

"Thanks."

"Listen, I'm going to give you advance notice of something
that is very good news for you."

"A bequest? I don't have any maiden aunts."

"Shut up. This is serious, not a chat on Broad Street after
your tutorial. An Arab, a young man, is going to confess to the
murder."

Ivor looked toward his window, where daylight was trying its
best to push through a pair of thin brown curtains.

"How do you know this?"

"As far as you're concerned that matters even less than how I
found you. But believe me, it's about to happen. My assumption
is that not only are you in the business of defending your clients,
but also you don't want to see two Jews convicted of murder any
more than I do."

"I don't want to see two innocent men convicted. I don't
care if they are Jews or not."

"You can tell Baron he doesn't have to worry. In a few days
the case will be thrown out. It will never come to trial."

Ivor knew he should have been delighted with this news, but
he wasn't. Gross's tone was combative, not merely instructive or
enlightening, and in the nonchalant request that Ivor pass on the
information to Baron, Ivor thought he also detected the whisper
of a threat, or at least the murmur of a warning.

"Why are you telling me this?"

"Because I don't trust you to do the right thing. You're
capable of exhibiting a crippling naivety. I know you've been

doing some digging in Jerusalem, I assume on behalf of your clients. . . ."

Ivor raised his eyebrows and let out a small sigh of exasperation.

"The party . . . the party. We know who was there . . . that lot, the nicies and the goodies, the ridiculous Canaanites, the stalwarts of the Painters and Sculptors Association, same Bohemia all over the world."

" 'We'?"

"Never mind. The important thing is that you need to stick to your guns. You're persuadable, you always have been, and frankly I'm not convinced that you can be relied upon to abide by the principles that guide your profession."

Ivor understood very well what Charles was saying. For him it remained the most vexing aspect of the law, something he had struggled with throughout his studies, the defense of men you knew to be guilty. He had learned the mantra: You were never really defending the men, only the law, the right of the accused to a fair trial and so on. And this was his first case, his primary test. He was still hoping for certainties, hard facts, evidence that would acquit beyond a doubt. And now here came Charles with something that already sounded shady, as if Charles knew that the defense of Stavsky and Rosenblatt was going to need propping up, or more than support, a knockout blow to the other side.

"They're all for a conviction," Charles said, "your new Jerusalem friends, and they'll try to do whatever it takes to get one."

"And you are doing the opposite."

"Absolutely. It's all as clear as daylight, and broad daylight as soon as the confession comes out."

"And remind me how you know about this?"

"I didn't say."

Ivor sat with his hands on his knees. Where had Charles developed this sense of him as unreliable, malleable? Perhaps it was true. He had never quite felt that the law was for him, and from his midteens on he had felt his father's hand in his back pushing him not so gently in the direction of the profession that he had made his own. Ivor had been drawn, in dreamier fashion, to the works of literature, novels and poetry, that his father had little time for, enthusiasms that led Edwin Castle to refer to his son's "unfortunate romantic inclination." At Oxford he had shared a picnic on Port Meadow with Clara Halsted, and as the sun set behind a row of poplars and grazing ponies bowed their heads like shy swans, he had recited Yeats's "When you are old and gray" to her. To his consternation she had remained singularly unmoved.

"What I'm advising," Charles continued, "is to take the gift that will be offered to you and don't think about it too much, and don't listen to the chorus of doubts that will inevitably arise from your new friends in the Holy City. You know damn well that Stavsky and Rosenblatt didn't murder Arlosoroff. And now you'll have more proof than you'll ever need."

"And what if I discover to the contrary?"

Ivor knew that this was not a question that he was permitted to ask, and yet he did. Charles's dubious resolve had rendered him oppositional.

"Don't be a fool," Charles said, then stood and took three steps toward the door. "I have to get to the bank."

"One last time," Ivor said, "how do you know, days in advance, that this event is going to occur?"

For the first time since their conversation had begun, Charles smiled.

"Oh," he said, "we bankers know everything."

Days passed. No unusually urgent cries rose from the newspaper boys selling *Haaretz* and *Davar,* no calls came from Baron
with the extraordinary news of a confession, no denizen of the
Casino, wild-eyed, arrested Ivor's progress as he made his way to
the bar with a "Have you heard . . . surely you must have heard?"
Instead, the longueurs of his daily routine stretched inexorably
until he could make his way back to Jerusalem to meet Tsiona.

At Baron's request he read, once again, all the documents
pertaining to the case, but this time, seated at the small desk in
his room, he paid acute attention to the affirmations and deni-
als surrounding Sima Arlosoroff's supposed mention of Arabs
to three different individuals in the immediate aftermath of
the murder. First there was Constable Shermeister, who was
telephoning from the Jaffa police station. What actually took
place there when that conversation was going on was by no
means clear. Sima later denied the suggestion that she had told
the constable the assailants were Arabs, or that she said that
Arlosoroff had been "shotten" or shot by Arabs. In this ver-

sion a garbled account of what occurred appeared to have circulated in the police station, leading to a log entry to the effect that "somebody" had been shot by an Arab "in some street." Then there was the journey to Hadassah hospital in a motorcar where a conversation took place between Mrs. Arlosoroff and her driver, who remembered her saying that she was "ninety percent or one hundred percent sure" that the attackers were Arabs. And finally, the third episode, when, in the middle of the night, a detective had shown photographs of a number of Jewish suspects to Mrs. Arlosoroff and she was alleged to have said, "These are Jews; show me photographs of Arabs." And yet in each instance Mrs. Arlosoroff had denied, or retracted, or, as in the last example, attributed her request to the confusion of someone whose memory was as yet sieving blood and sand. That memory recovered, its occlusions swept away, like the clouds that scudded across the Mediterranean sky only to be chased off by the relentless electric blue of the day, what remained was the vivid certainty in Mrs. Arlosoroff's imagination that Stavsky and Rosenblatt had murdered her husband—executed him, in fact, for what they perceived as crimes against the Jewish people—and that whatever she may or may not have mumbled incoherently about Arabs, the faces of those two Jewish Revisionists, her husband's stark political enemies, were, in the bright currency of her mind, embossed like the king's head on the half crown from the year of his birth that Ivor kept in his pocket for good luck.

He hadn't mentioned a word to Baron of his meeting with Charles Gross, partly for fear of looking a fool if the confession failed to materialize, and partly for the awkward position it might land him in if it did. For now, he preferred the role of the dutiful assistant, bland, trustworthy, the incandescent passion that burned within him invisible to the naked eye.

When he grew tired of reading, Ivor wandered the streets of Tel Aviv. He was searching for Tsiona, of course, even though he knew that she was not there. His peregrinations had a twofold purpose: to obliterate the memory of the man she was with (a task that he abjectly failed to accomplish) and to imagine her, having departed Safed early, journeying through his neighborhood on her way back to Jerusalem, stopping for coffee at one of the small cafés that he had determined, through nonchalant conversations at the bar of the Citadel, to be the local haunts of the Bohemian crowd: the Sheleg Levanon café on Nahlat Binyamin and the Cassit Café on Ben Yehuda at the corner of Mendele. There he encountered small animated groups gathered at separate or joined tables, exchanging sketches done on empty packets of cheap cigarettes while downing shot after shot of cheap medicinal cognac. At night, as the alcohol percolated through their bodies and the heat and humidity lubricated songs in their throats, the poets and painters sang out in Hebrew and sometimes in Russian. Ivor stood on the fringes, an awkward figure, scanning the lively, talkative regulars as their voices rose in strength and they gestured ever more wildly to get across some salient point or other. She wasn't there, why would she be?

On the return journey to his boardinghouse, now listening only to the sound of his own shoes on the pavement and the rumors of nearby waves lapping the shore and making their presence felt in the salt air, he found a way to leave the city entirely. There he was in London, it was winter, they had emerged from the lobby of the Tate Gallery after wandering through the rooms of the Burne-Jones exhibition, it was snowing softly, and the last light of the afternoon was trapped and held for a moment in an icy curtain as they crossed Millbank to look over the Thames. Tsiona, transported to this chilly clime, wore a black coat with a fur collar and a red wool felt pillbox hat. She held his arm and inclined her head onto his shoulder. Later, he imagined, they would hop on a bus and he would bring her to meet his parents. He thought he would never feel so happy again.

Back in his room he lay awake until the hours pulled the black sails of sleep over him.

9

He arrived in Jerusalem early on the day that Tsiona was due to return. The bus had taken him through clusters of citrus groves on the outskirts of Jaffa. In a couple of months, the woman seated next to him had said, the air there would be pervaded with the scent of orange blossom, the intoxicating, overwhelming aroma of the winter fruit.

He wasn't ready to knock on her door. In his mind he was giving her other lover, who for all he knew was not her lover and was still in Safed or somewhere else entirely, time to depart. Instead, he went first to the Hasharon Café, on Jaffa Road, where, wittingly or not, Tsiona had sketched Stavsky and Rosenblatt. He wanted to see the premises for himself.

The corrugated shutter was only halfway open, and a small boy dipped under it, back and forth, setting chairs and tables in the street. Ivor ducked under the metal frame and into the main room. Although the place did not appear to be ready for business, two men in workman's clothes, wearing flat caps, were already seated at a narrow table playing backgammon. When Ivor appeared, they looked up from their game.

"Is the proprietor here?" he asked.

One of the men simply lifted his hand and pointed toward an arch and narrow passageway that presumably led to the kitchen. When Ivor hesitated to advance, the other player adjusted his round spectacles, stared hard at Ivor, then yelled, "Yossi!" into the back.

A man with a thick walrus mustache, a dropsical stomach, and a head of curly brown hair approached, wiping his hands on the front of his apron.

Ivor held out his hand. "Ivor Castle. I'm the legal assistant to Phineas Baron, the Stavsky case. I just wanted to see the place. Hope that's all right? I know you've already had the police here."

Yossi shrugged.

Ivor looked around. The walls were covered in posters, illustrations accompanied by Hebrew writing that he could not understand. Only one was fully accessible to him, a white gull, wings extended, filling an azure sky over what looked like the domes of Jaffa and beneath it the words GUIDE TO THE NEW PALESTINE.

Ivor had seen posters like this before, occasionally in London and most prominently pinned to the otherwise bare walls of Charles Gross's room in Corpus Christi. One he remembered in particular, a bucolic setting, young pioneers resting after a hard day's work in the fields, the woman as vivid as the man, pictures of health, bales of hay, neat fields in shades of green and yellow stretching to the horizon, and the beckoning caption COME TO PALESTINE. Ivor had remained indifferent, then as now. He was here by chance, not design. He hadn't come to build a state, only to dismantle his own torpidity, or find a person, not a country, he might love and—a tougher assignment he now saw—who might love him back with equal ferocity.

"I have a friend," Ivor continued, "a painter, Miss Tsiona Kerem, she's here almost every night, you must know her."

Yossi pushed out his lower lip and shook his head.

"I don't," he said.

"Yes, you must, she sits here and sketches. In . . . well . . . it must be this corner, I believe." Ivor turned and gestured toward a table that the boy was in the process of setting up.

Again, Yossi shook his head. "I know the regulars," he said, "British, Jews, or like you—a bit of both."

Ivor felt his face redden. In response he launched into a detailed description of Tsiona, intending to omit the superlatives that he wanted to include, but then, of course, he slipped a few in.

"She was here on the night of the murder," he said.

"How do you know that?"

At this, the attention of the two backgammon players was drawn away from their game. Ivor was about to mention both the police report and the sketches but, sensing that he had already said too much, now said nothing.

Yossi took a moment before he settled on a response.

"If she was ever here it was only once," Yossi said. "A woman as beautiful as you describe I would have remembered." He smiled. Ivor didn't know if Yossi was teasing him or telling the truth.

"Come on," Ivor said, "she comes here all the time. She told me."

"Then she is not telling you the truth. You can come back and check with our customers if you like. She was here once . . . and I'll tell you how I know. Of course, I remember her. The police let her go that night. I never saw her before, and I never saw her again."

Ivor was silent for a moment. The backgammon players returned to their game and Ivor heard the click of dice in their rosewood cup, the slide of the stones on the board, the fealties to chance and skill amplified in sound.

"You don't, I suppose, remember how long she was here?"

Yossi opened the palms of his hands upward and spread his fingers in the universal gesture of blissful ignorance.

Why would she lie to him? It would have to be the first thing he asked her, but when she opened her door, smiling, excited to see him, already kissing him and tugging at his shirt before he could get a word out, the world outside scattered and shrank until there was nothing except their naked bodies and the bed.

He was sitting up, a pillow wedged between his back and the stone wall that functioned as a headboard. She lay curled in the crook of his arm, half-asleep. Ivor, spent, kissed the top of her head. Moments earlier he had whispered, so low it was almost as if he didn't want her to hear, "What do you want, Tsiona?" And she, without hesitating, had replied without opening her eyes, as if reporting from the depths of a dream, "Tenderness."

Three feet from the foot of the bed Tsiona's easel still displayed her color-saturated portrait of the man from Safed. She stirred and extricated herself from Ivor's clasp.

"Tell me who he is," Ivor said, lifting his glance in the direction of the painting.

Tsiona turned on her side and faced away from him.

"You don't have to worry," she said, "we're not deeply attached."

Her reply both was and wasn't what he had been hoping to hear.

"What exactly do you mean by that?"

Tsiona sighed.

"The lover," she said, "is supposed to be fun. If you're not going to be fun, then we shouldn't see each other. You shouldn't have come to Safed."

Ivor ran his finger down the length of her spine.

"I had to see you."

"And I have to be free to do what I want to do."

"I understand," Ivor said, but his comprehension registered only as profound disappointment and hurt.

Tsiona rolled over to face him. She was smiling.

"Do you know why I tease you?"

"No."

"Because you're so easy to tease."

The morning light poured into the room undeterred by the odd drugged cloud that endeavored to block its path. Through the open windows the scent of oleander rose from the garden to mingle with the cloying smells of turpentine and pungent linseed oil that permeated Tsiona's apartment. A heady air that seemed to capture Ivor's confusion of desire, jealousy, and suspicion. All he had ever known before Tsiona was that one night of awkward struggle at Oxford with Mary Buss, an experience so clumsy that Mary, barely more proficient than he was, had needed to guide him in with her hand.

Ivor looked once more at the reproachful painting on the easel, silent inanimate witness to their recent ecstasy and his good fortune.

"You still haven't told me who he is."

"He does bother you, doesn't he? He's my friend. A painter.

He thinks I'm a genius, and I think he's a genius. I'm right, and he's not. We share that little studio in Safed. It helps that we split the rent."

She reached for the pack of Atid cigarettes on her bedside table, sat up, and lit one.

He wanted to pursue the topic, press her for more information, but something in her tone closed the door on his inquiry. She had a way of saying things that brought him up short and brooked no response, as if, like on an old map, the message was "Go no farther, for there dragons lie."

"The proprietor at Hasharon says you're not a regular, says he's only seen you there once, on the night of the murder."

Tsiona's face twisted into a grimace. "Now you're really going to make me angry," she said.

"I just . . . I just want to understand. . . ."

She rose from the bed and walked naked to the bathroom. When she emerged, she was wearing a thin white shift and her face was set in stone against him.

"Please," he said, "tell me when you did the sketches. It's all I need to know. Everything else, everything, is your business."

Tsiona stubbed out her cigarette in the ashtray on her kitchen table.

"I did them," she said, "days after the murder. From the Wanted poster the police left with me, not from life. Are you happy now?"

"But why?"

"I don't know why . . . because their faces interested me. That's why."

He didn't believe her, not for a second, but from the moment she began to withdraw her affection from him he was incapable of challenging her. The woman who wanted "tenderness" had evanesced, and the taut figure who stood in her place was armored, impenetrable, unknowable.

"Your friends all think our clients are guilty, don't they?"

"And what do you think?"

"It's not my business to judge, only to help defend."

"That's very convenient," she said.

"Baron may want you to testify."

"That wouldn't be wise."

"Because you know when they left the café. You know they had time to get to Tel Aviv."

"I don't know anything."

"Then why wouldn't it be wise for you to testify?"

"Trust me."

He didn't trust her, not at all, neither about the "genius" nor the sketches. He hardly knew her, yet when she turned the klieg lights of her full and substantial attention upon him, he felt impossibly happy, but when she withdrew, instant darkness, her mystery preserved.

Ivor had thrown off the covers and was sitting on the edge of the bed. Charles Gross's information was pressing on him, a pressure he could only relieve by passing it on. He wanted to tell her, to say, "What you may or may not have witnessed doesn't matter. An Arab is going to confess. So, you can tell me the truth."

She came, stood before him, pulled her white slip over her head, and pushed him back onto the bed; the morning's aureate light filled the room.

"Your clients are murderers," she said. "I'm sure of it."

10

Ivor, seated in the lobby of the King David Hotel, watched as Baron made his entry and walked purposefully toward him. He was all business, unsmiling in his creased gray trousers, navy blue blazer, white shirt, and blue tie. True-blue, Ivor thought, but perhaps, in the end, loyal to no one but himself.

They moved to a table by one of the long French windows that overlooked the newly planted garden: shrubs, four palms, and a grove of narrow cypress trees. The late afternoon light flattened before them and cast long shadows across the brown patch of grass that, back in the spring, had begun as an attempt to seed a lawn. Baron glanced quickly at the menu, appeared to decide that food at this moment was a waste of time, and launched right in.

"Castle, your coup de foudre regarding Mademoiselle Kerem is going to turn our case into a farce. Did she or did she not sketch our miserable and much-maligned clients at an hour that precludes the possibility of their arrival in Tel Aviv in time to commit foul murder on the beach?"

"She insists they were not drawn from life."

"Then what the hell were they drawn from, the deep well of her imagination?"

"No, the identity portraits on the Wanted posters that the police left with her."

"She sketched from the sketches?"

"That is what she says."

"And you believe that nonsense?"

"I don't know what to believe."

Baron gave Ivor a look of disdain.

"What's her game? She should be a stalwart for the prosecution; luckily for us that doesn't appear to be quite so. Odd, as she is undoubtedly an entrenched Bohemian and her entire set never saw a fully formed Jabotinskian Revisionist with dreams of restoring King David's Greater Israel that it didn't want to string up. She's not interested in the truth; she has some kind of agenda; no different from Mrs. Arlosoroff's with her revolving myopia: They were Arabs! No, my mistake, they were Jews!"

"I wouldn't put her in that category, sir, she seems very much her own woman and perhaps she's simply an honest one."

"Oh . . . oh . . . here we go . . . please don't tell me that you're sleeping with her."

"Of course not."

"Believe me, I understand the attraction, I gather she has quite the following, but that would really take the cake."

Ivor felt the blood rush to his cheeks.

"How much longer, sir, before we go to trial?"

"It could be weeks; it could be months. In fact, now that I come to think of it, nothing at all will get done until these damn holidays are over and done with. The Jewish part of our little fiefdom is about to shut down until mid- to late October and you can bet your life that as soon as our people have finished atoning for their sins and hanging fruit and two veg in booths, the Arabs will come up with some monthlong reason why they can't come to court. The Christians are much easier to deal with, a couple of days here and there, birth, death, and back to life and chop-chop, *finita la commedia*."

A waiter, in a white jacket and dark trousers, approached, and Baron, without even looking at Ivor, ordered gin and tonics for both of them.

"Helps the body fight against malaria," Baron said. "You know Kligler? Been doing an extraordinary job. Has it all figured out, got the population on board. They were dying in their droves until he got here. Places with no population, all of a sudden, acres of cultivatable land. Every university should have a Department of Hygiene, don't you think?"

Baron clinked his glass against Ivor's and knocked back his drink.

"So, young Castle, do you have plans for the New Year? You are welcome to visit with Mrs. Baron and me, but I imagine you have younger friends. You absolutely must, however, join us after Yom Kippur to break the fast, *tout* Jerusalem will be there, not that I shall have fasted, and I am guessing that if you are anything like your father, you will not have done so either. If . . . *if* you are to remain in Jerusalem during these days of awe"—and here Baron gave Ivor a look that somehow managed to be at once cautionary and marginally salacious—"then there are certainly synagogues in the Old City which are of considerable, shall we say, anthropological and architectural interest that you might find edifying to visit. The Karaites, for example, have a small cellar all to themselves. And, of course, there is the Wailing Wall, where you will find the denizens of the place inserting written messages to God in the cracks between the stones. I imagine that many are confessional in nature. If we had access to them our job would be made much easier. I understand that in Japan almost every accused confesses, court exists for sentencing and little else. Here in the West, and to the farthest reaches of our empire, it is quite the contrary. Everyone is innocent, everyone has a story to tell, and as my old mentor Lord Justice Lockley used to say, if there is one fact you can be certain of in a court-room it is that everyone is lying."

A second round of G and T's arrived, although Ivor had not yet drained his first. He had forgotten the approach of the Jewish New Year, had not noticed the increased activity on the street, crowded markets, shoppers busier than usual, a world bustling to prepare, clean, and clarify. Ivor recalled his family's Rosh Hasha-nah visits to St. John's Wood Synagogue. His father, wearing his best suit, took his hand and led him out onto Hamilton Terrace, where they merged with the residents of the other nearby Jewish homes as they spilled into the adjacent streets in hats and over-coats, each man carrying his own blue or brown velvet bag for his prayer shawl, some marked with the Star of David.

In the weeks running up to the festival his father would always make the same joke when asked where he planned to spend the high holidays—"The Orthodox is the synagogue that I do not attend"—but then a residue of ancient duty coupled with the results of pressure from Ivor's mother (an arm-twisting that he clearly enjoyed) would settle upon him and he would relent.

Inside the packed synagogue, under the magnificent chan-deliers, the wardens sat in their brushed top hats and tails while the rabbi and the cantor, dressed all in white, urged the congre-gation to settle so that the service might begin. Ivor had loved the theater of it, the tinkling bells on top of the Torah scrolls; the aspirational voices of the hidden choir; the hierarchy of seating that allowed the Castles to occupy a front row even though they only attended three times a year; his mother above them in the ladies' gallery, gesturing to Ivor to smooth his hair; and best of all the moment when the children were invited onto the bimah, where the priests waited to bless them. Ivor and his friends jostled and crowded under a canopy of broad prayer shawls while these men, transformed from their day jobs as plumbers or electricians or fishmongers, swayed above them and sang in Hebrew, "May the Lord bless you and keep you. May the Lord make his face to shine upon you and be gracious unto you. May the Lord lift up his face unto you and give you peace."

"Well," Baron continued, "you have a few days to yourself. Use them wisely."

"I intend to," Ivor said.

Abruptly, it seemed, the lobby had filled and waiters, all of them young Arab men, hastened from table to table, conveying drinks to the broadening set of British functionaries, bureaucrats, public servants, and military men. Close to Ivor's table a group of Arab businessmen, all crowned in the fezzes that symbolized their urban sophistication, had surrounded the Syrian Orthodox archbishop from the Old City and were deep in conversation with him.

The archbishop was an imposing figure, taller than his interlocutors and with an impressively sculpted black beard. Ivor's attention was drawn to the thick gold chain around his neck and the oversized medallion it carried with the pietà image of Jesus in Mary's lap.

Baron, dutifully disdainful, waved his hand in their direction.

"Sometimes it seems as if the whole of Mesopotamia is here," he said, and then, as if to find an exit from the region he had conjured, added, "Missing Oxford? Missing London?"

"Not so far," Ivor said.

Baron's eyes lit up. "She really has dug her nails into you, hasn't she? You know, when your father asked me to take you under my wing—"

Baron stopped in midsentence. Sir Douglas Wharton with a small entourage in tow had entered the lobby, and, as if in deference to an imagined misophonia on the high commissioner's part, his arrival hushed for a moment the clink of glasses, the clatter of dishes, the scrape of cutlery, and all conversation.

"Well," Baron continued, "I should probably go over and pay my respects to our commander in chief."

He rose from his chair, and then to Ivor's surprise, Baron offered a tribal communication in Yiddish, as if to undermine the ambient authority of the distinguished presence that had entered their midst: "If I don't see you before the holidays, I wish you *gut yontif*."

Ivor watched Baron hurry across the lobby, then made his way out into the dusty street. Feeling slightly tipsy from the gin and tonics, he walked in the direction of Jaffa Road.

He held two secrets now: his relationship with Tsiona, and Charles Gross's transmuting information, if that was what it was. He knew why he held the first one close, but the second he should surely have revealed to Baron by now. And yet he waited.

Tsiona sent him shopping near the Damascus Gate and instructed him not to return until well after dark. He had wandered for an hour in the sloping market inside the city walls on cobblestones polished by a rare late afternoon shower, picking up a jar of milk at one stall, oranges from a vine-leaf basket at another. He walked the narrow alleys in the company of Samaritans in long white tunics, Nazarenes in sleeves that ended in

rattling bouquets of sequins, men in floating black mantles followed by veiled women, one of whom carried on her head a basket of roses.

Here and there small groups of Hasidim made their way
quickly in the direction of the wall, their bodies draped in satin,
their heads crowned with round sable caps that seemed better
suited to a Polish winter than the near-relentless sun of the Middle East. And in case the spice-box delights of the city became
too seductive, there were reminders everywhere of poverty and
disease—old men dragging trembling limbs, legless boys on sliding carts, children whose eyes were enlarged and clouded by tra-
choma, overburdened donkeys lurching forward as they were
whipped up narrow stone stairways or chomping straw from
barrows while they dropped balls of shit in a haze of flies, and
over all the hircine stink that emanated from the alleyways.

On his way out of the Old City Ivor ran into a group of British soldiers, six of them squatting on a low stone wall, one adjusting his knee socks, another fidgeting with his helmet. Sweat
dripped from their faces and accumulated on their short-sleeved
shirts in dark stains under their arms. They held their gun barrels
straight up between their knees, stocks to the ground. The men
looked exhausted; two simply stared down, heads hung low as
if they might vomit. With the exception of their sergeant none
of them appeared to be much older than Ivor, and one or two
maybe younger. The soldier seated a little way off from the rest
of the bunch, his nose red, his neck burned above the collar, had
the pocked face of a teenager. He was writing in a small notebook with a pencil, licking the lead tip occasionally to secure a
darker line.

As Ivor approached, two of the soldiers glanced his way.
Immediately, and with absolute certainty, Ivor knew that they
knew he was an English Jew. He had been aware of this instant

registration on the faces of English strangers ever since he was a child. Their antennae were highly sensitive and allowed them to pick up signals from Semitic features even when, as in Ivor's case, they were not particularly evident. In London, as a boy, he had been called a Jew more times than he could remember, sometimes the shout coming from so far across the street that it seemed impossible to have had his facial and bodily characteristics discerned.

Ivor noticed the wry smile on the faces of the two Tommys who had locked eyes with him. One of them looked as if he were about to say something when the sergeant hollered, "All right, you lot, get moving."

The soldiers stood reluctantly and began to collect themselves, taking last swigs from their canteens of water and shouldering their rifles. Only the boy at the end stayed put, scribbling energetically, oblivious to the order.

"Gates, you fucking idiot, what are you doing, writing a novel?"

"It won't have any good bits, Sarge," one of the men said, "he don't know what they are. He's lacking experience." There were a few laughs and Gates, unfazed, closed his notebook.

As the squad prepared to move on, and while the sergeant was looking elsewhere, one of the men touched Ivor on the elbow.

"Got a fag for later?"

Ivor touched his shirt pocket, searching for his pack of cigarettes, but he had left it in Tsiona's flat.

"No smokes?" the soldier said, and then added, almost under his breath, "Shouldn't you be down at the wall doing some wailing?"

There it was, the inevitable moment. Before he could reply (and what really was there to say?), the squad, that small but potent reminder of who ran the show in dusty Palestine, had moved on up the hill in the direction of Jaffa Road. Ivor felt the sting of the remark, but then, as so often, came the mitigating thought: Why should he be aggrieved? All the advantages had been his, the beautiful home, the expensive private school education, Oxford. If England had cursed at him, it had also blessed him. It seemed to him self-evident that, whatever barbs might come his way, he was more at home among the gentiles in the country of his birth than among the Jews of the Promised Land.

He followed the troop at a distance up al-Zahra Street, past the Notre Dame center and the French hospital. At the corner of Jaffa Road, he paused while the cindery dusk gathered around him. Against Ivor's expectation the setting sun brought no relief from the heat. Perhaps he should delay his return with a drink at the bar of the Hotel Fast? He hesitated a moment by the revolving door beneath the draped Union Jack and the new German flag with its arrogant swastika, before walking on. Why risk bumping into anyone and having to account for his presence in Jerusalem?

As the first three stars appeared in the sky, he returned to Tsiona, holding the string bag that bulged with his purchases: flatbread, fruit, the milk, ripe tomatoes, goat cheese, oranges, and two bottles of wine.

They were sequestered now, walled in by the night as the noise of the city subsided to a murmur. Only the loud wail of stray cats and the occasional cough and spit of an engine starting up punctuated the silence.

She was sitting on the floor drawing in charcoal on a large piece of paper; lines of varied thickness and intensity resolved into hills, houses, a distant minaret, tiny figures in the foreground.

Ivor dropped his shopping bag to the floor, moved behind

her, knelt, and kissed the nape of her neck. Her hand continued to move on the paper but then she stopped and turned to kiss him on the mouth. The heat shunted in waves through the open windows; she touched his face, left a black smudge on his cheek, and then his beautiful, utterly compromised witness reached to unbuckle his belt. Ivor closed his eyes.

They lay entangled on her bed and he breathed in her hair. When she stirred and turned on her back, he propped himself up on his elbows and kissed her eyes. She smiled, keeping them closed, and rolled back onto her side.

Ivor rose naked from the bed, made his way to the toilet, lifted the hard wooden seat, and pissed. Through a narrow window he saw a combustible dawn spread across the sky. Next to the window his unshaven face, eyes red and puffy, crease lines from the sheets etched into his cheeks, stared at him from her mirror. He flushed the toilet and stood back. He barely recognized himself, as if the events of the last few weeks had altered his physiognomy, in addition to redirecting his inner life. Until his arrival in Palestine, he had imagined that he knew, with varying degrees of certainty, where he was going. Now he was adrift without a compass.

The taps squeaked when he turned them on, and the pipes gurgled. Ivor splashed his face with water, spread a line of toothpaste on his finger, and applied it to his teeth and tongue. On the tiled floor next to the sink a small wastebasket held a cache of Hebrew and English newspapers. Ivor had noticed these necessary reserves elsewhere in Palestine: Toilet paper was not always that easy to find. He plucked a copy of *The Palestine Post* from the basket. There, on a front page dated two months earlier, was a photograph of Arlosoroff's body lying on a long slab and covered in what appeared to be a striped blanket, although it might have been a prayer shawl. Three men stood at attention over the corpse. Deeply tanned, they all wore short-sleeved shirts that bore different but indecipherable insignia and flat caps. One of these honor guards, dressed all in white, wore a belt whose buckle was a metal Star of David. The men stared straight ahead and not down at Arlosoroff's head where it rested on a pillow, the only part of his body that was exposed, mouth open, eyes closed. A long bouquet of wildflowers stretched almost from Arlosoroff's chest to his feet. In a corner of the room two women sat. Ivor imagined that they were Arlosoroff's widow and his mother, but their faces were blurred in the photograph and he couldn't be certain.

He brought the newspaper with him, sat at the kitchen table, stared at the photograph, then read down. The official police blotter describing the suspects had been reprinted in the paper.

> The one who held the flashlight: *Suspect Number 1:* Male, taller than average, large build, age 30–40, clean shaven, full face, light skinned, tough expression, brownish-reddish hair, stands with legs apart, has a duck-like walk. Wearing a dark suit in a European style—black or dark blue—and the stitching may be in a "double-breasted" style. Collar or long tie. Wearing shoes, speaks without accent.
>
> The one who shot the gun: *Suspect Number 2:* Male, short, stout body, age 30, dark Oriental type, long nose, unshaven, tough expression, dark hair, wearing a

dark suit in a European style with irregular
stripes. We think that he is wearing a gray
hat and shoes. He makes Oriental movements with his hands.

The police were offering a five-hundred-liroth reward to
anyone with information about the suspects. The Jewish Agency
was pitching in with an additional thousand.

Ivor had read this information before, but for some reason
he had never seen the photograph. Baron had oddly omitted
to mention its existence. But what was there to glean from it?
Only, from Ivor's admittedly skewed diasporic experience, its
strange secularity; where was the rabbi, and the *shomer,* who (he
knew from the funeral of his grandfather) should have been sitting with the deceased to recite psalms? And the flowers, Ivor
remembered very well that there were not supposed to be any at
a Jewish funeral; flowers, his father had once explained with his
favored ironic sweep, were how the gentiles tried to pretty up
death instead of facing it head-on. But here in Jewish Palestine,
the state-in-waiting inside a state, different rules applied. Post-
mortem Arlosoroff belonged to the socialists.

Ivor looked across the room to Tsiona's sleeping body. Did
it even matter that she withheld information, presented half-
truths, concealed more than she revealed? She offered, he felt,
small rounded certainties that existed inside the larger circle
of her fabrications. In the end, nothing she said, true or false,
had any effect on the scope of his passion. In any case, if Charles
Gross was right (and how Ivor wished that was the case) they
wouldn't need her in court. And then what would he do? Stay in
Palestine forever? Never leave this flat?

"Too early," she murmured when he returned to the bed.
He watched her as she fell back to sleep; for a few moments her

hand moved on the mattress as if she were executing a dream sketch and the sheet were her drawing pad. Then she turned into him, curled under his arm, and rested her head on his shoulder.

"I was in Tel Aviv that day," Tsiona said, "the day after the murder."

They sat opposite each other in her kitchen area with what remained of breakfast on the table before them. Tsiona looked again at the photograph in the newspaper that Ivor had retrieved from the wastebasket and returned to her attention.

"The crowd was enormous, it felt as if every home in the town had emptied out."

"The police said seventy thousand to one hundred thousand; that is double just about everybody, isn't it?"

Tsiona laughed. "There must have been a few more like me who came down from Jerusalem. They arrested Stavsky the next day."

Ivor tore off a piece of flatbread, then took a sip of his tea. "Yes," he said, "the immigration clerk Halutz identified him from the photo on his exit visa petition, said Stavsky had been there on the day of the murder, that he wanted to withdraw his application. You watch, Baron will make mincemeat of him in court."

Ivor felt no qualms now about discussing the case with her. In for a penny, in for a pound.

"Do you understand," she said, "that everyone in the country is watching this case? Do you realize what this means for anyone who testifies? I am a very private person. You don't think so, but I am. I enjoy my solitude, I value it; that is one reason I was so angry that you followed me to Safed."

"But you weren't alone."

Tsiona sighed. "He doesn't bother me. We do our work."

"And you would choose solitude and anonymity over saving the lives of two innocent men?"

Tsiona hesitated. Outside two black and white hoopoe birds swooped across her balcony, settled for a moment in the plum tree that hung over the climbing geraniums, then took off again. The morning uncoiled in its ambient quiet. In London, in Oxford, the Jewish New Year had been just another day lost in the cacophony of transport and busyness, and the local Jews made their way to synagogue through the melee of city life, but here you didn't hear a car horn or a police whistle, no squeal of brakes, no tram or trolley sparks, only the occasional clops of a donkey's hooves, which, as it diminished, only served to amplify the silence.

"If I thought they weren't guilty . . ." Her voice, almost a whisper, trailed away.

"Do you *know* they are guilty? Do you know that for a fact?"

She looked away from him. "I can't remember when I drew them. I'm telling you the truth."

"So, they are not sketches you made from the police photographs."

Tsiona let out a small cry of exasperation. "You know I was just saying that. I wish you would leave me alone."

But he couldn't. He knew enough, however, to shift the direction of the conversation. She was volatile, and he was afraid of her anger.

"What made you attend the funeral?"

Tsiona smiled at him, the reward, he knew, for allowing her to evade questions that she didn't want to answer. "I was curious. I was neither in mourning for Mr. Arlosoroff nor there to show political solidarity, although I do have it. I simply wanted, well, *to see*."

"And what did you see?"

Shortly after Ivor's arrival in Palestine, Baron had described to him, with some excitement, the river of people that had meandered behind the pallbearers; the scalding heat of the sun and the way it had been deflected by an admixture of umbrellas, pith helmets, caps, and what Baron had referred to as "funny hats"; the eight wreaths, each one borne by members of a different political or trade union group; the British ministers keeping up appearances in their dark suits or military outfits; the Zionists, informal in short-sleeved shirts and some of them even in shorts. "Bit disrespectful really," Baron had said, his register suggesting the way that, in this branch of the country, those who were supposed to be building it up continued to let him down.

Tsiona had risen from her seat and now she presented Ivor with a large loose-leaf sketchpad. He flicked through; there were the umbrellas viewed from above, the serpentine crowd, and even a page of figures in loose tunics and "funny hats," which turned out to be fezzes with black tassels.

"Where were you?" Ivor asked.

"At a friend's apartment, on Allenby. She had a room that looked over the street."

Ivor took his time with each sketch. Only the last one brought him up short. There he was again, her "friend" from Jerusalem and Safed.

"He was there with you?"

"Shouldn't he have been? Did you even know me then?"

"Was he also curious?"

Tsiona removed the sheaf of drawings from the table and carefully slid them into a cardboard portfolio.

"Enough," she said.

.   .   .

Two white burning days. While half the city prayed communally in the hope that their names would be inscribed in the Book of Life for the coming year, his own temple was a bed.

In the early mornings when he opened the door to the flat's broad balcony he could see her in the garden, barefoot in a white dress with a red sash around her waist, sprinkling plants with an old watering can. The sun rose watercolor pink over the deserted art school next door, its courtyard dotted with benches and gnarled olive trees.

Bread on her kitchen table, sprinkled parsley, and olive oil dripped on tomatoes and cucumbers—the most basic food tasted ambrosial to him. Tea was nectar. When he lay half-asleep on the bed in the torpid afternoon, she asked him not to move, sketched him rapidly. He closed his eyes, felt himself borne up by waves, floating. And on those occasions when, after making love, he woke before her, he simply sat in the wicker chair by her bed, watched her, and waited.

From time to time, he selected a book from the shelves at the far end of the room; his choice of volumes in English was limited, and in any case, he preferred the thin catalogs that she had acquired in France, which featured painters he had never heard of, some wild and expressive, others masters of geometric constructions, angles superimposed on clear-cut rounded lines. But he could only concentrate weakly on these images before turning his attention back to the sleeping figure in the bed: her face, half-turned into the pillow; her hair, which he had stroked, tugged, and raked his fingers through, tousled and covering one eye; the curve of her breast above the sheet.

He knew it couldn't last. As night fell on the second day the ram's horn would sound in synagogues all over Jerusalem, to both announce the end of the New Year and break his trancelike state. The city would come alive in a crescendo of activity: The whir and sputter of engines, an orchestra of carpet beaters out on their balconies spanking the dust from household rugs, guttural street calls, buses hurtling through the streets, the rumble of handcarts—everything would conspire to cut him off from her.

"What now?" he said.

Once again, they faced each other across the kitchen table. It was the first time since Ivor had entered the flat that they had both been fully clothed.

Tsiona cut an apple into wedges and pushed the plate toward him.

"You'll come back," she said.

"Do you want me to?"

She looked away from him and murmured, unconvincingly he thought, "Of course I want you to." But then, as always, the beguiling smile, and his anxiety was smothered, contained.

"When?"

"When the trial is over."

"I can't wait that long."

"Oh, Ivor, are you going to pine for me? You're a sweet man."

He didn't want to be a sweet man. He wanted her to love him as much as he loved her. He wasn't sure if she was capable of it; he saw how she bridled at attachment or what she conceived as any kind of demand for reciprocation. Drained but deliriously happy, he had made the mistake as they lay in bed of whispering the magic words. She had been happy to hear them, but she was not going to repeat them back to him. "Yes," she'd said, "you love me."

"Come to Tel Aviv," he said. "You came for the funeral, why not now?"

"I have work to do and I *don't* want to be disturbed. I'm having an exhibition at the end of October, at the Herzliya Gymnasia in Tel Aviv. It's my first solo exhibition. I'm not even close to ready."

"What will you show?"

"You want to know if you will be there on the wall, lounging in my bed?"

"No . . . I wasn't thinking about . . . I mean . . ."

"It's portraits, all portraits."

Ivor looked around the room. The man with the orange hair had not moved from his position on her easel.

"So . . . he . . . ?"

"Yes, that will be in it."

"What's his name?"

"It won't help you to know."

A divisive ray of sun ran a gold line across the floor and bisected the table. Tsiona lit a cigarette and Ivor watched its violet smoke twist upward.

"Tell me."

"Yosef."

"Everyone here is called Yosef."

Tsiona shrugged and, as if to make up for her insufficient response, added, "I'll come to you before the show. You can help me to bring over the paintings."

"Is that what I'm good for?"

She laughed. "You should go," she said. "Your Mr. Baron will be wondering where you've been."

"He will, and he'll want to know what you told me. He's invited me to his house to break the fast on Sunday, more an order than an invitation, and I'm sure he'll corner me then."

"Let's say it wasn't them, let's say it couldn't have been, that I drew them right at the moment that the shots were fired. Let's say Sima Arlosoroff was wrong to pick them out in a lineup, that they had never heard a single speech in which a Revisionist politician called for Haim Arlosoroff's assassination, never saw the fist and heard the shout, never read the manifesto of the Sicarii that was found in Stavsky's room. Do you know about that? It was written by the Jewish assassins from Masada who murdered Jewish leaders accused of consorting with the Roman enemy. Let's say all this was the case, and still it wasn't them. Then I want to ask you, who was it?"

Ivor cradled his face in his hands and stared at her. "We'll find out," he said.

"You know that Arlosoroff refused protection, don't you? Do you know why? Do you know what he said?"

Ivor shook his head.

"He said, 'No Jew would kill me.' But he was wrong, wasn't he?"

"I don't know," Ivor said. "Perhaps he was right."

Tsiona pushed the plate with the quartered apple away from her in annoyance. "What do you want from me?" she said.

"I want you to tell me the truth."

By the time Ivor arrived in Rehavia, the front room of Baron's ground-floor flat on Rambam Street was already crowded and noisy. A table had been set for the hungry, and those pretending to be—orange juice, sliced bread, cheese, olives, smoked salmon, and, in a nod to both solemn observance and colonial merriment, wine and whiskey.

As soon as Baron spotted Ivor he came across the room, took him by the elbow, guided him into a corner, and began to identify the guests. *Tout* Jerusalem turned out to be significantly different from Tsiona's Bohemian set: women in dowdy frocks; men in dark suits, white shirts, and ties; Europe's dress code a futile act of resistance to Middle East weather. There were politicians, stalwart members of the legal profession, academics and their wives, British Jews whose names were familiar to Ivor—men, by and large, who wielded power in the Mandate administration, in the courts or at the university, and yet men whose status was always somehow cautious and provisional, dependent, as it was, on the perception that they remained unbiased, evenhanded, neutral, and dispassionate in their treatment of Palestinian Jews and Arabs alike.

Baron had a word to say about most of his guests, quick summaries that he offered to Ivor sotto voce. "There's Bentwich, lost the attorney general position a couple of years ago, some colonial undersecretary accused him of 'perceived Zionist bias,' 'unsuited to the peculiar racial and political conditions of Palestine.' Bentwich more or less gave us a new rubric for Palestinian law, added a British inflection, and got rewarded with a brush-off. Problem is Jabotinsky's lot don't like him any better than they like the Arabs, they think he's soft on them; naïve; lover of peace, harmony, and rapprochement. Powers that be shunted him into a chair of international relations at the university. And talking of which, there is Judah Magnes, that august institution's chancellor; perhaps you've heard that our people's presiding genius, Professor Einstein, does not exactly hold him in high regard. Called him 'weak and incapable,' 'a failed American rabbi,' resigned from the board in protest at his appointment. That tall woman in the prim dress he's chatting with is Bentwich's sister Margery, and in the spinsterish outfit, her constant friend the violinist woman, can't remember her name, they call the two of them the Believers, can't for the life of me remember why. I suppose they must be fanatical about something or other. Oh, and there in the corner is my favorite philo-Semite, Clarissa Barlow, yes, sister of the poet, holds literary soirées with the local German-speaking Jews, she's a Christian Scientist, so don't get ill in her house, you'll never come out."

Baron was clearly enjoying himself, and never more so than when he introduced Ivor to Hillel Schosberger, a tall, stick-thin, stooped individual with a shock of white hair, interrupting him at the point where he had just taken a bite of his smoked salmon sandwich. "I believe, if I'm not mistaken, that the good doctor here was analyzed by Herr Freud himself. Perhaps you'd like to take this opportunity to relay to him some of your more notable and striking dreams, Ivor? His office is a stone's throw from the railway station." Schosberger, who had clearly been ribbed by Baron before, fixed him with a cold eye and said, "Perhaps you should make an appointment to visit me yourself, Phineas."

Unlike Tsiona's party, where Ivor had been relentlessly pestered about the Arlosoroff case, Baron's guests, whether out of politeness toward their host or a common commitment to a certain kind of proper behavior, strictly evaded the subject of the murder. In fact, with that topic so assuredly off the table, they evinced such little interest in Ivor that he soon found himself quite alone.

He moved toward a window and pushed it open, breathed in the night air. Baron's flat was only a five-minute walk from Tsiona's. Exiled from her presence, he had thus far accepted the terms of their agreement and had suffered through eight dull, aimless days in Tel Aviv before returning to Jerusalem at Baron's behest. He could leave now and run to her. Surely, she would let him in.

Someone tapped a knife on a wineglass and the room subsided into silence. Dr. Magnes, chest puffed out in the waistcoat of his finely tailored gray three-piece suit, stood before the food table as if to bar access. He began by graciously thanking his hosts, especially Mrs. Baron, and then, with an actor's—or perhaps it was a conjurer's—flair for the dramatic, announced that he had something to say that would thrill everybody present. There was a soft murmur of anticipation in the room, yet Ivor could tell that among the British guests there was already an established sense that "thrill" was going too far, an unfortunate expression of American overexuberance.

"I'm delighted to let you know," Magnes began, "that within

days we shall have thirteen new professors arriving from Germany, distinguished gentlemen all, scientists, linguists, philosophers, mathematicians, and two historians of the Hebrew Bible, who will become, I'm sure, immediately valued colleagues of our very first professor of Jewish mysticism, Professor Gershom Scholem, whom you all know." Here, Magnes stopped and looked around the room in search of the great scholar of Kabbalah, but it seemed that Professor Scholem had preferred to break his fast elsewhere. Slightly peeved, it seemed, Magnes continued on, "All these men are German Jews who have been callously removed from their academic positions on no other grounds than that they happen to be Jews."

Ivor listened but his mind was elsewhere. Magnes explained the sources of the funding, the untangling of bureaucracy—everything that had gone into enabling this event that was at once an act of rescue and a blessing for the university.

Now, Ivor thought, as soon as Magnes ends his speech, I will leave, but there was no escape. Baron was at his side, pressing a tumbler of whiskey into Ivor's hand.

"And this," he said, "is why our shining university on a high mount will forever be known as 'the last great German university.' Einstein is for enlisting young scholars, you know, not the old and famous. Nevertheless, of course he wouldn't oppose, can't let these people languish in Hitler's Germany if it's at all possible to get them out, can we?"

From across the room Mrs. Baron waved at her husband, her urgent gesture appended to the peal of a telephone from another room. Baron disappeared, only to reappear by Ivor's side within moments, clearly agitated.

"You have to return to Tel Aviv immediately," he said.

Ivor felt the night fall in on him. "Tonight?"

"Yes, tonight. You can't wait till tomorrow, in case there's some delay come morning. You have a meeting at the Jaffa police station first thing. Something urgent has come up and they can't tell me what it is over the phone because the officer in charge has gone home, only that it's bloody important. So, you have to be there. As soon as you find out what's going on, you let me know. Now, off you go. Don't worry, I'll say your goodbyes to Mrs. Baron for you."

Ten minutes later Ivor was standing in Tsiona's walled garden under her dark plum tree, staring up at the tangled geraniums in her window boxes, all the intoxicants of the night returned. There was no light visible in her flat. Surely, too early for her to be asleep. He took the steps up to the second floor at a run and knocked on her door. No answer. He waited, listened, thought he heard someone moving inside, then knocked again, louder this time. Suddenly, his jealousy was exasperated to the highest pitch and he was sure she was in there with Yosef. He banged once more on the door, but she didn't answer.

12

Ivor had been waiting for Duncan Prendergast, the only British officer at the Jaffa station, in his small office at police headquarters for more than an hour. Outside he could see the sky dropping lower, ready to release a rare autumn rain. Before entering he had spent a few moments staring over the milky-blue sea trying to collect his thoughts while gulls wheeled and dipped overhead, their cries almost lost in the crash of waves.

There was a copy of *The Palestine Police Magazine* on the desk, and Ivor had already picked it up, perused it, and thrown it down three times. He stared at the plaster walls, striated brown, as if someone had emptied their morning cups of tea onto them from an elevated position. A photograph of the king in uniform, sashed, tasseled, and bemedaled, his thin hair parted, gray beard carefully trimmed, hung on the wall behind the desk. Next to it a desultory Huntley and Palmer's Biscuits calendar dangled askew from a nail. The image on display showed Tower Bridge shrouded in mist. Ivor rose from his chair to take a closer look: *London in the Fog* by Lesser Ury. Ivor had never heard of the artist.

Apparently, Prendergast had stopped flipping the pages several months ago; he was stuck on March.

The telephone rang twice, then stopped. Ivor couldn't wait like this any longer. He needed to find out what was going on, but as he opened the door, he almost bumped into Prendergast on his way in.

Prendergast oversaw a mixed company of Jews and Arabs as they went about their business fulfilling the duties of a constabulary. Now he skipped deftly past Ivor, took his seat behind the desk, placed his white police hat with its black brim in front of him, took out a pack of cigarettes, repositioned the glass ashtray, lifted his overstuffed briefcase to the desk, removed a folder of documents, and set it down.

"So, Mr. Castle, I am obliged to show you these, and please read in the order I give them to you."

Prendergast, who was probably only a few years older than Ivor, had already developed an enviable air of authority. He sat up very straight, his hair smoothed down with Brylcreem and bisected in the middle, his blue belted tunic impeccably pressed, the silver buttons and the insignia on his round collar burnished to a shine. Only the bags under his gray eyes betrayed the toll that keeping order in Mandate Palestine must have taken on him, while the eruption of freckles across his nose and on his cheeks lent him the look of a schoolboy who had ignored his mother's warning to stay out of the sun.

He extracted several pages from the folder and pushed them across his desktop to Ivor, then leaned back and lit a cigarette. "You'll see that what you have in your hands is a confession. Don't say anything yet, just examine the document. I can't let you sit here all day so please read as quickly as you can. I've already had carbons made for you to take away."

Ivor, startled, suppressed his desire to question Prendergast and began to read, his attention steady and fixed. "Statement of Abdul Malik el-Hindi el-Boukhari of Jaffa, aged seventeen years, a mechanic." Abdul Malik was in the Central Prison in Jerusalem pending trial on a different recent murder—not Arlosoroff's, but the knifing and shooting in Jaffa of someone named Lufti. Nevertheless, he was taking this opportunity to put the record straight on Arlosoroff. He described how, accompanied by his former friend Issa Kurkar on a random seashore walk, he had waylaid "the Jew and the Jewess" on the Tel Aviv beach. Abdul Malik's story, in its particulars, more or less reiterated what was already known, albeit with a slightly different cast of characters: It was a starlit night, the two assailants had passed "the Jew and the Jewess" twice earlier in the evening, the torch, the question about the time; Abdul Malik had stopped to urinate near the Muslim cemetery, then, not far past the Casino, he had become tired of walking and wanted to go home. According to Malik, it was Issa who'd fired the shot that killed Arlosoroff, and then they both ran away in the direction of the cemetery. After they escaped the scene Malik asked Issa why he had shot the Jew. Issa replied that he "intended to frighten him by pointing the revolver at him so that he might run away and leave [them] alone with the woman," but on seeing Dr. Arlosoroff advance, although they didn't know it was Dr. Arlosoroff at the time, he thought that he would attack him, and he fired.

As if to add a coating of authenticity, Abdul Malik's confession was flecked with color, a feature entirely absent from other reports: Malik was wearing a blue jacket, blue trousers, striped shirt, multicolored tie, old black shoes; he didn't remember whether he had removed the rubber heels from them or not; he was bareheaded. Issa sported a khaki jacket and khaki trousers; Arab shirt, striped, unbuttoned at the top; native black shoes (balga); and an old faded hat that had lost its shape without band and no lining.

There were several more pages, and Ivor, both disturbed and excited, barely took it all in. At the bottom the statement was signed in Arabic and dated September 6, 1933. Mr. Zvi Rosen, a clerk in the Criminal Investigation Department, confirmed that he had accomplished the translation into English.

In Ivor's imagination the night on the beach coalesced in bruised darkness; once more, he could hear the waves lapping as the shot was fired, smell the clean air of the open sea. Here, it seemed, was the end of the case. But Prendergast was pushing more pages across the table.

"Before you say anything, read this one."

The new document that Ivor now held in his hands was dated the seventh of September 1933 and its location was noted as the same jailhouse in Jaffa where Abdul Malik had been held when, only a day earlier, he had confessed to murdering Arlosoroff. Now he offered a fresh statement that began quite differently:

I was in Jaffa lockup when a Jew came to my cell and introduced himself to me by the name of Stavsky. He asked me, "Did you admit the murder of Lufti for which you are charged?" I told him yes, that Issa and I had committed the offense together. He said, "All right, as long as you have confessed of this, if you had killed ten or one it is all the same." He continued, saying, "You resemble me and your friend resembles a friend of mine, a short man. You will admit that you have killed Dr. Arlosoroff and we will pay you money. We will give you money and we will appoint you advocates from abroad." I told him I would see later and think the matter over. The next morning, I accepted on condition that they will give LP 1,000 to me and my friend Issa. I told him, "If we say that we killed Dr. Arlosoroff, how could we relate the story?" He told me what to say.

Ivor read on. What followed was a detailed description of the narrative passed on to Abdul Malik. "They even made a sketch of the scene and explained to me the position of the cemetery and the public way." Occasionally, he interpolated an additional exculpatory detail: "I do not even own a torch light." The retraction concluded: "Read over to him and certified correct." Signed, witnessed, and dated.

After he turned the last page, Ivor broke into a heavy sweat. A young Arab man had confessed to the murder and then, within twenty-four hours, he had retracted. It felt as though the walls of the room were perspiring too, as if at any moment the office itself might metamorphose into King Kong's jungle and Ivor would be lost in the undergrowth, hunched under broad fronds with his back against a tree, soaked by curtains of rain.

"This is absurd."

Prendergast offered a thin smile.

"And why didn't you inform us on Sunday?"

"Jewish holiday. My understanding was that Mr. Baron and yourself were not to be contacted until after sundown last night."

"A man confesses to the murder of which our clients are accused, and you don't get in touch. It's unconscionable."

Prendergast shrugged. "But as you see, the same man retracted his confession shortly afterward."

"Well, precisely. What the hell is going on here? We should have been alerted to his confession immediately."

"Mr. Castle, I certainly wasn't going to send one of my Muslim policemen rushing into a synagogue on one of your holy days shouting that an Arab had owned up to shooting Haim Arlosoroff."

"I wasn't in synagogue."

Prendergast raised his eyebrows. "Naughty, naughty. I won't ask where you were. Was known to skip chapel on occasion myself."

"Who is this Abdul Malik character?"

"He's a short-, soon to be long-term, resident of our facility or another one just like it. He recently got involved in a fracas with a young man who had apparently propositioned his sister in an unseemly manner, and he stabbed him to death. The claim is self- and self-righteous defense, but good fellow that he is, and as you see, he has owned up to the killing."

Ivor's head was spinning. Charles Gross's face—expanded, puffy, laterally sliced by a shaft of light—orbited into view. He had given Ivor advance warning of the confession to come, and here it was, but despite his oracular certainty, he apparently had no idea that a retraction would follow on its heels twenty-four hours later.

"Can I meet with Mr. Malik?"

"Not now, I'm afraid. They carted him off to hospital for an X-ray."

"Is he ill?"

"No. It's standard procedure with someone in his situation. We're not quite sure how old he is. He says seventeen, but we haven't been able to track down a birth record. No death penalty for the under-eighteens, as you must know. Lucky bastards. We're checking his bone age. Quick look at the wrist, hand, and fingers and the docs can more or less pinpoint your birthday. It's been scheduled for a while."

Ivor held up the pages. "I'll need to keep these."

"Not those. I'll fetch you that set of carbons."

"And when can we see him?"

"I imagine you'll have to ask his lawyers about that. I suspect they'll want to be there, don't you?"

"Have you told the prosecution?"

"I have informed the attorney general, Mr. Cunningham, and his assistant Musa Effendi el-Alami (OBE, I might add)."

"How long have they known?"

"Oh, longer than you, by what? A day and a half."

"So, you reported to them after the confession but before the retraction."

"I believe that is correct. No synagogue problem, you see."

"And what was their reaction?"

"I seem to remember that Mr. Cunningham laughed."

"And after the retraction?"

"He and Mr. el-Alami both laughed."

"Well, it's extremely serious."

"Didn't you say it was absurd?"

"Absurd that you didn't notify us immediately."

"We do our best to respect religious beliefs. I mean, if not here in the Holy Land, then where? All our Jewish policemen had the days off."

Ivor shifted uncomfortably in his chair. Prendergast had turned on his desk fan, angling it carefully away from his papers. The cool air caught the side of Ivor's face. For all of Prendergast's glib self-assurance, Ivor wasn't persuaded by his story. Surely there had to have been a way for him to contact Baron, if not Ivor, over Yom Kippur. Someone had engineered those extra days for the prosecution, and the prosecution was the government.

"And where is Mr. Malik's friend Issa, his supposed accomplice?"

"As I'm sure you're aware, we are somewhat undermanned at

this garrison. But we're looking for him. Probably hightailed it into Transjordan sporting his proud tarboosh."

"Unless he doesn't exist."

"That's also a possibility." Prendergast stood up and extended his hand. "Apologies, but duty calls. I have no doubt we'll be meeting again soon. I assume I don't need to remind you of the need to keep this matter confidential. We don't want a riot on our hands."

Ivor nodded, and then to his surprise Prendergast added, "Perhaps we could get a drink sometime? We few, we happy few . . . and so on."

Ivor mumbled a half-hearted affirmative response; his mind was elsewhere, far from any notion of a pleasant evening socializing with Prendergast.

He waited for the desk sergeant to bring him the carbons and then he walked slowly down the long windowless corridor and out into the clarifying air. The rain clouds appeared to be maneuvering into position to burst but for the moment held off. Ivor walked north away from Jaffa. The sea to his left had turned gray and threw up steams of spray over the shoreline wall. He passed soda kiosks and rest stands. Hardly anyone was around; the dullness of the day seemed to have driven the local populace indoors. Two men on horseback cantered past him on the dunes, their rides kicking the sand behind them into a dance, and then, with the exception of a small fishing boat heading out toward the horizon, he was alone.

13

Ivor had an hour to kill before his scheduled meeting with Baron. He sat on his bed, back against the headboard, the sheaf of carbon papers scattered around him. The gray clouds had lifted and through his window Ivor watched fresh wisps of white emerge against a background that grew bluer by the minute. First and foremost, he had planned to seek out Charles Gross at the Anglo-Palestine Company, but by the time of his arrival at the building on Herzl Street Charles had departed for the day and no one knew where he was.

He shuffled once more through the pages and began to reread them, this time slowly and carefully. If Ivor had not already known about the retraction that followed, the attention to detail in the confession would have been exhilarating, the greatest gift the defense could wish for, and yet, as it was, it only came across as utterly baffling. On the one hand it seemed impossible that anyone could have "learned" to describe the events leading up to and including the murder if they hadn't at the very least witnessed them: The story was too intricate, the match with so many aspects of Sima Arlosoroff's account of that terrible night irresistible. And yet, the retraction was equally persuasive, entirely plausible, and to compound the problems, both accounts appeared to emerge from the darkest conspiratorial alleys, where ominous forces that Ivor could hardly begin to comprehend congregated in the shadows.

On the Friday night in question Abdul Malik and Issa had attended a show of the Egyptian athlete Mukhtar Hussein at the Muslim sports ground at al-Barriyeh in Jaffa. At the oddly precisely defined time of five-thirty p.m. (odd because they had no watch), the two young men had begun their walk to the Neve Shalom Quarter and on toward Tel Aviv. Their landmarks ticked off: the Eden, Ophir, and Mograbi cinemas; the Casino; the seashore opposite the baths; the Muslim cemetery; and, near this last site, yes, they had passed "a Jew and a Jewess" walking together. From then on everything proceeded as Mrs. Arlosoroff had described, including Abdul Malik's stop for a piss, except that the players were two young Arab men instead of two not-quite-so-young Jewish men.

It was already dark; Abdul Malik took a poetic turn, stating, "Midsummer, we sat near a wooden house." Yes, Abdul Malik asked Arlosoroff in Hebrew for the time, and the Jew obligingly allowed him to illuminate his watch with his torch. Malik saw a wave of fear pass over Arlosoroff's face, for behind him Issa held a revolver in his hands. "I shone my torch on Issa. The Jew stepped forward and I was frightened and stepped backward. Issa fired a shot and ran toward the cemetery and after a moment I ran away too in the same direction." Exigently, his path to escape took the same route as the footprints identified by the police, across the Abd al-Nabi cemetery and into the vineyard before they stopped at the asphalt road near Sarona that would return the killers to Jaffa.

And now Ivor noted more details that he had somehow skipped over, hurried as he had been, in Prendergast's office: The gun was a black "Nickel Roos" revolver, and the rounds were "Nickel Roos." Neither assailant knew that the man they had murdered was Dr. Arlosoroff. Three-quarters of an hour elapsed (so precise!) from the time when they first saw Dr. Arlosoroff and his wife until Dr. Arlosoroff was shot. No, Abdul Malik could not describe the victims, it was dark: "I don't know if he had glasses or not . . . stouter than you. He was wearing a European suit. The lady? A little shorter than I. It was dark, I saw nothing. I don't know if she was fat, I think medium build. I cannot say how the woman was dressed, whether she had a hat or not. I don't remember the color of her dress. The Jew was about my height. I don't know if he carried anything, stick or anything else. I don't know if his clothes were light or not." No, he would not be able to identify photographs of Dr. Arlosoroff. Once more Ivor read the chilling ending to the confession: how Issa had pointed the revolver in order to frighten Arlosoroff, "because he wanted his wife and perhaps the man would run from her and Issa would have intercourse with her," but on seeing Dr. Arlosoroff advance, "he thought he would attack him and he fired."

A black cockroach the size of Ivor's thumb scuttled across the floor and disappeared under the bed. Ivor dropped his papers and, in a futile effort to crush it, leaned down, picked up one of his shoes, and chucked it after the insect. There were moments, and this was one of them, when he hated Palestine and felt shudders of resentment toward his father for having recommended that he come out here. He was aware that the place distorted certain personalities. He could see, for example, how a kind of astringent misanthropy had settled upon Baron, and he hoped that wouldn't happen to him, but the stifling humidity, as if the swampy malarial heat from the country's north had gifted its residue to Tel-Aviv-on-Sea; the political turmoil; the seething resentments of Arabs and Jews glued together in a manner they absolutely didn't want to be by their British supervisors; the heady infusion of religion that rose up from the country's various and competing spiritual omphali as tendriled smoke, then unpredictably ignited into flame—all this had spawned a shouting, gesturing, argumentative bunch of individuals who couldn't keep still.

Tsiona's home, of course, was a parcel of delights, but so many others that he had seen were just crowded and impoverished. Meanwhile, back in London his father sipped tea on the lawn of his Hamilton Terrace garden, mastered the *Times* crossword puzzle, and observed the roses in their second bloom, everything temperate, the worst that could happen a light shower to send him scampering indoors.

He attempted to plump the thin, lumpy, and entirely inadequate pillow provided by the rooming house and ended up folding it in two to shove between his neck and the headboard. "Like my room at Oxford, only much worse" was how he had described his new domicile to his mother in a letter home—a missive that she would probably never receive. The post office on Allenby, as Ivor surmised from observing its operations over a period of weeks, acted more like a terminal letter drop than a conduit. The mouths of its postboxes functioned like the cracks in the Wailing Wall, where you left your scrawled message to God and hoped for the best.

His eyes rested on the enigmatic end to the confession.

On Saturday we went down to the people who sell
sivziv from the river. We had a lemonade and then Adel
el-Ghalayim, who had a notice on the table, read it, and
explained its contents to us, and said that two persons,
one spoke to Dr. Arlosoroff in Hebrew and the second
approached him and shot him, and if there is a person who could give information against these two persons the Government will pay him 1,000 pounds. Adel
el-Ghalayim told us, "The fishers are in danger to be
caught by the Government because they pass through
that way less be caught [*sic*]."

Ivor had no idea what Abdul Malik was talking about; what
was "sivziv" and why should the "fishers" be afraid? Were they
involved in smuggling of some kind? Were the police running
around all over the neighborhood disrupting their lives and
their livelihoods? For a moment it seemed, Issa, Abdul's mys-
terious accomplice, worried that Abdul Malik might tell Adel
el-Ghalayim the truth about what had happened and that he
would then inform on them and claim the reward. Or worse,
perhaps Abdul Malik would himself go after the money and turn
his friend in. But Malik reassured him:

I did not speak about the matter to Adel el-Ghalayim
or anyone else. I said to him, "No." And the reason
for which I did not inform the government and get
the 1,000 pounds is that I was hearing the people say,
"Whoever gives an information is put in prison." I was
afraid to speak lest I shall be put in prison, and this is my
statement.

A note had been typed at the bottom of the page:

Read over to him, he certified it saying it was recorded accurately.

> Sgd. Abdel Malik el-Boukhari
> Accused
> Jaffa 6 September 1933
> Recorded by me and in my handwriting
> Sgd B. Shitreet, ASP CID

Baron, with a misty beer bottle in his hand, was waiting for Ivor at a table set under a large red umbrella in the garden of the San Remo Hotel. He had chosen a spot at some distance from the other guests, far enough away not to be overheard. Baron wasn't alone. A man in perhaps his early forties, either an Arab or a Jew from an Arab country—Ivor couldn't really tell them apart—occupied the seat next to him.

"This is Fawzi Bahri, and this is my intrepid assistant Ivor Castle, née Schloss."

Fawzi greeted Ivor with a broad smile and a handshake.

"Mr. Bahri," Baron continued, "owns and operates a bookshop, a *maktaba,* in Jaffa, and he is going to help us. In addition to scholarly and cultural books in Arabic and foreign languages, he also sells periodicals and journals, school and business supplies, pens, paper, gifts, toys, and certain invaluable household aids. Anything I've forgotten?"

"The gramophones and the typewriters." Fawzi smiled again, apparently pleased with Baron's iteration of his stock.

"Ah yes, indispensable."

"English typewriters?" Ivor asked. "I could certainly use one."

"English, Arabic, Hebrew—whatever you want. Come to the store. We'll find what you need."

"Very good," Baron said, "but our purpose here is to tap

into Mr. Bahri's considerable network of friends, relatives, and acquaintances, not to mention the gossiping customers who frequent his shop in numbers large enough to have turned him into a wealthy man."

"I wouldn't say that."

"Suffice to say that I am envious of his home, which overlooks the sea and offers a view which makes you understand why some people call Jaffa 'the darling of the waters,' and if, Castle, you are lucky enough to receive an invite chez Bahri, I would suggest that you accept with alacrity."

A waiter who had been meandering in the shade of the garden's umbrellas replenishing drinks and receiving new orders now arrived in front of Baron.

"One more of these," Baron said, waving his beer glass in front of him. "And what about you?" He looked across at Ivor. "Tired from your exertions, need a pick-me-up?" His inference was unmistakable, but Ivor let it pass.

"Yes, coffee please, if you have it."

"Fawzi is going to be our eyes and ears and help us sort through the miasma of twisted, competing narratives that our case appears to have become."

Ivor glanced from Baron to Fawzi. The shopkeeper had a pleasant face, Ivor thought, a slightly bulbous nose, but appealing large dark eyes that appeared magnified by the lenses of his horn-rimmed glasses; his hair was thin, and his mustache too seemed undergrown, aspiring to some Platonic ideal of a mustache, but the overall effect was of an entirely decent individual. It seemed far too hot for the two-piece chalk-striped navy suit that he wore, especially with his shirt collar buttoned to the top and his knotted tie held tight to the collar.

"I am happy to help you, as always."

"Now, Ivor, tell us about Mr. Malik and his crimes."

Ivor, taken aback, faltered for a moment. He looked from one man to the other.

"Well," Baron said, "we're waiting."

"I was asked by Deputy Superintendent Prendergast not to talk about it to anyone, to anyone except for you, that is."

"Young man, if I have asked you to relate what you have learned while Mr. Bahri sits here next to me, you can assume that Mr. Bahri is a gentleman of impeccable character and absolute trustworthiness, not at all the kind of person who might, for example, compromise an important witness, or ignore specific instructions to stay away from same. Otherwise, I would not have asked you to reveal a single word of what passed between you and the good superintendent, now, would I?"

Baron's voice had risen toward the middle of his response, locating a point somewhere between irritation and anger before flattening out at the end, a wave losing its strength as it ran up the shore. He removed his jacket and Ivor noticed the patches of sweat that had accumulated under the arms on his white short-sleeved shirt. The eminent barrister picked up his napkin and dabbed at his brow. "Well?"

Ivor took the carbons from his briefcase.

"No, no, give us the summary. I can read through these pages later."

Ivor parsed Abdul Malik's confession as best he could, looking down to check the typed account. He was interrupted by a series of staccato questions from Baron, as if Ivor himself had taken the witness stand.

It seemed the coffee must have been brewed in Cairo, because it was not until twenty minutes had passed and Baron had exclaimed with a laugh, "Not Nickel *Roos,* Nickel Ross, what idiot took that down?" that a small sweet cup of Arabic coffee was set before Ivor.

"Excellent," Baron said as Ivor concluded his summary of the confession. "We have our killers, case closed. Now let's hear about this ridiculous retraction."

Mr. Bahri, who had remained silent until now, removed his glasses and cleaned them on the as-yet-unused cloth napkin before him.

"Yes, yes," he said, "the athletical show, by Hussein el-Kasri, it was in the 'Barrick' open space behind Iskander Awad Street. My son had wanted to go. Perhaps he did. At least that I can verify."

"Ask him if he saw two young men loitering with intent to murder the most controversial political figure in Palestine."

Fawzi laughed. Ivor wondered if Baron's aristocratic nonchalance was a pose. A role he could easily fill in Palestine, where Jewish identity was fluid and could merge into British as the occasion demanded, especially when there were no gentiles around. Or perhaps he had already acquired his studied dispassion along with his lancing wit at the Inns of Court in London.

"Come on," he said to Ivor, "spill the beans."

"In a nutshell, sir, Abdul Malik was bribed, paid to confess."

"And how was that nefarious deed accomplished?"

"He says it had been in the works for a while. Stavsky apparently came to his cell, asked him if he'd already confessed to the murder of the man who had insulted his sister. When he confirmed that was indeed the case Stavsky said"—and here Ivor paused and shuffled through his sheaf of papers—"'All right, as long as you have confessed of this, if you had killed ten or one it is all the same,' and then he said, 'You resemble me and your friend resembles a friend of mine, a short man, you will admit that you have killed Dr. Arlosoroff and we will pay you money.'"

"Well, the story is certainly direct and to the point, I'll give him that."

"Abdul Malik was to receive a thousand."

"And how did they conduct this jailhouse conversation?"

"In Hebrew, through the bars of the cell."

"In Hebrew?" Baron looked across at Fawzi and both men smiled. "Sounds a little unlikely. I'm sure Mr. Malik has more than a smattering, but our own clients perhaps not so much. They seem to prefer Yiddish or their native Russian."

"Stavsky also promised 'advocates from abroad.'"

"Did he, now? I wonder whom he had in mind. And Mr. Malik agreed, just like that." Baron snapped his fingers in the air, and the waiter, misconstruing the gesture, began to hurry toward the table but Fawzi waved him away.

"No, he thought about it overnight . . . *then* he agreed."

"And there was considerable to-and-froing between cells?"

"There must have been."

"And who facilitated that?"

"It's not clear."

"All right, go on, let's hear it."

"Stavsky tells him exactly what to say."

"Which is the content of the confession."

"Precisely."

"He also tells him that he doesn't have to worry about being executed because he's underage."

"And is he?"

"He's undergoing an X-ray right now."

"But not for the Arlosoroff murder?"

"No." Ivor shifted awkwardly in his chair.

"Meanwhile it seems our clients had the run of the jail, is that right?"

"Yes. Other prisoners were always in their cells, but our men were out of their cells from morning to evening. They were even permitted access to the kitchen."

"And how is this explained?" Baron asked.

"Because they were foreigners."

"Exceptional treatment for foreigners."

"Yes."

"What a nice and polite prison system our colonial officers have established here. I wonder how that would go down in England. 'Here you go, Dr. Crippen, you're an American, please enjoy our special hospitality during your stay at Pentonville. The kitchen? Absolutely, make yourself an omelet, three eggs, no problem.'"

Ivor glanced down at the pages. "Are you sure . . . ?"

"No, go on. I'll read them myself later."

"He mentions that his Hebrew is better than Stavsky's."

"Good for him and good for us."

"But in any case, a translator shows up, chap called Subhi Zabalawi, knows Hebrew, 'married to a Jewess.' He's also on the inside. Together they cover all the details, right down to where he got the torch that he shone on Arlosoroff's watch."

"And who took all this down?"

Ivor glanced down. "An Inspector Nazem Husheimi."

"Do you know him, Fawzi?"

"I know the family, yes."

"Very good. Well . . ." Baron spread his hands wide and Fawzi took this in the way it was intentioned. He stood up from the table. "Everything and anything," Baron said.

"Understood."

After Fawzi had left, Baron took the carbon sheets from Ivor, put on his reading glasses, and began to leaf through. After a few minutes he looked up. "I defended one of Fawzi's sons, you know. He was rowing about just outside the territorial waters of the port of Jaffa in the close vicinity of a felucca laden with hashish: wrong place, wrong time. Two gentlemen from Beirut, captain and mate, were arrested along with a Lebanese barber who was on the boat with them. Never been quite able to figure out why. At any rate, I was able to extricate Khalil Bahri from this unfortunate mess. Does hashish interest you, Castle? Fawzi seems to feel that he is forever in my debt."

Baron turned his attention back to his reading before Ivor could answer. Prior to his arrival in Palestine hashish had not interested him, in fact, he didn't even know what it looked like, but perhaps he would find out now. Undoubtedly Tsiona or one of her friends would be able to aid him in that endeavor.

When he had finished perusing the statements, Baron turned to Ivor. "A question: Did the family indeed access any funds post-confession?"

"On the Friday? I suppose that would be important to know."

"It certainly would, important to know if there even was a deposit." Baron lowered his voice. "But don't look too hard. This might be a search that we should leave to the prosecution for a while, a good long while."

Ivor drained the dregs of his coffee, its sweetness turning bitter on his tongue. "What will happen now?"

"Unfortunately, we will have to request an identification parade."

"Why unfortunately?"

"Because I have no confidence that Sima Arlosoroff will wish to recognize the Arab or Arabs who she initially assured the police had waylaid and shot her husband. Although, of course, she denies it now. She is, to put it bluntly, and I shall argue this strongly, in the pocket of both the Mapai, Ben-Gurion's Labour Party lot, those stalwart Zionists of the factory and the land, who wish to damage beyond repair their Revisionist opponents, and our beloved Mandatory power, who would much prefer some infighting between Jews to an all-out conflict between Jews and Arabs."

"But will we have to support the identification parade?"

"Of course. We would look extremely foolish if we did not. How could we possibly pass up an opportunity to quickly and easily exonerate our clients? In fact, I shall ask for the matter to be expedited. I shall say we want it done this week, if they can tear themselves away from scrutinizing Mr. Malik's radiated bones, that is."

Baron glanced at his watch and drummed his fingers on the table.

"The money," he said, "the inducement to confess, that's the key. More important even than your putative inamorata's timeless sketches."

Ivor spent the late afternoon in fitful sleep, tormented by mosquitoes that penetrated the netting on his window, buzzed his ears, and left small red bite marks on his arms and legs. In his broken dreams he inhabited a local landscape formed thousands of years before kings and prophets, eons before fences and roads and electricity, when the land belonged to no one at all and only some ancient dromedaries awaiting domestication dragged their sad humps through the dunes, sand sliding into miraculous and ever-shifting patterns around them.

When Ivor woke in a sweat he felt, for a moment, utterly lost, as if his personality had been fully erased by the environment his sleeping self had conjured. Two quick bursts from a pneumatic drill on the street outside his room brought him back to the present. He dragged himself from bed and headed for the bathroom to splash water on his face.

For the next three days he more or less kept to his room, venturing out only at mealtimes and for a quick evening stroll late at night when the streets began to empty and the air cooled sufficiently to enable him to walk a hundred yards without breaking into a sweat. He read through both the confession and the retraction repeatedly, wrote letters home, and listened to the radio that Baron had loaned him, handing it over with a great flourish during their first meeting. The set may well have been purloined army issue, as a line from the king's Christmas message, typed on paper browning at the edges, had been glued to the back: "For the men in His Majesty's Forces so cut off by the snow, the desert, or the sea, that only voices out of the air can reach them."

The salient voices, of course, were the plummy but nonetheless steadfast and reassuring tones of the good old BBC Empire Service, which Ivor could pick up if he fiddled around with the shortwave dials for long enough. Sometimes, adjusting the knobs for better reception, he accidentally tuned in to Hitler ranting from Berlin, transmitting his invective around the globe; his voice would come in, wobble on the airwaves, and then be gone.

Otherwise, he eschewed the endless chatter in Hebrew (of which he understood nothing) from Radio Tel Aviv and tuned in to music from the Egyptian capital. He lay naked on his bed as the sun set while drum, tambourine, and a series of beguiling voices held him mesmerized in a way that seemed to make the darkness, when it came, even more intense. He could meet her in the street; he could meet her in a dream.

Late on Thursday afternoon, word came from Baron, via a telephone call he was summoned to take in his landlady's front room, that the identification parade had been scheduled for the following morning at eleven-thirty a.m. Ivor's presence was both requested and required. More than this, the police had located

Abdul Malik's phantom friend Issa. He was real enough to have been dragged out of his aunt's home not a mile from the police station. He had denied any and all knowledge of and involvement in the Arlosoroff murder. "Perhaps," Baron added, "the bribe wasn't sufficiently impressive for him." But he too would participate in an identity parade.

The evening stretched before him. Ivor thought he might go to the cinema, take his chance with whatever was playing. In a worst-case scenario he could always buy another ticket for *King Kong*.

It was almost dark when he made his way down the stairs. On Allenby the asphalt smell of a newly laid stretch of road hung in the air. Ivor stopped at a kiosk, bought a glass of Tizer, and planted himself on a nearby bench where the newly risen dull orange moon cast its light through the branches of a pair of scraggly acacia trees.

Across the street he observed a small crowd of men form, then disappear inside what appeared to be some kind of community hall. More and more individuals, some in uniform, some not, made their way through the open doors, and then he saw, heading toward the building in a slightly grubby white suit, Charles Gross with a young woman on his arm, her face partly obscured as she turned toward her companion, a yellow rose pinned on the collar of her dress. Charles was laughing, tugging the girl closer as they walked. Ivor shouted across the rush of traffic, but Gross either didn't hear or chose to ignore him. Ivor quickly swallowed his drink, returned the glass to the kiosk to be washed out, and dodged his way across the street.

A narrow poster affixed to the door advertised in bold letters BOXING TONIGHT, PALESTINE POLICE FORCE VERSUS 2ND BATTALION THE SEAFORTH HIGHLANDERS AND OTHER CONTESTS!

Entrance was one hundred mils for a reserved seat, fifty for unreserved. Soldiers and airmen in uniform could be admitted at half price. Ivor produced the necessary coins from his pocket and then he was inside, part of the crowd in a packed, dimly lit, smoke-filled auditorium where a temporary ring had been set up.

He searched the room for Charles and his friend, but the lights went down before he could distinguish their faces. A single intense blue beam focused on the ring announcer, a ranking officer from the Seaforth Highlanders. To the usual mix of jeers and cheers, he introduced the fighters, two short, wiry bantamweights, each one sparsely tattooed on his arms. When a series of spotlights illuminated the entire ring, Ivor noted the boxers' odd piebald appearance, each one with brown face, lower arms, and legs and an unhealthy-looking pasty white on his chest.

When the bell rang, the crowd greeted its respective champions with a barrage of obscenity, some of it inventive, the rest more direct and to the point as each camp vied to outdo the other in both encouragement and insult. At the end of a first round in which neither boxer had managed to land so much as a solid punch, and which was greeted with a fresh round of creative insults, someone yelled out.

"Tone it down, lads, ladies present!"

The response, "Talking about yourself, Sarge?," got a big laugh.

The air in the room grew foul and three slow-turning overhead fans did nothing to dispel the accumulating stench of sweat and smoke. The little Scotsman began to pummel the English policeman, got him in a corner, and drew blood with a straight left to the nose. The Highlanders roared. And then Ivor saw Charles stand up from the second row and offer a couple of demonstrative uppercuts of his own before his girlfriend tugged on his jacket to pull him back down. Charles's behavior, Ivor thought, was of a piece with the image that he had cultivated at Oxford, the tough Jew, belligerent, not taking crap from anyone.

At the end of the third and final round, by which time the policeman's legs were wobbly and his face was a bloodied, crumpled mess, Ivor saw Charles heading for the exit and moved to cut him off.

"I need to talk to you," he said.

"Right now? Not a good time."

Charles was holding his girl's hand and looked almost to drag her past Ivor.

"I'm Ivor Castle. . . . I'm sorry to interrupt. I just need a minute with Charles," he said to her.

"Come on, Susannah," Charles said, "we're late."

"Well, you were the one who wanted to see the fight."

"Oh, you're American," Ivor said.

"I am."

She was pretty, Ivor thought, with darting hazel eyes. Her light brown hair was fashionably cut, a part in the middle and pinned back in a way that made her look styled, finished, and altogether incongruous here where everyone and everything else seemed like a work in progress.

"Ivor is working on the Stavsky and Rosenblatt case," Charles said hurriedly. "He's assisting Phineas Baron."

"How fascinating. Well, perhaps you'd like to join us for dinner and tell us all about it?"

"That's very kind but—"

"My father is a lawyer and my mother a gold-star gossip, so I'm sure they'd both be thrilled to meet you."

"Your parents are here?"

"Yes, visiting from Baltimore, as am I."

Charles, increasingly impatient, took Ivor by the elbow and

steered him a few feet away. He stood with his back to Susannah, a soundproof wall.

"What is it you want?" he hissed.

Ivor stared at him. "How did you know?" he said. "About the confession. How did you know?"

Charles's face lit up. "So, it happened. When?"

"I think you know."

"I have no idea."

"An Arab confessed and then a day later he recanted. I'm telling you this in absolute confidence. Understand?"

"Recanted?" Charles's face looked for a moment as if he had taken a solid punch from the pugnacious Scotsman.

"Yes. Now tell me." Ivor gripped Charles's arm tight. "How did you know what was going to happen?"

"We all knew it was an Arab, it was just a matter of time, wouldn't surprise me one bit if he wanted to be paid before he'd admit it."

"Is that the case?"

"How the hell should I know?"

"Did you arrange that payment?"

"Don't be ridiculous."

"Was he paid to confess or to murder?"

"I don't have time for this, Castle."

"And why would he recant?"

Charles stared at Ivor, and a look of disgust passed over his face. "Why don't you ask your girlfriend's boyfriend?"

"What?"

"You heard me. You don't even know who he is, do you?"

"He's not . . . he's not her . . . and he's a painter."

"A painter? You fool! What's he painting? Deals with the Nazis? He's part of the whole damn thing."

Susannah took two steps forward and tapped Charles on the

shoulder; he wheeled around as if he might erupt, then made an effort to control himself.

"Let's go," he said, and pulled her across the street, the blare of a car horn sounding behind them as they dashed to the other side.

Ivor watched them hurry away. From the doorway of the community hall came the sound of breaking glass, and then a fight broke out, and there didn't seem to be any police around to stop it. They were all inside.

He walked aimlessly, desperate and hopeless. It had crossed his mind to make for the Casino and drink himself into a stupor, but he couldn't bear to be in company and so he eschewed the waterfront and made his way north down side streets, past new blocks of flats rising rapidly on half-empty lots, and beneath the watchful gaze of families, new arrivals by the looks of it, in clothes and hats redolent of old Europe, out on their balconies to enjoy the warm night air.

The city was crowded with Jews now. Each day more and more poured off the boats, Germans, Poles, the persecuted horde with no place else to go. Each landing of an immigrant ship was trumpeted enthusiastically in the Jewish press while the Arabs observed the new arrivals with suspicion and anger and the British paused in their offices and mess halls, lifted their pens and their mugs of tea, gazed from on high over the proceedings, and thought, How the hell are we going to manage this?

At some point Ivor found himself on Rothschild Boulevard and remembered that Tsiona had grown up there. But which house? She had mentioned two stories, but that applied to several of the homes. Perhaps she was relaxing in one of them now, his betrayer, visiting her parents. He would burst in and she would look up in horror, accuse him once more of stalking her, and he would stutter and capitulate and ask for her forgiveness when it should have been the other way around.

He walked on through the residential quarter of Lev Tel Aviv, on to Ben Yehuda Street and Nordia, where a large sign in Hebrew and English announced with a flourish the construction of homes on land owned by the Jewish National Fund: "Tel Aviv. First town in the world built and populated entirely by Jews. Elected Municipal Administration. Population 46,000 and growing!" There seemed to be no discernible pattern at all to the town's buildings, which featured a medley of design: houses with red, pink, ochre, green, and blue walls; curves, columns, and pediments; turrets and pointed arches. Two hotels on Allenby boasted silver domes. Almost all Ivor's initial impressions of Tel Aviv had been of an unregulated place, free from its moorings. It wasn't only the floating eclecticism of the architecture—the houses frequently had no numbers, women smoked in public or wore bathing suits on the bus, all bourgeois inhibitions swept away. In England he had been closed in by taboo, a suffocating mix of British reserve and Anglo-Jewish restraint. Here he was free, the muddle of his identity of a piece with the town itself.

As the darkness deepened, lights dimmed or were extinguished all across the nascent city, and it was well past midnight when Ivor passed through Tel Nordau and the workers' quarter to arrive on the banks of the Yarkon River.

Here, on his first Sunday in Palestine, Larry Gedalia, an English cousin of the Oxford Stone twins out working in Palestine as a journalist for the London-based *Jewish Chronicle,* had taken Ivor boating along with a friend of his, Cecil Eastman, private secretary to Nigel Handyside, the chief law officer of the Palestine government. At Gedalia's urging the three of them had dressed in white brimmed hats with black bands (provided by

Larry) like the characters in *Three Men in a Boat,* pulling their skiff down the river from Kingston upon Thames to Oxford.

Now, alone in the darkness on the bank, the river before him narrow and muddied, the absurdity of that prescribed "jolly" afternoon struck Ivor. You couldn't just import England here and plonk it down, no matter how hard you tried.

And then Ivor recalled the most awkward moment of that day, when Eastman, languorous in the bow, his boater tipped forward over his nose, had recounted the way in which he had found Tel Aviv to be "a perfect freak in Palestine without any flavor of the East" and talked of the city as "gruesomely go-ahead, everything bubbling over with expansion," and then, as if he had completely forgotten with whom he was sharing his afternoon, added that these "trodden people from the ghettos had a right to be proud" but said it was "rather nauseous in a way—and absolutely unscrupulous." Ivor, new to the country, kept his thoughts to himself. Gedalia looked disturbed, but Eastman continued on about how unattractive Jewish crowds were, how they spoke not a word of English and how that very morning he had forgotten to pay his bill at a café and been pursued down the street by "a horrid little Yid waiter."

At this Gedalia had muttered, "Steady on, old chap," and Eastman, realizing that he had careened off the rails, pushed up his hat and enunciated, "So. Terribly. Sorry."

Ivor turned from the river, its flow almost stagnant in the windless night. The memory of that Sunday afternoon funneled into a surge of resentment, and while Eastman certainly deserved it, he knew that his anger was truly directed against Tsiona.

Was it possible that she had simply used him to cull information and pass it on to whoever her "boyfriend" really was? That would be the ultimate implication of Charles's message. If so, Charles was right, and he had been an utter fool. Had her body lied then, even during their moments of greatest affection, when she lay half-asleep in his arms? Everything appeared suspect to him now.

But what could have been so important for her to discover that she would give herself over to Ivor as she did? A few tidbits about the case that Baron was building? It seemed impossible. And what "boyfriend" would encourage her to do what she did? If it had been up to Ivor he would have erased her past entirely, removed every lover she had ever known, made himself the first and the only. And surely, she knew that she could have slept with him once, or not at all, and still kept him on the hook.

On Yarkon Street an hour later a barefoot prostitute in a cheap blue silk dress cut low to expose her cleavage stepped out of the shadows to accost him. Before Ivor could wave her away another girl with garish painted lips appeared, the dark of her blond hair visible at the roots, her nipples pushing through her thin muslin blouse, but what transfixed Ivor's attention was the small gold Star of David around her neck.

Grabbing him by the arms, the women tugged Ivor toward a dilapidated garage next to a warren of tin shacks, one with its door flung open. They whispered in his ear, pressed their breasts against him, played with his hair, and tried to slide their hands into the pockets of his shorts. Together they cajoled him, teased him, spoke in a Babel of tongues, and into the mix threw a broken-English menu of what was on offer.

Ivor shook himself loose, quickened his pace, heard their taunts and then their laughter following him down the street. He felt for his wallet, which mercifully had evaded their prying fingers. Above him the moon swung amber in the night sky as if the entire world were a bordello.

After another half an hour, with the sea surging to his side and his mind burning with its heady mix of anger and desire, he arrived on the outskirts of Jaffa port. There, his legs weary and feeling almost ready to collapse, he came across a moonlight swimming party, a dozen or so of his compatriots, young men and women, laughing and splashing in the waves, then running to warm themselves at the fire they had lit on the beach. Ivor stood at a distance, close enough to discern the English accents but too far away to be recognized. He observed this happy congeries of individuals, flirting, smoking, toweling one another off, breaking into couples and strolling down the beach: his life turned upside down, but the world the same.

He woke stretched out on the deserted shore. The swim-ming party had long since departed. Ivor roused himself, sat up, brushed the sand from his face and his clothes, and stared bleary-eyed around him. Steadily the sky became brighter and then the first rim of sun appeared as the day broke. Ivor stood and walked to the water's edge. He had removed his shoes and socks before falling asleep and now he allowed the dregs of the surf to lap over his feet. He waded a little farther in, dipped his hand, and splashed water onto his face. The salt stung his eyes, and he lifted the corner of his shirt to wipe them dry.

When the port came into focus, he noticed that away to his left a sizable cruise ship, the *Roma,* had docked and was pres-ently disgorging its many hundreds of passengers down two wide gangplanks: tourists to the Holy Land, of course, heading undoubtedly for a day in Jerusalem.

Not a dram of alcohol had reached his lips the night before, and yet he felt hungover, destined for a morning with his head under a pillow, keeping the light at bay, if only he could make it back to his bed.

There was sand in his hair and in his mouth. Perhaps he

could approach one of the pilgrims, if that's what they were, and ask for water, and yet he didn't want to startle them with his appearance—unkempt, unshaven, lips sore and cracked, red-eyed, some half-formed creature that the waves had tossed up on the shore.

The kiosks and local shops would not open for an hour or two; he had no choice but to make his way back to his rooming house as best he could, but twenty minutes later, his mouth parched, he could go no farther. The salmon steeple of a Russian Orthodox church rose above the stone houses that surrounded it, and a yearning for shelter drew Ivor toward the sanctuary.

He pushed through a green gate and walked down a long avenue shaded by mulberry trees. The door to the church was partially open; Ivor went in and was instantly embraced by the coolness of the stone. No one was around as he dipped his face into the fonts and stoups set by the door and sucked up the holy water intended for congregants and visitors to sprinkle on themselves as they entered.

His thirst quenched, he stepped into the last pew and lay on his back. Above him, while onlookers gazed in wonder, a bearded figure in blue and scarlet robes with a halo around his head raised a woman swathed in white from what must have been her sickbed. In the adjacent panel a winged angel appeared to be lifting the same man from the ground, imploring him to do something, or maybe elevating him to his final reward.

A visit to Westminster Abbey and a school trip to Canterbury Cathedral were among the rare occasions that Ivor had been inside a church. Not much had stuck with him from those days except fun and games on the coach traveling from and back to school. Now, as he lay staring at the ceiling, it struck him how paltry and reduced the synagogues he knew were in comparison with the great edifices where people worshipped Christ. It was a wonder, given the spectacular quality of Christian architecture, that more Jews didn't convert. But they didn't, and it seemed axiomatic that the vast majority of them never would. Not his father, who didn't believe in God, and not Ivor, who had neither God nor the barest allegiance to ritual. So, what was it then? Why remain a Jew? Why not shuck it off and announce himself as an atheist? The Jews he had met in Palestine didn't appear to be much interested in God themselves. They were either social-ists who preferred Trotsky to Moses, or Revisionists who wanted an expanded Israel on both banks of the Jordan, but the whole contrary lot of them agreed on one thing: They wanted a place where nobody would bother Jews anymore. And was that why Arlosoroff had been shot, because he'd done a deal with the peo-ple who were bothering Jews the most? It was Baron's job, and his job, to argue against that.

The angel on the ceiling spread her gilded wings, lifted her hand, and stretched it out before her. "How many lovers has she had?" Ivor asked. "Five?" The angel laughed and brought her hand higher. "Fifteen? Twenty?" The angel raised the level again, raised and raised until she held her hand far above her head; she showed no mercy at all.

At the far end of the church the portal to the vestry swung open and a priest in a high black hat, with a thick shovel beard to match, stepped through. Ivor jumped to his feet and made for the church doors. Within moments he was down the path and through the gate, the taste of stolen holy water on his tongue.

"Mr. Castle? Ivor?"

He was standing in the shade of a leafy ficus tree with his back pressed against its trunk. He didn't know how long he had been there. After escaping the church, he had crossed the street and settled to catch his breath close to the walls of the Tabitha Mission.

The woman who approached him now, holding a racket and in blinding tennis whites, a knee-length skirt, a sleeveless cotton top, and a broad headband, looked as if she had stepped directly from center court at Wimbledon onto the hot and dusty Jaffa street.

Ivor shielded his eyes against the sun.

"Susannah, Susannah Green. We met yesterday evening." She laughed as if the possibility that Ivor hadn't remembered her was fully explained by his disheveled appearance.

"Of course," he said, "I'm so sorry. What are you doing here?"

"Looking for a tennis partner."

"Oh, I . . . I haven't played in years."

She laughed again. "No. I'm not really in the habit of waving my racket around Jaffa and hoping someone will come to join me."

"Of course not. Stupid . . . sorry."

"Stop being so sorry. I'm meeting my friend at the mission. Among the amenities on offer there for the weary traveler is a lovely well-kept court. John Loxton, who is working on the Survey of Palestine, told me about it. Do you know him? He's also a friend of Charles's."

"I haven't had the pleasure. Is that who you're meeting?"

"No."

"Then Charles . . . you're meeting Charles?"

"I do have other friends!" She lifted her hand to stop him before he could apologize. "And in any case Charles, I'm afraid, is in a bit of a huff."

"Why is that?"

"He got into an enormous argument with my father last night at dinner. I thought for a moment he might punch him."

"What about?"

"Politics, of course! Does anyone here talk about anything else? Daddy is a great fan of Ben-Gurion, whereas Charles, well, I'm sure you know."

"And you?"

"And *I* am looking forward to breakfast before my partner arrives. Come on, Mr. Castle, tea and toast. An irresistible combination for an Englishman, no? And I'm buying."

Inside the mission's restaurant the full panoply of colonial effects was on display: Arab waiters in elegant uniforms, tables covered in spotless white tablecloths, elaborate polished silverware, heavy square Minton ashtrays featuring approximations of royal imprimaturs, and overall a sense of decorum aspiring to that of an exclusive London men's club. Through the long French windows Ivor could see out to the tennis court, its red clay surface surrounded by high walls designed to protect from prying eyes and probably, given the mission's location on the border between Jaffa and Tel Aviv, stray bullets as well.

He had washed himself in the bathroom as best he could, but after splashing water on his head and face and scrubbing up his body all he could do was reprise the shirt and shorts in which he had slept. A razor, toothbrush, and toothpaste would have been nice, but none of these items was available. He checked himself in the mirror; his thick black hair was flattened on his head as if it had been dipped in tar, and there were circles under his eyes and a day's growth of beard on his face. "You're a handsome boy," his mother used to tell him, holding his face in her hands. "If only you took care of yourself better. Comb your hair once in a while. Stand up straight. Don't hunch. You're over six foot and you come across as nothing better than average height." Reflexively, at the memory of her words, Ivor pulled his shoulders back, puffed his chest out, and assumed a military bearing, like the men who had stood guard over Arlosoroff's body. For a moment he felt coursing through him a sensation appropriate to those who inhabited the role of the New Jew in the ancient homeland, as if by standing straight Ivor could put behind him the entire bent and crooked history of the Jewish Diaspora.

Susannah lifted the teapot and poured through the strainer for both Ivor and herself before removing her headband to run her fingers through the stylish cut of her chestnut hair.

"And what brings you to this charming neighborhood so bright and early in the morning? No need for an answer if you don't wish to provide one. Probably none of my business."

She was being kind, Ivor thought, behaving as if the way he looked signaled no more than the tolerable, and indeed almost desirable, eccentricity of the Englishman abroad. Nevertheless, he felt the need to dispel any thoughts she might have entertained that he had spent a torrid night with a lover, or worse, in some local brothel.

"I'm trying to retrace the steps that our clients are accused of taking en route to the murder of Mr. Arlosoroff."

"And they were here at some point?"

"Well, that is the accusation."

"To play tennis?"

Ivor laughed. "I'm afraid I shouldn't really say too much more."

Two cups of tea revived him, and he had to hold himself back from wolfing down the toast before Susannah had buttered a single slice.

She glanced at her watch. "My partner must be held up."

"Speaking of partners, if you don't mind my asking, how long have you and Charles . . . ?"

"Charles?" She broke into a broad smile. "Oh no, Mr. Castle.

You have the wrong end of the stick. Charles is my cousin. A distant one to be sure, I believe his grandfather was my grandfather's cousin, or perhaps it was my grandmother's. Either way the family made the same journey from Germany and then diverged. One half didn't get too far and stopped in London while the other sensibly carried on to Baltimore."

"Perhaps Charles's lot couldn't afford the full fare?"

"That's a distinct possibility. I shall have to ask him."

The waiter arrived with a second round of toast. Ivor felt that for the first time in weeks he was enjoying himself in a manner both relaxed and undemanding. And if he was honest, he had to admit to a sense of relief. Charles as Susannah's chaste relative was far preferable to Charles as her lover.

"And remind me why you are in Palestine?"

"All these questions," Susannah said. "You're not being very English, are you?"

"I know. Something's happened to me here. Must be the sun. I'm like my grandmother in her last years, disinhibited. She started swearing like a sailor, and I'll say anything to anyone and I won't even apologize."

"I am here because my undergraduate studies are complete, I did not particularly wish to return from Cambridge to Baltimore for anything more than a couple of weeks, and my parents offered me this delightful vacation among the warring tribes."

"Cambridge?"

"Cambridge, Massachusetts. Yours is not the only one on the planet, you know."

"I'm sor—" Susannah raised her eyebrows and Ivor checked himself.

"In any case, it seems my father has some business to attend to in Tel Aviv and Jerusalem. He spends most of the day holed up at the hotel deep in conversation with someone he refuses to introduce either to my mother or myself."

"Who is this person?"

"According to my father he can be filed under the heading 'authorized purchasing agent.'"

"Authorized by whom? To purchase what?"

Susannah turned and scanned the room. The tables around them were filling up, official-looking members of the British hierarchy sitting down to conduct the pressing matters of the day with local prelates and Arab businessmen. For a moment Ivor thought that he spotted the Russian Orthodox priest who had interrupted his alarming reverie, but no, the cut of the beard was different, the hat with its high cylinder soft sided.

"I have no idea whatsoever and to tell you the truth I am not much interested."

Ivor sat back in his chair, his attention held for a moment by the sparkle of Susannah's two small diamond earrings. She was exactly the kind of girl his mother would have liked him to bring home: younger than Ivor but not by too much; pretty but not threateningly beautiful; intelligent but in all likelihood apolitical; from a wealthy but perhaps not oppressively wealthy family; and most important, Jewish, but not too Jewish! A modicum of observance would satisfy. His mother wouldn't need any more than that. Susannah's glaring deficiencies—American and from an unheard-of place called Baltimore—could be overlooked if those other attributes were all in place. In fact, all things being equal, even her committing mass murder, as long as she left no trace of it, could probably be disregarded.

Susannah turned to scan the room and the hallway that led to it.

"I didn't mean to pester you," Ivor said.

"You didn't. And now, as it appears that my dear friend Ruth has ditched me for tennis, I suggest that you, Ivor from Oxford, act like the gentleman I take you to be and join me on the court."

"I'm hardly prepared for that."

"Don't be such a bore. We'll fit you up with all the necessaries. You'll be a regular Fred Perry."

Someone had left a copy of the day's *Palestine Post* on the seat next to Ivor's. He picked it up and glanced at the front page: six prominent Arab leaders joining forces to protest against Zionist advances in Palestine, tension building, rumors the Arab Executive committee would call for a general strike.

"Anything of interest?" Susannah said.

Ivor folded the paper and set it on the table.

"Not a word about tennis," he replied.

From somewhere in the bowels of the mission she secured for him a racket, a pair of long white trousers, and a white short-sleeved shirt. Unfortunately, plimsolls that fit were impossible to procure and Ivor stepped onto the red clay court in his entirely inappropriate shoes, slipping and sliding as Susannah, whose graceful form, Ivor imagined, reflected years of expensive coaching, sent him scampering from one corner to the other. Perhaps, if he had slept longer than two hours, and in a bed rather than on the beach, he might have conjured a few returns that would not have completely embarrassed him. But as it was, his ineptitude combined with Susannah's competitive and serious attention to the task at hand (what was it with Americans and sports? They didn't seem to get the "fun" part at all) turned their rallies into ludicrous demonstrations of her overwhelming superiority.

After Ivor had been trounced, 6–0, his magnanimous opponent led him back inside the mission and insisted that he at least allow her to arrange for a room with a shower where he might wash up. He resisted, of course, but then a quick glance at the clock in the vestibule reminded him that he was due at the Jaffa police station in less than two hours and he capitulated.

He watched Susannah get into the taxi and impart the name of her hotel. As the engine idled, she leaned a little out of the back-seat window.

"Well, shall we see each other again?"

Ivor, taken aback, hesitated only for a moment, but it was long enough to notice the instant hurt in her eyes.

"Of course," he said quickly, "I'd love that."

He sat on a narrow bed in one of the small monastic rooms originally designated as rest spots for pilgrims en route to Jerusalem. The shower had run cold almost immediately, but that was probably for the best. He lifted one of two thin, rough towels from a wooden stool, the room's only other furniture, and dried himself off. He had no change of clothes and was obliged to dress himself once more in the shirt and shorts in which he had slept on the sand.

He wouldn't have to see her again; he simply had to say that he would. After that, all manner of unpredictable occurrences could get in the way of their meeting: a suddenly requested journey to Jerusalem, long days in court, the time-consuming work that Baron demanded of him, and beyond these entirely reasonable excuses the event that he could never mention to Miss Susannah Green: Tsiona's arrival in Tel Aviv, when she would explain everything, dispel his worries, fall into bed with him, ask him to hold her in his arms and kiss her eyes.

· · ·

Three electric bulbs, one of which flickered and threatened to go out, lighted the room. The CID officer called out a list of names and ten young Arab men filed into the room.

"Majid Tukboub, Abdel Rachman Eid, Faiz Kaddoura, Wodiek Akal, Saleh Abdullah Saleh, Akram Medani, Khalil Hamis, Abu Hatoun, Elish Sliman, Yousef el-Hayek."

Ivor and Baron watched as Abdul Malik was placed among the others. On arrival Baron had cast some inquiring looks in Ivor's direction, clearly taking in his soiled shirt and shorts and generally disheveled appearance. There would be questions, and Ivor had no idea how he would answer them. He had not even released the bottled-up truth about Tsiona to Baron, let alone the fresh news about his lover's lover. Ahead of him lay disgrace, disbarment, and in all likelihood banishment: In no time at all Ivor would be on a ship back to England, his career over before it had begun, and he would carry within him the heavy baggage of a broken heart that he knew might never heal.

"You can stand wherever you want," Prendergast was saying. "If you have any objections to the arrangements, tell me now." Abdul Malik placed himself in position number seven. Prendergast glanced from the prisoner toward the two sets of lawyers, neither of which expressed any concern.

The room was unbearably stuffy. A decision appeared to have been made to keep the windows closed during the identity parade, a genuflection toward secrecy. Baron wiped his brow with his handkerchief. Attorney General Cunningham and Mr. el-Alami maneuvered themselves beneath the ceiling fan, which revolved slowly and ineffectively.

"In a few moments I am going to bring in Mrs. Arlosoroff. I confirm that the identifying witness has been kept all this time in another part of the building. It has been impossible for her to see any of the persons paraded or any of the arrangements made.

I ask you to make no remark or indication whatsoever to the identifying witness. At the end of the proceeding all the persons paraded will be taken out and placed in the Fingerprint Office."

Sima Arlosoroff entered the room. Her hair was pinned up carelessly and she wore a simple black dress. It was the first time that Ivor had seen her in the flesh; she was much thinner than in the newspaper photographs, as if she had lost the weight of her husband. She must have been around Tsiona's age, but she looked a decade older. Ivor glanced quickly at Baron, who had fixed Mrs. Arlosoroff with a hard stare. He didn't trust her; Ivor knew that "the lady," as Baron had told him, offered "completely different stories according to the convenience of the moment." Nevertheless, if she were to identify Abdul Malik now the entire prosecution case would instantly collapse and their clients walk free.

"Mrs. Arlosoroff," Prendergast began, "we ask you to look at those present and to say whether you recognize any of the paraded persons as one of the persons who took part in the murder of your husband. If you do recognize him, you should indicate him."

The young men stared straight ahead. Mrs. Arlosoroff walked up and down twice, stopping carefully before each individual.

"Can I see them walk?" she asked.

"You may."

One by one the young men in shabby clothes walked the length of the room and returned. Mrs. Arlosoroff took a breath.

"I recognize nobody. Except that number nine is similar in type to the tall person who attacked us, but he is not the man."

A fresh parade was performed with ten new faces, then Issa Kurkar was brought in and issued the same instructions given to Abdul Malik. He raised no objections and placed himself in the number five position. Again, Sima Arlosoroff looked twice at the parade, passing along the line and returning, and again at her request each of the paraded walked the length of the office and returned.

"I recognize nobody," she said.

Baron offered a weak smile, as if he had known all along that this was the inevitable result of the parades. He looked toward Cunningham and el-Alami, who had already begun to make their way toward the door but paused to let Mrs. Arlosoroff pass through first.

"Well, Ivor," Baron said, when only they were left in the room, "we shall have to make our case without her. We do, if memory serves, have eight—no, nine—independent witnesses who will swear that our incorruptible Sima Arlosoroff, when her memory was fresh, described her assailants as Arabs. If the court is prepared to find they are telling the truth, then the prosecution's case is at worst punctured, riddled at several points, and at best the result, I submit to you as I shall to them, is its destruction."

Ivor could barely keep his eyes open. He made his way back to the mission, past the Arab farmers' market, where, close to their owners, dozens of camels sat with their legs splayed, the heavy bags on their backs split open to exhibit fruits and vegetables resting in beds of straw. At the edge of the market six mounds displayed an abundance of watermelons that sat like giant eggs in their broad straw nests. As he walked the vendors hawked their wares, calling out to him, some grabbing his arm to pull him close or direct him to the produce spilling from the back of their ox- and horse-drawn carts.

Ivor felt heat drugged, exhausted, and he almost stumbled

down the narrow avenue lined by lemon-scented eucalyptus trees that led to the mission. He managed to get his clothes off, then collapsed on the bed in the room that Susannah had secured for him.

Close to dusk, he was back at the port waiting for the bus that would return him to his rooming house and the change of clothes that awaited him there. White smoke spumed from the twin funnels of the SS *Roma,* its three decks already crowded above its hanging lifeboats with departing visitors taking their last looks at the Holy Land. A stream of late-arriving passengers headed up the gangplank, and more made their way toward the ship from a line of tourist buses parked nearby.

Ivor watched the bus closest to him empty out, returnees from Jerusalem, tired from walking the Via Dolorosa, but hearts full, no doubt, with the love of Jesus. He saw two women with large olive-wood crosses around their necks and then a man and a woman together as they stepped from the bus, the woman in a blue head scarf, the man in the dark tunic of a Catholic priest clutching a small suitcase to his chest, his silver cross caught in the leather handle. Their faces were turned away from him but when they shifted direction to head toward the ship, Ivor saw, clearly and without any possibility of error, that the priest was Tsiona's "boyfriend" Yosef—only this time his hair, while not bright orange, was significantly lightened away from the black that Ivor had first observed while looking down on Tsiona's doorway in Jerusalem.

Ivor's bus arrived, spewing fumes, interpolating itself between Ivor and the tourist bus and blocking his view. He tried to skirt the bus, pushing through the line of passengers eager to get on board. In Palestine, despite the British presence, the idea of a queue held no purchase. Jostled between two heavyset women with large overflowing shopping bags, he almost flung one of them over in his rush to get free. In the commotion someone grabbed at his shirt and he felt the neck rip. And then he was loose and running toward the ship, his heart pounding.

He had lost sight of them, but then there they were, making their way up the gangplank. Was it her? If only the woman would turn around. Ivor sped down the quay only to be blocked by two young Italian sailors at the foot of the walkway.

"I don't have a ticket," he snapped. "I just need to talk to those people up there."

The Italians shrugged and when Ivor tried to push through, they shoved him back.

The priest and his female companion had reached the top of the ramp.

"Tsiona!" Ivor cried out, her name almost lost in the sounding of the ship's horn. He called again at the top of his voice. As the priest stepped onto the deck he turned around and locked eyes with Ivor just as he had done in Safed, only this time instead of waving he put his finger to his lips before pivoting on his heel and disappearing from view.

14

October

$\smile$

The trial was scheduled to begin a week after the long interregnum of the Jewish holidays had ended. Now it was the festival of Sukkoth. Ivor had spent the past few days mired in misery, oscillating between hot spurts of jealousy and the degradation of self-pity. Now he had been dragged, unwillingly, back into the quotidian, by Susannah Green and her proposal that they travel to Jerusalem to wander the Orthodox Jewish neighborhoods as dusk fell and see the hastily constructed booths with fruit and flowers hanging from trellised roofs open to the sky. "We'll observe how our ancestors lived," she'd said, as if they were a pair of anthropologists about to realize their neighbors as a newly discovered tribe.

They walked in the narrow streets of Mea She'arim under an opalescent sky while shopkeepers hastily shuttered their stalls and Hasidim in wide-brimmed fur hats scurried home. The approaching darkness was slowed by a full moon that rose, as always, to coincide with the first night of the festival: One shining planet (was it Jupiter?) hung below the flat silver disk like a pendant while, earthbound, the flimsy outdoor booths were irradiated with flickering candlelight. Susannah took Ivor's arm, led him down cobblestone alleyways, where they stopped occasionally under narrow balconies and listened to murmurs of benediction and prayer quickly followed by a clatter of cutlery as the evening meal was served.

An hour later they were seated in the central hall of the King David Hotel waiting for Susannah's mother to come down from her room. Susannah had omitted to mention that her parents were presently in Jerusalem and Ivor felt that a trap had been set, although why she had wanted to catch him this way was not immediately apparent.

Here and there people were gathered at round tables nursing drinks and dipping into small plates of food: upper-echelon British officers, Mandate officials, church dignitaries, well-off tourists, and a group of dignified Arab men in stark white robes. The night air was warm and every time the swing doors opened it rushed in to check the cooling effect of the room's ceiling fans. Beyond the open rear windows Ivor could see late-blooming autumn roses, red petals closing for the night.

Mrs. Green appeared, tall and imperious, in a midnight-blue silk dress, her dark hair carefully curled in short waves. When she shook Ivor's hand, he couldn't help but notice the impressive diamond on her finger and the sparkle of smaller stones in her necklace. She had the same hazel eyes as her daughter, but her accent had a strong Southern twang. Susannah registered Ivor's surprise.

"Are you appalled?" she said. "My mother grew up in Georgia. If you press her, she'll tell you how the Jews arrived in Savannah. It's one of her favorite stories."

"Well, they did come from England, you know, so Mr. Castle might be interested."

"Perhaps you're related," Susannah said.

"Well, perhaps we are."

Mrs. Green laughed and Ivor, at least momentarily intrigued, was happy to take his seat next to her as she began to unfurl the events of her day, which she had spent, it turned out, totally alone as her husband had been off somewhere attending, she said, his "endless meetings."

After a round of liqueurs Mrs. Green reached into her handbag and produced what looked at first like a theater program, its paper worn and slightly stained at the edges.

"Oh, for God's sake, Mother," Susannah said, and tried to snatch it away from her, "not again."

"Why, darling, I'm sure Mr. Castle would love to see this."

"His name's Ivor."

"Yes, please, I should have said, call me Ivor."

Susannah made another effort to grab the program, but Mrs. Green had already maneuvered to hand it over to Ivor.

"You're so embarrassing."

"I'm sure Ivor would love to know something of our world."

Ivor read the cover page: HARMONY CIRCLE 1860–1928 HOTEL BELVEDERE WEDNESDAY NOVEMBER 28TH, 1928. Inside, inserted between the two-page menu of a multicourse meal, he found a double-columned newspaper clipping with the headline BALL HELD BY HARMONY CIRCLE: SEVEN DEBUTANTES MAKE INITIAL BOW IN ANNUAL SOCIAL FUNCTION AT HOTEL BELVEDERE. Accompanying the article was a photograph of Susannah in a long silk gown.

"Doesn't look a day older than she did then, does she, Ivor?"

"You're being ridiculous." Susannah stood up. "I'm going outside to get some air."

"N-no," Ivor stuttered, "she doesn't."

He didn't know what to do, follow Susannah or stick it out

with her mother. Almost involuntarily he began to read the article. The Harmony Circle, it appeared, was a Jewish simulacrum of the debutante balls he had previously thought were reserved only for the Anglo-Christian upper classes. There had been former debutante girls at Oxford, but they were entirely out of his orbit, and in any case, he had no idea that America, that splendidly egalitarian republic, even went in for that kind of thing. Clearly, he was wrong. Wrong too, he now realized, about Susannah's being rich but not too rich: Her reflected wealth glittered brighter than the desert stars.

He read the rapturous account of beauties in velvets and brocades of every hue swarming the floor of a lofty ballroom flooded with golden light while Fisher's orchestra played. In the banquet hall, a mass of palms and smilax was relieved by bright splotches of rose and gold. A huge golden basket of pink chrysanthemums, with a rose light and a fairy fountain playing in the center, and garlands of pink chrysanthemums marking each place, formed the decoration of the debutantes' table. And here, as the dancing began, came the formal announcements: Miss Myra Stern Metzenbaum, niece of the Misses Stern of Callow Avenue, in a hooped gown of orchid velvet and silver lace. Miss Hilda Brager, daughter of Mr. and Mrs. Lewis L. Brager, gowned in Alice-blue velvet, with a pearl bandeau. On down the list until at the very last, and the only one to be pictured in the newspaper, seventeen-year-old Miss Susannah Green, daughter of Mr. and Mrs. Henry Green, in a gown of jade-green chiffon brocaded with silver flowers and made over silver cloth.

In the last paragraph, which was careful to note that the Harmony Circle was the "oldest social club in Baltimore," came a dutiful list of the board of governors, not the titled aristocrats Ivor would have expected at home, but men with names like Levy and Wallenstein, a Rabbi Wessel, and yes, there at the very end, even a Schloss! Could any celebratory event be further removed from Tsiona's birthday party? Miss Tsiona Kerem, not seventeen but thirty, daughter of who knows who, in a simple white short-sleeved dress embroidered at the neck and cuffs, and surrounded by her cohorts, a bunch of men in baggy khaki shorts and worn blue shirts.

Ivor handed the program and clipping back to Mrs. Green.

"It's a beautiful picture," he said. "You must have been very proud of her."

Susannah had reappeared beside them. "Is the humiliation over?"

Mrs. Green took one last look at the clipping. "Such a pretty dress," she said, then unclasped her bag and replaced the program. "Now," she continued, "tell me something about yourself, Mr. Castle."

As he spoke Ivor felt he heard Mrs. Green's brain clicking like an abacus, totting up, running beads in quick lines, making additions and subtractions, until she reached a final account of the sum of his being.

Meanwhile, Susannah ordered a second round of drinks, toyed irritably with her bracelets. "I think that's enough," she said as Ivor concluded a brief summary of his home life and education. "And please don't ask him about the trial, we'll be here all night."

"As it happens, I'm not allowed to talk about it."

"Well, as it happens, I would like to take a walk in the garden while it's still warm."

Susannah rose, and Ivor with her, glad that the gate had opened for his escape.

"Oh well," Mrs. Green said, "I suppose that the story of Savannah will have to wait."

Ivor shook her hand. "I'll look forward to it when we next meet." He was fairly certain there would be no next meeting.

Outside an unexpected chill had crept into the air. Susannah shivered and Ivor felt that she expected him to put his arm around her, but he didn't.

"Perhaps we should go back in," he said.

Susannah crossed her arms and rubbed her shoulders. "It seems my parents have booked me a suite here for the night. You don't have to go back to Tel Aviv. You could sleep on my couch. They wouldn't know."

"It's very kind of you, but I couldn't trouble you like that."

"But you could, and it wouldn't be trouble."

Ivor sensed her disappointment, just as he had done when they had first parted after tennis in Jaffa. He felt now that he must give her *something*.

"How about this?" he said. "I'll find a nearby room for the night and tomorrow we can explore the Old City together?"

Susannah brightened at his offer, once more slid her arm into his. "That would be lovely," she said.

The receptionist at the front desk recommended a small rooming house near Herod's Gate. "British owned," he announced. "A number of our guests' acquaintances have stayed there."

Ivor walked parallel to the crenellated walls of the Old City. He passed through a gate and into a small courtyard. When he knocked on the door it was opened by a thin, pinched figure, a woman wrapped in an oversized red cardigan, her hair entangled as if she had just woken up. To his surprise Ivor recognized her. She was the Christian Scientist Baron had pointed out at his break-fast, the sister of the famous poet.

"Yes?"

"I'm looking for a room and at the King David—"

"Yes, yes, come in. The attic is free. How long will you be staying?"

"One night, perhaps a little longer."

"Well, you need to be sure or if you decide to extend your stay you may find you've lost the room."

"I'll let you know tomorrow."

"And you are . . . ?"

"Ivor Castle. Actually, we've met before. At Phineas Baron's break-fast."

Clarissa Barlow leaned back a little, as if to get a better look at Ivor. "I don't see that well in the dark," she said, "but I'll take your word for it."

There was nothing very poetic about the attic, a cold, sparsely furnished room with a narrow, hard bed. To reach the bathroom Ivor had to descend the stairs, go back out, and cross the gray-stoned courtyard. Inevitably, there was no hot water. Miss Barlow must have forgotten to light the boiler.

He lay on the bed and stared up at the ceiling, then rose, pulled back the dusty curtain on the dormer window, and looked down to where two Arab women in traditional dress but with heavy Wellington boots on their feet made their way toward the city gate. He wondered, not for the first time, why he had agreed to his father's suggestion that he take a position in Palestine, some yearning for adventure, to find an exit for himself from the seductive comforts of home, more dangerous in their way than the conflicting factions at war with one another here. Or maybe he just wanted to test his allegiances. In England, at school and at Oxford, he always felt that the foregrounded thing about him was his Jewishness, and often, much too often, the subject of it arose in some grotesque form. Here, at least half the population simply thought of him as an Englishman, while for the local Jews he wasn't Jewish enough. He lay back down on the bed; from the great mosque at the center of the Old City the muezzin issued the day's last call to prayer, timeless, lingering in the air, and, he thought, no more or less intimate and strange than the pellucid notes of Evensong he'd heard issuing from college chapels in Oxford as he returned at dusk from the library to his room.

In the morning as he began to cross the courtyard, Miss Barlow waylaid him.

"If you're going to be here tonight," she said, "I need to tell you about the water. Until the rains come it's in short supply and that places a severe responsibility on all my guests. You'd be surprised, or maybe you wouldn't, how wasteful people can be. Whenever possible we use the same water a number of times, secondhand bathwater to wash the floor, that kind of thing."

"I'll do my very best," Ivor said, eager to get away, but Miss Barlow wasn't done.

"It all comes from Solomon's Pools a couple of miles south of Bethlehem, and there's a reservoir in the Old City. Now, some people are very lucky, they have underground cisterns which store the rainwater that runs off the rooftops. In the newer buildings, and this is one of them, the water's stored in tanks on flat roofs. I can't protect it! Do you know I've had children using my tank as a swimming pool?"

Ivor didn't have the heart to mention the lack of hot water on the previous night. Again, he reiterated that he would follow the rules of preservation.

"Oh, and when you return, you'll find a candle in your room, electricity failures are not infrequent."

As soon as Ivor arrived at the King David, he spotted Susannah dressed as if for a hike in long diamond-patterned socks, shorts that extended just below her knees, a thin cardigan, and a jaunty yellow scarf. Immediately, she shepherded him over to a corner of the central hall where four men were gathered in animated conversation around a small table. As Ivor and Susannah approached, the men fell silent and one of them stood up. Clearly, it was the turn of Susannah's father to meet and assess Ivor.

"Daddy, this is Ivor."

Henry Green extended his hand. He was tall and distinguished looking, with prematurely gray hair neatly parted at the side, handsome as could be and clearly he knew it. His voice, when he introduced himself, boomed across the room. To Ivor he looked and seemed every inch the full-blooded American, almost a parody of the type, and not one he was familiar with in the world of the Jewish Diaspora.

Unlike his wife, Henry Green showed little interest in pressing his daughter's eligibility on Ivor. Quite the reverse—he was impatient to get back to his conversation with the three men, none of whom he bothered to introduce. The table was cluttered with coffee cups and the glass ashtray at its center full of cigarette ends. From the expressions on the men's faces Ivor gathered that he and Susannah had interrupted a serious discussion.

"Well," Henry Green said, "off to see the sights?"

"We're taking a car to the Dead Sea, with a stop at the Monastery of Mar Saba."

Ivor turned to Susannah. "I thought, you know, the Old City."

"Oh, this will be much more fun. Consider it an adventure."

"Well, enjoy yourselves," Mr. Green said. "Say hello to the monks for me. Oxford, is that right?"

"Yes."

"And working on the Arlosoroff case? We're going to have

to have a conversation about that. Perhaps tonight when you return."

Ivor offered a weak smile. He wondered whether he would be able to resist if Mr. Green pressed him for information. He seemed a formidable force.

As they walked away Susannah whispered, "They're all German Jews, Zionist émigrés."

"And what are they up to with your father?"

"Don't ask me. Ever since he retired, he's been acting like a spy. Secret meetings all over the place. It sounds exciting but my guess is it's all terribly boring."

"Retired? Isn't he rather young for that?"

"We owned two department stores in downtown Baltimore— well, he did, inherited from my grandfather. He sold them both not long before the crash. Clever of him, wasn't it?"

The car descended into the Kidron Valley with Ivor and Susannah occupying the back seat. After an hour or so, as heat rose in waves off the desert, the monastery came into view high on a cliff above the barren wilderness that surrounded it, an arid landscape of mountains gray as elephant hides and narrow escarpments. Susannah nudged him, pointed, then spoke directly to the driver.

"We'll take the car as far as we can go, Mr. Awad, and then we'll walk up?"

Ivor, without a change of clothes since the night before, was dressed in a white shirt and dark trousers more suited for dinner at the hotel than a hike up a cliff. The same went for his shoes, brogues that had felt a half size too tight for him since the day after he had bought them.

"Perhaps," he ventured, "we could just content ourselves with a long look from here, then move on to the Dead Sea."

"Oh, don't be such a spoilsport. Look at it, stunningly beautiful, we have to get up close. And don't worry, I brought canteens of water for both of us."

By the time they reached the monastery gate Ivor was sweating profusely while Susannah had somehow managed to retain both her composure and her unblemished complexion. Then, in an awkward and unfair reversal, Ivor was rewarded for his lack of enthusiasm. For it turned out that women were not permitted to enter the monastery; this had been the case for more than a thousand years and no amount of Baltimore bravura could change it. Susannah, however, was allowed to access and climb the exterior tower, from which vantage point she would be able to see into the promised land that she was forbidden to enter.

"I'll stay with you," Ivor said, but Susannah insisted that he go in by himself.

This was the second time in recent days that he had found himself in the settled silences of a Christian Orthodox setting. If he couldn't keep his passions in check, and clearly where Tsiona was concerned he couldn't, then perhaps this was where he was destined to end up. He could grow a beard, try to find Jesus on his own.

The Sabaite monks largely ignored him, and Ivor, eschewing the chance to view both relics and an ancient library, found a bench under an almond tree, happy to be in shade and able to catch his breath. All around him were pink stone walls creviced with dark entrances to cells and hidden rooms, stones so ancient that it almost looked as if the ridges of purple rock beyond the walls were the latecomers to the landscape. He drank in great swigs from his canteen and had the desire to pour what remained of the water over his head, although it felt unseemly to do so, a secular baptism that no one would appreciate.

The porter monk who had admitted Ivor and banished Susannah to the tower emerged from behind a blue door. Unlike his fellow monks, who dressed uniformly in black, his pantaloons, deep-pocketed tunic, and cylindrical klobuk were all green, the color chosen for the intermediary tasked with meandering between the inner and outer world of this city of monks. He held before him a tray carrying small objects that glinted in the sun. Ivor began to feel in his pocket for coins, but the monk passed by and Ivor saw that what he carried was a set of keys.

He looked up at the tower and imagined Susannah staring down, trying to pick him out. Or perhaps she was looking farther southward to the sea that was the lowest point on earth and not really a sea at all, and beyond that, how far could the view take her? Maybe all the way down to the Gulf of Aqaba, where he imagined brilliant blue waves backed by hills in every shade of mauve and pink, green stone slashed with blue, some color spectrum that in its unattainable beauty resembled his improbable future.

They returned late to Jerusalem, having floated in the Dead Sea and clambered up to Ein Feshkha, where they had bathed in its freshwater spring, Ivor in a pair of swimming trunks that Susannah had brought with her in case he needed them. As the car ground its way up the last inclines toward the city, Susannah laid her head on Ivor's shoulder and fell asleep. Ivor noticed Mr. Awad look quickly into his driver's mirror and Ivor, for some reason feeling that he owed him an explanation for the intimacy he was privy to, said, "She's my friend." Later, he thought they might have been the most ridiculous words he had ever uttered.

For the rest of the week, while the observant Jewish residents of Jerusalem prepared for Simchat Torah, the last holiday of the seasonal cycle, Ivor and Susannah pursued their chaste alliance. At the vast new Edison Cinema, where only a small fraction of its fifteen hundred seats was filled, they saw Loretta Young in *Zoo in Budapest* and marveled less at the film, in which a young zookeeper rescued both a beautiful orphan girl from the clutches of a cruel orphanage and animals released from their cages by his sadistic boss, than at the building's air-conditioning, the first oasis of its kind in the heat of Palestine.

Together they hunted the Old City's bazaar, where Susannah, importuned by shopkeepers everywhere she walked, decorated her wrists with heavy silver bracelets and bangles, picked up Armenian pottery, allowed bolts of fabric to be unwound before her, and tried as hard as she could to drive a bargain, while Ivor, "hopelessly English" as Susannah said, stood silent and ready to pay the first price offered so they could move on and out of these embarrassing negotiations. His relief when they exited the Damascus Gate was palpable. On Jaffa Road, a mile from the Old City walls, Ivor bought a change of clothes in a shop run by two Romanian brothers who Susannah insisted had inflated their prices because they sensed that Ivor felt it beneath himself to bargain. "It's not snobbery," Ivor replied, "I'm just no good at it. The whole business makes me uncomfortable. And anyway, you can't bargain in the Jewish shops."

"Of course you can," Susannah said. "We're all Semites, you know, it's part of the tradition."

In the evenings they dined together, once at the King David with Susannah's mother and the rest of the time in small, inexpensive restaurants recommended by Miss Barlow, who, to Ivor's surprise, turned out to be something of a gastronome.

Susannah's father was nowhere to be seen. Her mother sim-

ply reiterated that he was "away on business" with no amplifica-
tion as to where or what that business might be. Ivor felt relieved
by his absence; an interrogation undoubtedly had been coming
his way and the looming Arlosoroff trial was the last thing he felt
like discussing.

There was no denying that he enjoyed Susannah's company:
She was lively and funny, confident and up for banter, independent minded and, to her credit, clearly a reluctant debutante.
It didn't hurt that she was pretty and, of course, that she liked
him. He didn't know what he wanted from her beyond compan-
ionship; her own desires, he thought, although perhaps it was
vain of him to do so, required less clarification. Thus far he had
somehow persuaded Susannah to accept the constraints on their
relationship—they hadn't so much as kissed—imposed because,
try as he might, he was unable to betray the woman who had
betrayed him. Not that Susannah was aware of this, of course.
He hoped she simply found him overly polite, a perfect exemplar
of British repression, but he knew this couldn't last.

After the turbulence of his time with Tsiona, these days with
Susannah had a restorative smoothness, as if Jerusalem itself,
home to so many ugly animosities, had calmed down in Tsiona's
absence, but then, overnight it seemed, Ivor felt the city coil
once more like an animal and prepare to spring.

They were sitting in a café inside the Damascus Gate shortly
after six, the sun dipping its head toward the horizon, when all
around them Ivor and Susannah heard the shuttering of metal
doors yanked from ceiling to floor and then the clink of pad-
locks. The lockup appeared coordinated, not the usual haphaz-
ard end to the day. The storekeepers were in a rush, and Ivor
and Susannah both felt a new and disturbing electric charge in
the air. Susannah pointed out that the women and children had
disappeared from view. Down the El Wad alley someone lit a

brazier and soon small fires were burning deep into the Muslim quarter. Suddenly, the café emptied out, and the waiters began their own swift cleanup of plates and cutlery.

A young Arab man crossed quickly in front of the Citadel and approached their table.

"You must leave," he said. "Leave now."

Susannah stood up. Ivor reached into his pocket, extracted a few crumpled notes, and left them on the table.

As they moved toward the gate a squad of British soldiers entered, fanned out, and began to pester the few stragglers still locking their stores.

"Get a bleeding move on. Curfew's at six, not six-thirty."

Ivor and Susannah pressed against the wall to allow the soldiers through. When the last of them had passed, Ivor called out, "What's going on?"

The soldier turned and seemed to weigh for a moment whether or not to speak.

"Didn't you 'ear? Two stabbings in 'ere last night. Going to make sure things don't get out of hand. Nip it all in the bud."

"Who was stabbed?"

The soldier shrugged. "Don't ask me."

Once outside the Old City wall, Ivor and Susannah hurried up the road in the direction of the French hospital and arrived as its adjacent clock tower struck six. "It's all the rumors," Ivor said. "Mandate authorities helping Jews buy land, German Jews flooding into the country. The Arabs are very angry."

"How do you know they're rumors?"

"You're right, it's more than that. An endless vicious cycle. Jews pressure the British government to the point where it feels it must open the spigot, in come these poor bastards from Germany, and it doesn't take long before the Arabs here are up in arms, something terrible happens, and the authorities close the spigot again. Then, once more, the Jews begin to agitate and the whole damn process starts over. You can feel the tension building now, can't you? Something's going to blow."

Darkness fell and as it did so, the voice of the muezzin rose once more, summoning the faithful in the day's penultimate call to prayer.

"We're no match for it, are we?" Ivor said suddenly. They had stopped near the entrance to the Hotel Fast to catch their breath.

"No match for what?"

"I mean our presence here. The British presence. It's a thin veneer. Mrs. Barlow at my boardinghouse, she made me breakfast yesterday, English tea, toast and marmalade, 'Lots of oranges here,' she said, 'excellent marmalade.' She'd made it herself."

"I don't understand what you're saying."

"I'm not sure either. I mean there is no 'English' tea, is there? It comes from China or India, and the oranges and the sugar for the marmalade, you don't find them in England. It's just a label, a claim, even a theft. Like our authority here. Just a slapped-on label, eventually it's going to peel away."

"And the Jews who are coming in from Germany. Are they slapped on too?"

"The Arabs think so, but they have nowhere else to go, and anyway they began here, didn't they? I mean the British haven't dug up any Saxon swords in the Palestinian countryside, but there's a whole Jewish world under the ground here."

"And which world are you part of? The one that's 'slapped on,' or the Jewish?"

"That's the problem. I think the answer is 'both and neither.' What about you?"

"Well, I'm positively happy I don't have to deal with the British part. I don't know what I feel. I wish I had Charles's and my father's certainties. I don't so much admire them as envy them. You know, I had a wonderful time at Radcliffe, but then at graduation I overheard the parents of one of my friends talking about me; she described me as 'one of the better kind of Jewish students.' I said nothing, of course. This kind of attitude wasn't new to me. Along with Radcliffe I'd also applied to Barnard in New York and received a letter from the dean informing me that unfortunately the Jewish quota for my year had already been filled. So, I understand Charles's fervor, his desire to fight back, and also my father's commitment to the cause. They're on different sides, but their passion is the same. Do you have a passion, Ivor? I'm beginning to suspect that you do. But it isn't me, is it?"

They had reached the triangle at the foot of Ben Yehuda Street, where the Café Vienna and the Café Europe were still crowded with tea drinkers and chess players, and a long line of ticket buyers, which was truly more of a scrum, pushed for entry into the Zion Cinema.

"Shall we join them?" Ivor said.

"What's playing?"

Ivor looked up at the hoarding. "*Life Dances On.*"

"How could we not?" Susannah said.

On the last night before the festival, they dined in a small vegetarian restaurant. Afterward, they took a walk, turned a corner, and began to stroll down the Street of the Prophets, which Baron had told Ivor was the most beautiful street outside the Old City. They stopped outside the consulate built by an Ethiopian empress with its rose-colored dome, yet under construction, peeking over the high walls that surrounded it. It was a warm, still night, the moon invisible behind clouds, the branches of tall eucalyptus trees spread dark and heavy in the pallid light thrown by streetlamps, some flickering, some weakly powered, and most not working at all.

"Look," Susannah said, "it's appalling, isn't it?" She pointed toward the swastika flag that flew over the German consulate.

"They've also got one up at the Hotel Fast. Did you notice it? I stayed there on my first trip to Jerusalem."

"How can they let them do that?"

"What choice do they have? There are plenty of people here doing business with Germany."

"Not only here. I don't think there's all that much antipathy toward the Nazis at home, except from Jews, of course. The student newspaper at Harvard wants the university to give one of them an honorary degree, he's an alum or something. At least that won't happen here."

Ivor thought he heard footsteps behind him accompanied by the tick, tick, tick of a bicycle, but when he looked back over his shoulder, whoever it was must have disappeared into one of the homes along the road and the bicycle was leaning against the wall of an overgrown garden.

Susannah touched Ivor's arm and froze in place. Twenty yards away, three men emerged through the consulate gate. Ivor heard Susannah's sharp intake of breath. One of the men, significantly taller than the others, was unmistakably Henry Green.

A black car swept past Ivor and Susannah and pulled up onto the curb. The men hurried in, slammed the doors; the car sped off and disappeared around a corner.

There was no time to delve into the activities of Henry Green even if Ivor had wanted to. For, almost as soon as they returned to the King David, Susannah bursting with the news, Mrs. Green dismissed her with a firm, "You must have been mistaken, darling, your father hasn't been in Jerusalem for days." When Susannah insisted that it had to have been him, her mother responded, "Well, I spoke to him on the telephone only an hour ago and he was in Tel Aviv." And then, to compound matters, Ivor received a message of his own: Phineas Baron had contacted Beatrice Green; he knew (of course he knew!) that Ivor was a daily visitor to the hotel, and he'd asked her to ensure that Ivor get in touch with him immediately. "Such a charming man," Mrs. Green affirmed, in her honeyed Southern burr, although Ivor was starting to think that she laid it on a bit.

Baron's instructions were quick and to the point. Fawzi had gathered important information about Abdul Malik, and Ivor was to head to Jaffa and hear him out. The court date was imminent, "perhaps as soon as these damn holidays are done with." Ivor had realized some time ago that urgency was Baron's favorite means of exerting power, but he had no choice save to obey. Baron would hardly allow him to drag his anger and his bruised heart down the Via Dolorosa one more time before he left or nurse his secret misery in the cafés of the Triangle.

"I'll come with you," Susannah said when Ivor announced his planned morning departure. Mrs. Green gave her a long, hard look and Ivor wasn't sure if Susannah's enthusiasm was for him or an escape from her mother's company.

"And where will you stay?" Mrs. Green was quick to ask.

Susannah hesitated for a moment, long enough, Ivor thought, for her mother to imagine her daughter in Ivor's bed, but then she thought of something even better to goad her. "Well, if you tell me where Daddy is, I'll book into the same hotel."

Her implication wasn't lost on Beatrice Green, and so she rebuffed it with a bravura show of confidence: "I believe he must be at the San Remo." It was clear, however, to everyone present that she had no idea where he was.

15

Ivor allowed Susannah to come with him on one condition: While Fawzi spoke with Ivor she would absent herself; there was plenty to see on the streets, a vibrant market to explore. He would pick her up at the San Remo, from where her father, registered as a guest, had mysteriously disappeared before Susannah's arrival. Ivor had spent the night in his boardinghouse, risen early, and taken himself to a café, where he sat now with a glass of mint tea and read *The Palestine Post*. Everywhere in the country, it seemed, tensions were ramping up, small fires stoked toward a conflagration. The Arab Executive had called for a general strike.

Meanwhile, the enmities stirred by the Arlosoroff case had temporarily receded, except that the trial fed into the problem in the strangest way. All the Jews in Palestine agreed that more Jewish immigration to Palestine was a good thing, a necessary thing. But his clients and their supporters opposed the deal that Arlosoroff had tried to make—the deal that would bring more Jews—as a pact with the devil. The Revisionists had their own proposal, some scheme to persuade hundreds of thousands of Jews to leave Poland. In any case, what if Stavsky and Rosenblatt *were* innocent, as both he and Baron were committed to affirming; what if Arlosoroff had been murdered by Arabs precisely because he was enabling the arrival of more Jews? But Abdul Malik had made no political claims at all. If anything, his friend Issa had had his mind set on a rape. But, of course, Malik had retracted. His confession was a fiction. Perhaps today the information that Fawzi had promised to reveal would shed new light on the matter.

Ivor put down his paper. On the opposite side of the road a European-style villa was under construction, framed by cypresses. The workers, whose sawing and hammering had filled the air with dust, were taking a short break, lounging with their backs against a half-built wall, enjoying the sea breeze.

Ivor tried to remember when he had first learned about Palestine. When he was about ten his parents had placed a blue and yellow tin Jewish National Fund charity box on the mantelpiece above the fireplace in their dining room. It had Hebrew lettering that Ivor couldn't understand superimposed on a map of Palestine; once he had traced his finger from the blue lake at the top and down the river to what he now knew was the Dead Sea. He couldn't remember anyone in his family ever dropping as much as a single coin into the box. It just stood there, unnoticed, ignored, largely forgotten, which is how the entire country stood for most of the English Jews that he knew. It was only when he got to Oxford and met Charles Gross that Palestine entered his consciousness as something more than a distant, impoverished place that had no more to do with him than certain equally far-off and even more disadvantaged outposts of the British Empire. And now here he was in the thick of things, bleary-eyed, getting buffeted around by forces way beyond his control, and sick at heart to boot.

They arrived in Jaffa early for Ivor's meeting, walked a little way inland, and sat in a small out-of-the-way café surrounded by the stubborn disorder of the town, a tree overlooking a crumbled wall, a stairway leading nowhere, an empty terrace, but then a line of white houses with flat roofs running from Andromeda's Rock to the sea. Susannah's turquoise brooch, pinned to her striped knit shirt, seemed to repeat the color of the waves.

"Better than Baltimore?" Ivor asked.

The sky was beginning to cloud over but Susannah still took her sunglasses from her bag, put them on, then leaned back and stretched out.

"I do like the sun, and with all this walking I think I've got my tennis legs back." She pulled her skirt up a little, so the hem rested a couple of inches above her knees.

Ivor wasn't immune to her gesture. She was alluring. He caught himself staring and turned to look out to sea. He watched the waves kiss the shore and a fishing boat advancing slowly out of the harbor.

"I want to thank you," he said, "for being such a good friend."

"A good friend? How dull. You're hardly the first young man in my life, you know. And you don't have to be so careful all the time about what you say to me. I'm not a prude."

"I'm sorry."

"Yes, you should be. At the debutante ball, you know, we were each assigned an honor guard. Mine was a willowy, entirely unimpressive Johns Hopkins freshman from the Phi Epsilon Pi fraternity, Leonard Dalsemer. He was utterly hopeless. He wanted to kiss me very badly, and I wanted to be kissed, but he got too nervous and when he tried our teeth just smashed together. I studied English literature in college but I wish now

I'd gone for anthropology. You know, mating rituals among the tribes."

Susannah was laughing and Ivor too, and suddenly he felt a great tenderness toward her that at any other time might have been the beginning of a great infatuation.

"Perhaps you'd like to try to be my new honor guard. You can't do worse than Lenny Dalsemer."

Ivor was tempted to say, "I wouldn't count on it," but the awkwardness of his Oxford days had been dispelled on Tsiona's balcony, and in her bedroom. Now, he thought, somewhat embarrassed by his own confidence, he could do better than poor Lenny Dalsemer. He knew that.

Eventually they made their way to Fawzi's shop, which was situated right on the central square. Fawzi wasn't there; the young man behind the till apologized, told them he had been delayed, and assured Ivor that Mr. Fawzi would arrive soon. They browsed through the stock of international books and magazines, then sat and read, happily ensconced under the feathery leaves of a jacaranda.

At first, neither of them noticed the other merchants on Fawzi's street shuttering their businesses, and when Susannah pointed it out, Ivor guessed it was some kind of regular early closing on this particular day that they were unaware of.

A line of policemen appeared on the far side of the square. Ivor hardly had time to wonder why they were there before the doors of two nearby mosques flung open and a great crowd poured out chanting and running toward the clock tower, massing in rapidly expanding numbers and wielding every missile they could lay their hands on. Suddenly, Ivor had his arm around Susannah, trying to shield her from the rocks, stones, and bottles arcing through the air, peeling back the gray sky as they fell; so stupid of him not to remember what he had read only that morning, a demonstration planned for Jaffa. He had thought, if he thought about it at all, it would be some minor affair. Now they were trapped.

Ivor urged Susannah forward; if they could get behind the line of policemen they might be able to free themselves. A bottle shattered at their feet, and then another; half the projectiles aimed at the police, it seemed, took some random trajectory and missed their target. A hail of misdirected stones smacked against the wall behind them, Susannah cried out, and Ivor saw a trickle of blood running from above her eye and down her cheek. He stuck his hands in his pockets, searching for a handkerchief he knew wasn't there.

She held her hand to her head, her fingertips quickly covered in blood. Ivor rummaged through her bag, pulled a handful of tissues from where she had stuffed them beneath her compact and lipstick, and pressed them to her forehead.

"It's not deep," he said.

Arms raised over their heads, Ivor maneuvered them in the direction of the district commissioner's office. Progress was slow, hampered everywhere by frenzied rioters colliding with one another in their eagerness to get into the fight.

The first baton charge sent the front lines of the crowd back in a wave. Through megaphones the police called in English and Arabic for the protestors to disperse, their exhorting voices barely audible in the general din. Dust kicked up in wild spirals stung Ivor's eyes, clung to the blood on Susannah's face. They lowered their heads and, now bent almost double, jostled their way through.

At the opposite corner of the square the thin line of policemen, no more than fifty or sixty, buckled and then re-formed. It seemed the ever-swelling crowd must overwhelm them, but one baton charge followed another, and the crowd rolled back like a withdrawing tide, only to recoup its energy and rush forward again.

Suddenly a unit of mounted police rode from a side street into the square, unarmed, using their horses as weapons as they attempted to cut a swath through to the Port Road. The protestors pulled back from the path of the rushing hooves. Ivor, looking up, saw one of the horses slip on the cobblestones; an enraged group of men fell on its rider, beating him with sticks, dragging him into their midst.

The blood ran down Susannah's cheek and onto her chin, flecked the collar of her shirt with small red dots. Ivor reached back into her bag, collected the last of the tissues, balled them into a wad, removed the dust-smeared and blood-sodden paper that stuck in small pieces to her wound, and pressed the make-shift bandage hard to Susannah's eyebrow.

"Almost there," he said, although they weren't.

Lifting his head Ivor recognized Duncan Prendergast, the captain from the Jaffa station, who drove his large bay horse into the crowd, urging his men forward for yet one more baton charge, but they were stuck, shields jammed against the rioters' front line as they battled to hold it back.

At the moment when it appeared that the cordon must break, Prendergast, red in the face, twisted in his saddle and shouted at the top of his voice. Immediately, a small group of police, hidden to this point, rushed to take up positions on the flat rooftop of the district police headquarters. Once more megaphone-amplified voices called for the crowd to disperse. If anyone heard they paid no heed. Prendergast barked an order, and three successive volleys of bullets flew into the mass of people.

At the sound of the first shots Ivor pulled Susannah to the

ground. They lay there now, wrapped in each other's arms, Ivor cradling her head, while men and boys stepped over them and scattered, detaching themselves from the panicked throng.

A narrow dark cloud crossed the sky like a small tugboat dragging larger black clouds behind it, and then the rain came, a few drops followed by a downpour, the sky emptying onto the dead and wounded in the square. The last bullet shot through the head of a fallen horse.

It felt like hours before they picked themselves up, and when they did, Prendergast was standing over them.

"What the hell . . . ?" he began, but then noticed the dried blood on Susannah's face. "Willis," he yelled, "over here, pronto."

The rain stopped as suddenly as it had begun; a streak of lemon-yellow light filtered through the clouds and held there like a bright scar. As corpse after corpse was stretchered away, an uneasy quiet settled over the square. Close by, a group of grim-faced policemen surveyed the square. One of them dropped his shield to the ground and the tinny clatter on the cobblestones drew Ivor's attention. He looked quizzically at Prendergast.

"*That's* what they had to protect them?"

"The baking pans? Ingenious, aren't they? No budget for riot control gear. One of our chaps, Harry Booth, came up with a solution. Welded handles and leather straps onto the pans."

Prendergast's voice trailed away as he spoke. He looked around. "Did the job, I suppose. Better armed than our adversaries."

Ivor felt ashamed.

Prendergast shook his head and waved his hand around the square, as if only now the magnitude of what had transpired was beginning to sink in. "Awful day," he said, "awful."

While Willis attended to Susannah's cut, Ivor ran back to Fawzi's shop. In their haste to escape the riot he had left his briefcase there. Inside it was a sheaf of documents relating to the case, including the notes he had taken from his first interviews with Tsiona.

Spirals of smoke drifted skyward over Salahi Road; Ivor's heart sank. He broke into a run and turned the corner only to reach an abrupt halt before the burned-out shell of Fawzi's shop, its roof still smoldering and crackling.

A small group of Arab men stood in a half circle a little way from the charred and collapsed half beams that now constituted the shop front. One of the men acknowledged Ivor's presence with a sideways glance; the rest ignored him. A pall of misery hung in the air.

"Do any of you know where Mr. Fawzi is?" Ivor asked.

In reply he received a shrug, but then one of the men turned toward Ivor, lifted his hand, and drew its edge across his throat.

Ivor, walking through ashes, moved the twisted metal that was all that remained of the till. He wondered which of Fawzi's roles, merchant to the English or informer to Baron and no doubt others, had brought this horror upon him. But what did it matter now? As for whatever Fawzi was going to tell him, it was lost forever.

Ivor located what remained of his briefcase under two skeletal blackened chairs where Susannah had sat only two hours earlier leafing through month-old copies of *The Saturday Evening Post* while he read the hopelessly inadequate sports news in *The Palestine Post*. The clasp on the case was stuck tight. Ivor pried it open with his penknife and removed the blackened, brittle pages from the shriveled leather: They disintegrated in his hands.

Susannah lay on the narrow bed in Ivor's room. Back in Jaffa, while the high-pitched cries of mourners rent the air around them, Willis had wound an extravagant bandage around her head, but her cut had bled through and now she looked like one of the wounded of the Somme. The night had turned warm, as if discarding the turbulence of the day, and a late breeze, lazy and dissolving off the sea, penetrated the windows, but Susannah shivered.

"Do you have a blanket?" she murmured.

Ivor opened his closet, home to his meager wardrobe. He removed a maroon candlewick bedspread from the top shelf and spread it over Susannah. Moments later she fell asleep.

When she awoke Susannah rose from the bed and straightened her clothes. Ivor, sitting in the room's ratty armchair, reached for his cigarettes from the side table.

"Have you been watching me the whole time I was sleeping?"

"Yes."

"That's kind of you. Did I talk in my sleep? Say anything I shouldn't have?"

"You cried out for Lenny Dalsemer."

Susannah laughed, then winced and touched her hand to her head. "I suppose I should call my mother."

"Yes, she must be worried."

"Oh, I doubt she's heard about the riot, and if she did she has no reason to believe that I was there." Susannah brushed herself down as best she could.

"Where are you going now?"

"Back to the San Remo."

"Don't you think you should see a doctor? You might need stitches."

"I imagine that guest services could provide one, but I doubt it's necessary. It's just a small cut."

"I'll come with you."

"No, don't. I need a little time on my own. Come later this evening."

"Of course. Whatever you want."

She took his cigarette, inhaled, and returned it to him. The bloodstain had settled into a Rorschach blot on her bandage.

"How do I look?" she said.

"Like a very pretty member of the walking wounded."

A donkey's bray, like the sound of a mad cello, intruded into the room.

"We almost died," she said.

Ivor hadn't even begun to process what had happened: to lie still among corpses and to find yourself alive.

He listened as Susannah clattered down the stairs, then observed from the window as she took a few purposeful steps down the street and hailed a taxi.

After she had left, Ivor lay on his bed for a long time staring at the ceiling. Fawzi's face kept floating into view like Banquo's ghost. The trial would be postponed now. He couldn't see how it could go forward. Not until the spinning world of Palestine had settled back on its axis. He would have to talk to Baron, of course, but he couldn't imagine that the attorney general would want to prosecute the case at such a volatile time. The dead, Mr. Fawzi among them, would have to be buried and mourned, the wounded tended to and nursed, the Arab leaders and the Muslim clergy somehow placated. And in the meantime, the Jews would continue to trickle or flood into the country (depending on whose side you viewed it from), while the Nazi flags on the German consulate and the Hotel Fast flapped in the desert wind that blew across Jerusalem.

He must have been searching for some peace after the horrible violence of the day because, on the edge of falling asleep, he found himself cycling down the towpath by the river from Oxford to Iffley, and then he was standing inside that village's perfectly appointed Romanesque church, looking up at its stained-glass oculus as the light poured in, and for a moment he experienced a feeling of great tranquility, until that other sensation came over him, the one that attached itself throughout all his university years: that he was in the wrong place, that the countryside he loved, the delights of bramble and thicket, rainsoaked meadows, profusions of wildflowers, and birds singing all the way through Oxfordshire and the college buildings he admired, with their exalted dreaming spires, were marvelous attributes of a county and a country that barely tolerated him, and if so only as an interloping guest. He wanted to lay a claim, but he couldn't. As a ten-year-old boy he had made a wooden sword and imagined himself as D'Artagnan in his favorite book, *The Three Musketeers,* but when he came up to Oxford eight years later, he was assigned a far less exciting and thrill-seeking role: second violin in the kosher quartet. On the other hand, his college had let him in, hadn't it? No one had slammed a door in his face and said, "No entry for Jews."

Would he have felt more comfortable if he'd grown up here in this parched landscape with its sudden intrusions of beauty, a place that on this awful morning had filled with dust and blood? The answer was almost certainly no.

At dusk Ivor set out for Susannah's hotel, but his route was indirect. The date of Tsiona's show at the Herzliya Gymnasia, and her promise (was it a promise?) that he could help her to move the paintings, had been imprinted as indelible marks in his consciousness.

He detoured to Herzl Street to walk past the high school's long wrought iron fence with the hopeless expectation that he

would somehow discover Tsiona before the buildings' high turrets and its arabesque windows, directing assistants this way
and that as they carried her framed canvases into the exhibition
hall for tonight's opening. Yet how could she be there? He had
seen her—and it must have been her, disguised—mounting the
gangplank of the SS *Roma* with her lover, bound for Cyprus or
Rhodes or Brindisi, someplace where whoever was after them
would not be able to find them.

Ivor stood now at the front entrance to the school. There was
hardly any movement on the street or in the shops on the other
side of the road. The sun lowered itself behind the tall cypresses
and spreading palms in the school's garden. The branches of
the eucalyptus trees cast their last long evening shadows. Ivor
opened the gate and walked down the short path toward the
building. Affixed to the door, a poster advertised the show
in Hebrew and English: THE HEART'S PLAYGROUND, with the
word "Cancelled" pasted across it. It featured one of Tsiona's
pencil drawings of a woman's head and had been partly torn
down, but the opening date remained visible. It was a date that
would be remembered, but sadly not because of the impact of
her art.

He was about to turn away when he heard a noise, a rustle
of leaves and foliage that could have been someone stepping
through the garden. If he could have willed Tsiona, she would
have stepped out now from between the whispering trees.

Ivor remained in the garden, waiting for her, until the sun's
crimson reflections disappeared entirely from the classroom
windows that held them and seemed to absorb the bloody shock
of the day.

A flicker of memory brought his own London school to life:
voices in the playground, a game of cricket played with a tennis

ball, a wicket chalked on a brick wall, a handbell ringing to summon the boys back to classes. And then it was gone, and England seemed so distant he might have been in Palestine for four years instead of four months.

To his surprise, when he arrived at the San Remo, Susannah's father was waiting for him in the lobby. Sharply dressed in a well-tailored dark suit with his white shirt open at the collar, he lowered his perfectly coiffed head as if he might charge at Ivor. His deep baritone, when he unleashed it, filled the lobby as if it were a concert hall.

"What the hell were you doing in Jaffa? Are you an idiot? Is this what they teach you at Oxford? Don't you read the papers? Didn't you know what was coming?"

He grabbed Ivor roughly by the elbow and guided him in the direction of an alcove that harbored three wing-back leather armchairs set against sky-blue walls. "Sit down."

Absurd to think, as Ivor did, Yes, we were reading the papers; luckily, he managed to keep his mouth shut.

Henry Green continued to berate him—"I should punch you right in the nose"—while Ivor mumbled apologies and tried as best he could to alleviate the situation. It was only when a waiter appeared before them that Mr. Green dropped his voice and suspended his barrage of insults. He waved the waiter away and threw one last dart.

"You don't seem to be taking very good care of my daughter, do you?"

"Susannah is extraordinary," Ivor said.

Mr. Green leaned back in his chair. He lifted his hand and gestured to the waiter to return.

"Enough," he said. "Let's have a drink. A friend of mine's

going to be joining us, we have something important to discuss with you. He'll be here any minute."

Ivor surveyed the lobby, which was also home to the bar. Under a sparkling chandelier, a dozen or so British sojourners, some in uniform, and quieter than usual, perhaps on account of the day's tragic events, raised and clinked their glasses, downed their whiskey chasers, returned to their beers. For a moment Ivor envied them, imagined himself among them, just an Englishman among Englishmen. They weren't bad people, probably lamented what had happened today as much as anyone. He could hear his father's voice, as he sat in a deck chair, newspaper on his lap, savoring the delights of a mellow summer afternoon in his St. John's Wood garden, the air absorbing the scent of lilies of the valley gathered at the foot of his favorite lilac tree. "England, best country in the world."

"If you're looking for Susannah, she's not coming down," Mr. Green continued. "That wound needed three stitches. She has to rest. Why the hell didn't you take her to a doctor?"

"I thought . . . I thought the medic had taken care of her," Ivor stuttered. Clearly Susannah hadn't mentioned her hourlong nap in Ivor's room.

"You didn't notice the blood seeping through? Are you blind?"

The arrival of a stooped older man, with strikingly large ears and brown eyes circled by a pair of glasses that rested uncomfortably on a bump in his nose, put an end to Mr. Green's interrogation. Henry twisted around in his seat.

"Ah, Georg, you're here. All right. This is Ivor Castle, the young man I told you about, presently dating my daughter, Susannah. Ivor, this is Georg Oberman. He's the director of the German Zionist Federation in Berlin. He was with me when I met you at the King David, but you probably don't remember."

"I don't think we were introduced." Judging by his stature, Georg Oberman could have been one of the men he and Susannah had seen exiting the German consulate.

"That's right. You weren't introduced."

"You're a lucky man," Oberman said to Ivor.

"You bet he is. Luckier than you know, he almost got my daughter killed today, not to mention himself."

"You were in Jaffa?"

"We were."

A look of concern spread over Mr. Oberman's face. Henry Green gestured for him to sit down. "Never mind that now," he said. He looked toward the bar. "Let's keep our voices down, shall we?"

Mr. Oberman sat, coughed, removed his handkerchief from his pocket, and coughed again into it. He had a great weariness about him next to which Henry Green looked the very picture of health. He's come from "there," Ivor thought, where storm trooper thugs beat Jews on the street, smash the windows of their shops, take their livelihoods away, and even resort to murder: He'd read about a Berlin man found with a swastika carved into his chest.

In the first weeks after Hitler had come to power, Ivor remembered, Jewish shop owners in London had put signs in their windows. Ivor had seen them in the West End and on the Finchley Road not far from his home—NO GERMAN GOODS SOLD HERE. Other Jews, upstanding members of the community, argued that Herr Hitler had no idea quite what the Nazi thugs in his party were up to, and even if he did, the better course was diplomacy, not the antagonism of a boycott.

Ivor suspected that his father had belonged to that latter group—at least for a while. And what did the rest of England think? Sitting on the tube, heading out on the Bakerloo line from

St. John's Wood, the man opposite him holding his newspaper so the headline was starkly visible to everyone in the carriage, JUDEA DECLARES WAR ON GERMANY. When the man exited at Baker Street and left the newspaper on his seat, Ivor snatched it up. Not a call to arms, of course, but a scold, those aggressive Jews at it again.

"What's going on?" Ivor said to Mr. Green. "What's this meeting about?"

"Just listen to Georg, and then I'll tell you what we'd like you to do."

"You are involved in defending Stavsky and Rosenblatt," Oberman said, his English heavily shaded by his German accent, "so I don't have to tell you that their accusers regard them as murderous representatives of the hostile elements here who opposed Mr. Arlosoroff's attempt to secure a transfer agreement with the Nazis. This is an agreement that we Zionists in Germany support. We have made that clear to the new regime and we are working in every way we can to repeat and supplement Mr. Arlosoroff's agreement. The Nazi Party wishes to rid Germany of its Jews and we yearn to see German Jews safe in Palestine and we will do whatever it takes to get them here. Now, would you agree that even if your clients are innocent, which I cannot believe they are, that would do nothing to reduce the danger for supporters of the Arlosoroff agreement or any agreement like it?"

"I suppose so, although I can't say for sure what that danger is."

"Please let me finish." Oberman leaned forward and Ivor noticed a pattern of brown liver spots on the backs of his hands. "For some time, since the beginning of March, and even before Mr. Arlosoroff began *his* negotiations, Mr. Green and myself, and others whom you do not need to know, have been conducting our own. What do you know about German currency exemptions for emigrants?"

"Nothing." Ivor had the impulse to add, "And why don't we leave it at that?" But Georg Oberman had the fixed intent of the ancient mariner. The facts and figures he was about to share were of the utmost importance to him; they represented lives, the beaten and reviled Jews' chance to find their footing outside a hostile or indifferent Europe and start again.

"Well right now, as you might imagine, these exemptions for those wishing to leave are very tight, for everyone, but for Jews there is a loophole. As things stand today, although we don't know for how long, every citizen of Germany has a right to emigrate, and our British friends"—here Oberman waved his hand in the direction of the bar—"have determined that every Jew who has a thousand pounds to his name and can thus be defined as a helpful 'capitalist' may enter Palestine. It's a lot of money but it is nothing compared to what the Jews must leave behind when they depart German soil. So, you will understand that what we needed to do was convince certain government officials in Hitler's regime to permit Jewish emigrants to remove one thousand pounds of their wealth from Germany and bring it to Palestine."

"And did you?"

Oberman turned to Henry, who had been staring intently at Ivor, as if still in the process of taking his measure.

"We did," Henry said. "You don't need to hear the details, but we were in a position to promise a dramatic increase for German exports, which, as you know, are already under strong boycott in some places and the threat of boycott in others."

"How is this different from Mr. Arlosoroff's deal?"

"It is not that different. We are a tributary of the river, if you like, but our deal is highly secret, very much in the shadows, and we would like it to remain there."

Ivor sipped the glass of water that the waiter had placed before him. He felt as if from the moment that he had stepped off his ship and into Palestine he had found not dry land but rising seas.

"What's all this got to do with me?"

"These are volatile times, Mr. Castle, you have seen what happens when Zionists like us openly admit that they are negotiating with Hitler for the exit of Jews."

"Have I? What if my clients are innocent?"

"Do you really believe that?"

For a moment Ivor was back in Tsiona's apartment, lifting her sketchbook from the floor, turning the pages, encountering unmistakably the faces of Stavsky and Rosenblatt. "We have plenty of evidence." He was going to add, "We have a confession from a young Arab man," but that was no longer true, and even if it was, the information was not for public consumption.

"Be that as it may, our urgent need is to make sure that our deal appears to have derived from a British initiative and not a Zionist one. Otherwise, the consequences will be . . ."

"More than one shooting on the beach." Henry Green finished the sentence for Oberman.

"How can you possibly do that?"

"This is where we need your help. It is a very small thing that we will ask you to do. You will not put yourself at risk in any way."

Ivor ran his hand through his hair and looked around him. Oberman, he guessed, had put himself at risk a hundred times, and yet he was the one who felt he had to reassure Ivor.

"Listen," Oberman said, raising his voice for the first time, "we have got to get these people out! And the sooner the better."

"Why can't they go to Belgium, or France, why do they have to come here?"

Ivor didn't quite know why he was saying this; something in

the daily balance of his allegiances appeared to have shifted, if only temporarily. Perhaps it was the aftershock of the riot, the sensation lingering within him that this was a place of violence and blood—or at least, a place of multiple clashing dreams of belonging—and that things could only get worse.

The two men fell silent, staring hard at Ivor. Henry Green's face turned beet red; he looked as if he might explode.

"Well, for a start," he finally said, "they can't take their money to Belgium or France, none of it."

Oberman shifted his chair closer to Ivor's. "We managed to convince the British embassy in Berlin to act as a conduit between us and the bureaucracies of the Third Reich in order to have their various offices confirm that the zero-currency restriction on Jews leaving the country is lifted and the one-thousand-pound limit set in place. But what we require now is a carefully worded letter from us, from the German Zionist Federation (and implicitly its American friends), that will thank the British, not for acting as our go-between but for having come up with the idea themselves and worked hard to persuade the Germans to implement it."

"But they didn't come up with the idea, you did, and they didn't manage to get it implemented, you did that too."

Oberman sat back, then turned to give Henry Green a look of absolute bewilderment.

"I didn't lie," Henry said, "he went to Oxford and he has a law degree."

Ivor, his pride dented, felt the need to redeem himself. "I understand," he said, "you need to cast the exemption not as a concession won from the Nazis by the German Zionist Federation but by the British so there will be no backlash against you here from those Jews in Palestine who oppose any deals with the living evil that is Hitler's government."

"Precisely."

"And I assume you want me to draft your reputation-saving, or as you believe, lifesaving letter, thanking the British for phantom accomplishments that are, in reality, yours."

"Not draft, that's already been taken care of. Edit, amend, improve if you can."

"And to whom will you send it?"

"Why, to the high commissioner here, of course."

"To Wharton?"

"Yes. You're a fellow countryman. You speak his language better than we do. We want to make sure we're sending a letter that's persuasive. Look, we're not asking very much of you, just a little Oxford polish on the German American shoes."

"But surely he will know that what you've written isn't true. He must be aware that the British embassy in Berlin has been helping you, passing along all your proposals."

"That is possible, maybe even probable, yes, but Sir Douglas is not a stupid man and he has extended his sympathies toward us on frequent occasions. We think he will understand what he has to do if he wants to avoid another Arlosoroff affair."

"After today, why would he want to incite the Arabs further against the police and the army? Why invite blame on the British for allowing more Jews into Palestine?"

"Because the one-thousand-pound minimum qualifying condition of entry already applies. All he will have to acknowledge is a remarkable coup for the British government, who have persuaded the Nazis to allow Jews, after all, to take some money with them when they leave."

"For Palestine."

"Well, that is the only place where their money will be waiting for them."

"And what if they don't have the money?"

"That is where Mr. Green comes in."

"We're raising it," Mr. Green said, "in the United States."

Ivor's head was throbbing; the events of the morning had caught up to him. The denizens of the bar grew rowdier by the minute, and now they gathered around the piano and joined together in a song: "Coffee in the morning, kisses at night." The dead, it seemed, were already forgotten.

"When do you need this letter?"

"Later tonight."

Ivor hesitated.

"Why can't you get Charles Gross to write it? He can manage a persuasive English sentence as well as I can. And he's related to you, isn't he? Aren't you cousins or something?"

"Don't be a wise guy," Mr. Green said. "That little shit can't be trusted. I don't know what game he's playing, but it's not ours."

"Then why trust me?"

"Because I trust my daughter, and from what she has told me about you I gather that you don't appear to have a game, do you, Ivor? You want to make up for what you almost did today? Help refine the letter for us. We'll give you the guidelines. It shouldn't take you long."

Ivor surveyed the faces of the two men, but whatever he was searching for in them was quickly lost as the lights in the lobby and bar flickered and then went out. The Tel Aviv power station, a local monument to modern life and progress with its magnificent façade of pseudo-columns, looked like an urban temple but unfortunately tended to keep provincial hours.

Henry Green had risen from his seat. In the half darkness the hotel staff ran to light candles.

"I think you should stay away from Susannah for a while. She needs to rest and when her head is healed, I'd like her to go up north with her mother. Apparently, Mount Gilboa is very beautiful at this time of year, not to be missed. There's also a hot springs near Tiberias, thermal baths on the shores of the Galilee, I expect them to do my daughter a world of good."

"Perhaps I could just say goodbye."

"I don't think that's wise. Why wake her? No doubt you'll see her when she gets back."

"We saw you," Ivor said. "We saw you coming out of the German consulate and we couldn't understand what you were doing there."

Henry looked at Mr. Oberman. The two men stayed silent while the noise from the bar, the clink of glasses, voices raised in song, raucous laughter, rolled over them.

"Well," Henry finally said, "now you do."

They led him to a windowless cell-like room in the bowels of the hotel that featured a low, unforgiving chest of drawers with a typewriter set on its flat mahogany top and a single chair. After a while a staff member knocked on the door and delivered a ream of paper. Ivor sat with his knees pressed against the makeshift table.

"We'll wait for you upstairs."

Henry Green handed Ivor an envelope. Ivor reviewed the contents and set to work.

We are very glad indeed to see that it has been made possible, through the good offices of His Majesty's ambassador in Berlin, for Jews wishing to leave Germany to settle in Palestine with the qualifying minimum of one thousand pounds. I should like to thank most sincerely P. J. Baker for his help in this matter, and I hope some means may be found of conveying to Ambassador Sir Douglas Clark

JONATHAN WILSON

*our warm appreciation of his assistance in obtaining this
most valuable concession. We ask for your permission to
publicize the Palestinian exemption as the remarkable British
accomplishment that it is. . . .*

Ivor stopped typing; twenty minutes had passed and thus
far his embellishments had included "good offices," "most
sincerely," "warm appreciation," "valuable concession," and
"remarkable British accomplishment." That was the extent of
his own remarkable British accomplishment.

An hour later he left the room, closing the door quietly
behind him. The envelope carrying the new letter was in his
hand. Oberman was waiting for him in the lobby. They walked
outside, then around the hotel to the garden, where only last
month Ivor had sat with Baron and Fawzi: Fawzi, who had paid
for his open friendships with his life. Ivor saw him at the table in
his broad chalk-striped suit, his deep brown eyes set in his pleasant, accommodating face. Ivor wondered if Baron knew that
Fawzi was dead. He must have heard by now. Ivor felt suddenly
dizzy, and the moon staggered across the sky like a drunk cross-
ing the road.

"I have to sit down," he said.

Oberman took the envelope from him and stuffed it hastily
in the inside pocket of his jacket.

"Imagine," he said, "if each immigrant could bring a *second*
thousand pounds to invest in Palestine."

At this moment Ivor couldn't imagine anything about Palestine at all, he only wanted the pounding in his head to stop.

"There will be a massive influx of liquidated Jewish capital,
and, of course, the money will be controlled by official Zionist
entities on behalf of the immigrant. We will bring the first wave

of moneyed Jewish citizens to this country, and it will deliver the investment capital needed to establish the Jewish state!"

Ivor wasn't listening. He was back in Jaffa's Clock Tower Square on his hands and knees crawling on the cobblestones over corpse after corpse, the stench of the bodies filling his nostrils, his body stained by the blood-soaked clothes of the dead. He retched and vomited, then vomited again. The stars fizzing and spinning like Catherine wheels slowed above him. When eventually he got to his feet, Oberman was standing next to him, his shoes covered in bile and puke.

16

Baron threw the files down on his kitchen table. Ivor had arrived in Jerusalem early in the morning and headed straight for Baron's house in Rehavia.

"Read through everything," he said. "Maybe I've missed something. Your own notes are gone, I understand."

"Yes, they burned. I'm sorry—"

Baron held up his hand. "You're not to blame."

Days had passed since the riot. Ivor had thrice returned to Jaffa. He'd taken to walking in the Arab souk past shopkeepers selling bright bolts of fabric or skirting a circle of women with armfuls of cut flowers, lilies and fragrant roses, as if somehow the mingled busyness and beauty of the place returned to life might occlude his memory of the horrors he had witnessed there. But his visits had the opposite effect. Each time he subsided into a deeper gloom. When Baron had summoned him to Jerusalem, he'd felt a sense of relief to be extracted from his self-mortifying ritual.

Baron seemed unusually relaxed, perhaps because the court

would not convene for weeks, not until the powers that be determined that tensions had subsided enough.

"It's an entirely new landscape," he said. "Mark my words, there will be a long, hard government review of immigration policy. They've let in thirty thousand Jews this year, direct response to Hitler's antics. But there won't be thirty thousand next year, not after what happened."

Baron, tieless in a short-sleeved shirt, looking, for once, more pioneer than English barrister, dropped three spoonfuls of tea into the pot, poured in boiling water, and stirred it.

"Mrs. Baron is out for an early breakfast with Helen Bentwich," he said, "perhaps you met her at the break-fast. Wife of our former attorney general, lovely woman, has taken to writing articles for the *Manchester Guardian,* the last one was about oranges. Also, a fine tennis player. Last year she played for Palestine in the Maccabead. Shame you weren't here then, we could have used you, something of a sportsman yourself, isn't that right?"

"I played football for my college."

"Half blue?"

"Not even, only for the college."

Baron let the tea steep, then poured it through the strainer for himself and Ivor.

"If you can believe it, there were only two teams in the football tournament, Eretz Yisroel—that's the local Jews—and Poland. The game was tied at two–two when they had to stop because it got dark. Can you imagine?"

Baron started to laugh. Ivor thought he was never so happy as when exposing the provinciality of Palestine.

"So, they replayed it a few days later, and the Poles won, three–two. But the Maccabiah authorities felt bad, I mean to have the Poles come all this way only to play a single game. So, they hastily arranged another one, this time against Mandate Palestine. Took place right here in Jerusalem. Of course, our English boys smashed them, four–two."

"I doubt I'd have made the team."

"Which one?"

Ivor reddened.

"I'm teasing you, young man. Eretz Yisroel had to march under the flag of Mandate Palestine, all red, with a little picture of the Old City in a yellow circle and a Union Jack stuck up in the left-hand corner. They weren't too happy about that. I'm not sure what I think about these Jewish Olympics. Good way to smuggle in Jews, I suppose. My bet is half the teams who'll come here next time will never go back."

"Hitler's got the next Olympics now, hasn't he?"

"Wonder if they'll let him keep them. Not if he carries on the way he's going, I suppose. Although I'm guessing they won't stop play in Berlin when it gets dark."

Ivor pulled the files toward him. "What exactly should I be looking for?"

But Baron was staring out of his kitchen window as a bird darted across his garden. It seemed he wasn't quite ready to get back to business.

"Have you visited the pet shop on Shenkin Street, in Tel Aviv?" he said.

"Should I?"

"The owner calls it a 'zoo.' He's a Jew from Copenhagen and on his way here he bought some animals in Italy. I happened to be in there the other day with Annie Landau, who was looking for pets to bring to her school to show the children, and do you know what I saw?"

"Tell me."

"A red squirrel. In a cage." Baron turned from the window.

"Can you imagine? There they are scrambling up and down every other oak tree in England having a fine old time looking for acorns or whatever it is they do, and here they're as exotic as tigers and wind up in a cage for the locals to gawk at."

"I suppose it's all relative," Ivor said. "Wouldn't an Indian be surprised to see a tiger in a cage?"

"Red squirrels' days are numbered," Baron continued, ignoring Ivor's question. "As soon as some foolish Victorians allowed their American cousins, those little gray bastards, into our parks, they were done for."

Ivor began to open one of the files as if some overlooked matter of extraordinary importance might immediately present itself to him.

"What kind of country has a pet shop instead of a zoo?"

Ivor wanted to say, "A poor one?" but he kept it to himself.

"All right," Baron said, taking a deep breath and reluctantly turning to the matter at hand, "for starters, three episodes to take yet another look at: Mrs. Arlosoroff's telephone conversation with Constable Shermeister, the further conversation on the journey to Hadassah hospital in the motorcar, and the third episode when she was shown the photographs of several Jews in the middle of the night and uttered the remarkable words that, extraordinarily, the prosecution simply finds aberrational and irrelevant, to wit 'These are Jews; show me photographs of Arabs.' I want everything wrapped up tight before this trial begins."

"I'll get right on it."

"And, Ivor, I don't suppose you have any word from our star witness in waiting. The young lady you appear to have lost touch with?"

Ivor tried as hard as he could to maintain a steady demeanor. "No word."

"And no idea where she might be?"

"None at all."

Baron nodded. "Well, if she should show up . . . and if she has something to tell us, it would be good to see her in court."

"I don't know where she is."

"No, but in the meantime, I heard a rumor that you've found yourself a gray squirrel."

When Ivor didn't respond, Baron added, "Come on, you know how it is here. You wake up in the morning, throw your windows open, and demand of your neighbor, 'Well, how am I this morning?'"

"Everyone knows everything?"

"Just about. I expect you'll be glad to be getting home when all this is over. Do you have plans?"

"No plans," Ivor said, and then added what he had most been wanting to ask: "Mr. Fawzi, did he have a family?"

Baron removed his glasses and began to clean them on his napkin.

"Tragic," he said. "Wife and several children, I believe. Never met them. Well . . ." Baron replaced his glasses and looked brightly at Ivor. "Bentwich is giving his inaugural lecture at the university tomorrow. Why don't you stay the night in Jerusalem and come along? Going to be quite the event. And listen, after you've looked at the files you should take a few days for yourself. In any case I shall be away, a week or so's R & R before final preparation for the big event. Mrs. Baron and I have been invited on a trip in the Negev and Transjordan. Our companions will be the education officer Jeremy Parfitt, he's a rabid Tory, but never mind that, and Eric Strong, one of the original Occupied Enemy Territory Administration officers—keen intellect, philosophical mind, all in all a stimulating fellow to travel with. He's all in on Balfour. Very popular chap with the Jews, as you might imagine.

So, take the opportunity. You've been through something, you know."

After Baron left, Ivor headed straight for Clarissa Barlow's rooming house, where he found her placing two small saucers under the mulberry tree to feed her cats.

"Oh, it's you," she said, glancing up. "You're in luck, attic's still available."

He sat on the narrow bed with the files distributed around him. The preliminary examinations had gone on for months and the sheer quantity of paper was overwhelming. He ran through the headings on Baron's notes, made in preparation for the speech that he planned to offer for the defense: "An atmosphere where evidence emanates from a political party interested in Conviction"; "Disappearance of Documents"; "Alibi Defense Approached with hostility by Police"; "No Evidence as would render Arlosoroff's Assassination by Revisionists reasonable, feasible, or conceivable"; "Prosecution have failed to prove motive"; "No possibility of Stavsky or Rosenblatt knowing A's Prospective movements of which A did not himself know"; "Fixing of Guilt on Revisionists would occasion Minimum of Political Inconvenience"; "Criticism and analysis of Mrs. A's Evidence . . . the lady tells completely different stories according to the Convenience of the Moment. . . ."

As he worked through the pages a deep quiet settled in his room, as if the entire city of Jerusalem had gone on strike and suddenly decided to take a walk into the desert.

As he searched out and underlined the stark contradictions in Sima Arlosoroff's statements to the police, Baron's question about his "plans" continued to disturb him. He wasn't quite sure where "home" was anymore. Palestine, he had read in the "Nature" column of the *Post* only that week, was a country of migration, millions of birds making their way from Europe to Africa in the winter and returning in the spring, starlings, cranes, storks, a continual flapping of wings. The Zionists liked to celebrate the triumph of return over exile but when he had read the article the pattern of the birds' movements suggested something else to Ivor, that ingathering and scattering was perhaps a necessary and perpetual rhythm of Jewish life. He had mentioned this to Susannah, who had laughed at the idea. "I didn't know you were so interested in 'Jewish life,'" she'd said. "I thought you told me you were an atheist." Yet Ivor felt like the man who, when he is in the city, yearns for the tranquility of the countryside, and when he is in the country misses his urban distractions. He is only truly happy on the train traveling between the two locations.

Ivor joined the throng of students filing into the Mount Scopus lecture hall. A host of dignitaries were on hand, senior British officials, and a number of the Jewish notables Ivor had seen at Baron's break-fast. The arrival of two policemen at the door signified that the high commissioner was about to enter the room. Ivor spotted Baron and his wife involved in what looked like a lively back-and-forth with Helen Bentwich, and then, high up in the rear of the hall, he noticed Charles Gross huddled with a group of students. He thought to make his way over to him, but Professor Bentwich was about to be introduced by Chancellor Magnes, and members of the audience were politely requested to take their seats.

"I'm delighted," Magnes began, "to have the high honor of introducing our new and first Montague Burton chair of international relations, Professor Norman Bentwich, well known to all of you as our former attorney general, to present the inaugural lecture of our new semester, 'Jerusalem, the City of Peace.' Professor Bentwich—"

But before Magnes could go any further a noisy disturbance erupted in the upper corner of the room, then spread across the hall. Students were throwing handfuls of pamphlets in the air, showering the people in the seats below them. One voice in particular stood out louder than the rest: "Go and talk peace to the mufti, not to us!" Ivor picked up one of the sheets of paper, a screed from the Revisionist Student Society objecting to both the subject of the lecture and the lecturer. Professor Bentwich, his bald head shining under the lights, his square jaw set, and altogether exhibiting a remarkable degree of aplomb, simply stood his ground and waited for the furor to die down. When it did Magnes concluded his introduction, but as soon as Bentwich began to speak the commotion erupted again and this time turned into a ruckus as stink bombs were launched like grenades from the rear seats and immediately filled the hall with sulfurous fumes.

Ivor heard Baron's baritone bellow, "Shame on you," and then the police were in among the protestors, dragging at least one of them away, and more police began to rush through the doors. Throughout it all Bentwich stood patiently by. As Baron later reminded Ivor, a former lieutenant colonel in Allenby's victorious army, Bentwich was not to be easily cowed by a bunch of ragamuffin students.

In time the room settled down and Bentwich delivered his lecture on peace with an armed guard positioned on either side of him.

At the conclusion Ivor looked around the room but Charles Gross was nowhere to be seen. There was a modest reception afterward in one of the rooms off the new library. Baron beckoned Ivor over to join his little group, which included his wife and a Dr. Kagan from the Jerusalem Conservatory of Music.

Baron was in full flow. "The Colonial Office thought Norman too Jewish to stay on as attorney general. Bad enough to be persecuted by our lot for being a Jew but it's worse to be persecuted by your fellow Jews for being the kind of Jew you are."

"And what kind of a Jew is Professor Bentwich?" Dr. Kagan offered a wry smile.

"Good God, he's a binationalist, and where has that got him? First an Arab shoots him, poor shot luckily, then the Colonial Office kicks him out of his job, and now he gets showered with stink bombs by a bunch of hooligan Jews. Doesn't do to be a moderate here, does it?"

"What will happen to the student the police took away?"

"Who? Stern? Everyone knows about him. He's a troublemaker. Suspension, I suppose, although he deserves expulsion."

When the conversation slipped into a discussion of the impending visit of the actress Sybil Thorndike, Ivor slipped away.

He stood outside the amphitheater and looked down over the Old City. There was a slight chill in the air and the meager starlight illuminated only a nearby coppice of trees and a few houses that appeared to be clinging to rock. Ivor thought he caught the bitter odor of invisible cedars. He didn't hear Charles Gross approach and only turned when he heard his voice.

"What are you doing here? I thought you were busy with my cousin. Or are you still mooning after the painter? You've turned into quite the Casanova, haven't you?"

"Hardly."

"Susannah would be quite a catch for you, you know. Rolling in it."

"It isn't like that."

"So, you are still pining. Waste of time. I heard Yosef Lombrozo has fled the coop. It's all going to come out, you know. Arlosoroff palling around with Goebbels, the loathsome under-belly of his agreements. I'm sure it was even worse than we thought. No wonder his sidekick skedaddled out of here."

So that's Yosef's last name, Ivor thought, "Lombrozo." Now he could certainly find out more about him if he wanted to, but he wasn't sure that he did.

"Did he take Ms. Kerem with him, I wonder?" Charles continued.

"I wouldn't know, but why do you care?"

"How did you meet her in the first place? Does she have something to do with the case?"

Ivor, lost in thought, stared into the distance.

"Well, does she?"

Ivor only now registered what Charles had asked him and he recognized a shift in his tone, as if this question was what he'd been building up to.

"I met her at a party. Now give it a rest, will you?"

Charles paused for a moment, as if weighing Ivor's response, then abruptly changed tack. "I'll tell you something. If you thought that little skirmish back there with Bentwich was ugly, wait until you see what happens if your clients are found guilty."

"Blood in the streets?"

"Something like that, yes."

"I think I've already seen enough of that. In any case, it's you who's going against the grain. Arlosoroff was much loved. Weren't you here for the funeral? Thousands upon thousands, so I heard, including just about every dignitary in Palestine, Christians, Muslims, and Jews of all political stripes, including your lot. Your brand of incendiary politics is in the minority, or hadn't you noticed that? The socialists run the show here."

Charles's response was quick and sharp. "Loved by the gullible and the naïve, loathed by anyone who truly understands the Arab threat. And did you hear that the German consul was in attendance?"

Ivor turned away and looked down once more toward the Old City, darkness sheathing its domes and minarets, the Temple Mount set in its blue enamel dream. It was a place to both seduce and disillusion the sentimentalist in him. History had come and grabbed him by the throat, when all he really wanted to do was lie undisturbed with Tsiona, disappearing from himself into her eyes and drawing in the fragrance of their first night together.

He began to walk away.

"We're on the same side, you know," Charles called out, "did you forget that?" When Ivor didn't respond he added in a low murmur, "Watch out for yourself," and then, raising his voice once more, "Do you want a lift back down? You can ride pillion!"

17

Ivor, lost in thought, missed his stop and, hurrying not to miss the next one, got off the bus near Jaffa Gate. He looked up at its pointed spikes and toward the austere tower of David with its gray barbican silvered by the moon. Why had Charles suddenly become so interested in Tsiona? Ivor hadn't told a soul about the sketches, except for Baron, and Ivor was sure that his lips were firmly sealed. Charles's question troubled him, and all the more so because he didn't know quite why it did.

Back in his attic room Ivor plugged in the electric lamp with its tasseled shade, provided by Clarissa Barlow, and once more spread the files around him on his bed. Sima Arlosoroff's testimony was at the heart of the case and that was where he needed to focus his attention—"The lady tells completely different stories according to the convenience of the moment." Baron's handwritten scrawl was Ivor's signpost.

Ivor opened his notebook and drew a line down the middle of a page. On one side he listed the salient points of the prosecution's likely case based on Sima Arlosoroff's statements, and on the other contradictory comments that she now abjured. To play and then to replay. How had she come to reshoot the film of her experience? The case for the prosecution was simple: Sima gave a detailed story. She and her husband had seen two persons on the beach in Tel Aviv, these two persons were Jews, these persons had followed them, one of them flashed a torch, the other fired a pistol or a revolver. She had specifically identified Stavsky and Rosenblatt as the two persons she saw on the beach. The story was perfectly clear, unimpeachable, except that it wasn't.

The other story, their story, like all origin tales, was murky. A tale of half-light and whispers, garbled conversations and shadowy encounters, it crawled out of the lapping surf and onto the sand, its shape and form undetermined, subject to distortion and mutation, and it was precisely these qualities that made it so attractive to Baron's defense.

For how, in the weak light (or was it the entire absence of moonlight), could Sima Arlosoroff have seen what she claimed to have seen? And even if she did, how could it be explained away that three times, *three times,* in the two and a half hours before her wounded husband died, she claimed that one or both of the assailants were Arabs?

As he read through the statements, the Arlosoroffs' night seeped into Ivor's. He stood on the beach, removed his shoes and socks, traced a line with his toes in the sand, felt the warm air, imagined the boot marks that had long ago washed away, then blood staining the sand and running in a trickle toward the sea.

On one side of the line were a bright starlit night and police officer Stafford, who, on the beach only a short time after the murder, could discern the features of a man on a camel as he spoke to him, and thus the light on the beach had to be sufficient, as Sima claimed, to see "reasonably well" and for her to be able to note the color of the killer's shirt. And on the other side the general point that corporal identification is unreliable even in broad daylight, and more specifically the certainty that Mrs. Arlosoroff was in a state of emotional distress, and most urgently her own description when the murder was fresh and vivid in her mind that the light was "dark and uncozy." Everything for the prosecution was starlit and bright, everything for Baron was dark and uncozy. Sima Arlosoroff set off in the dark and the prosecution dragged her into the light because they needed her testimony to match the forensics. Baron had underlined and written in the margin "Not in a fit nervous state to identify anyone," "Impossible to discern colors in the dark," and, as if more for himself than the court, "A melancholic and tragic promenade."

Ivor turned the page, drew another line. He'd arrived at the crux of the matter.

The first phone call came from Constable Shermeister at the Kaete Dan to Sima Arlosoroff. Ivor had walked past the seafront pension many times. The Kaete Dan wasn't exactly the Savoy. In fact, he thought, it bore the same relation to the Savoy as the buildings of the Hebrew University to Oxford's colleges. Sitting on the bed, Ivor quickly tried to cast his Baron-like snobbery away from him. One last review. The Kaete Dan: three concrete blocks, a couple of metal balconies, louvered blinds, a rough wire fence enclosing unruly undergrowth that circled a tall telephone pole. It was there that Constable Shermeister first learned from Sima that her husband was "shot by Arabs." A muddled version of their conversation reached the police station at Jaffa and was duly recorded as "Dr. Somebody had been shot by an Arab in some street."

Second, in the car on her way to Hadassah hospital, following the ambulance that carried her wounded husband, Sima told the driver that she was "ninety percent, or one hundred percent, certain that the assailants were Arabs."

Third, in the middle of the night at the hospital, the police showed Sima photographs of Jewish Communists or Revisionists, or were they simply Russian Jews? Picture after picture until finally, exasperated, desperate, exhausted, she suddenly said, "These are Jews; show me photographs of Arabs."

Three times, in the hearing of nine different people, all of whom were willing to testify that they had heard her. And yet later, after the surgeons had removed the bullet, after her husband had died and that little piece of lead mattered only to the police and the lawyers, she had denied it all, denied that she ever spoke of Arabs to anyone.

Ivor's light bulb flickered, hissed, and died. He moved the files off the bed, lay down in a full stretch, and stared up at the attic window crowded with stars. He remembered what Baron had told him: "If there is one fact you can be certain of in a courtroom it is that everyone is lying."

18

In the morning Ivor packed his bag and prepared to leave, but then Mrs. Barlow suggested that he take his breakfast at a small table she had set up in the courtyard, and, the autumn morning so bright and dry, he decided to stay in Jerusalem at least until the end of the day, take a walk, clear his head.

His review of the materials had disappointed him. He had hoped to impress Baron by discovering something that the great barrister had missed, but that hadn't been the case. After breakfast he took the stairs back up to the attic and, one last time, without expectation or hope, reopened a large file of press clippings that he had flipped through the previous night. And there it was, stuck to the back of an article about a proposed boycott of German goods, the front page of an American newspaper, the *Jewish Daily Bulletin,* which someone had clearly posted to Baron. The headline from Tuesday, June 20, four days after the murder, was unequivocal: ASSAILANTS NOT JEWS, ARLOSOROFF BELIEVED. The accompanying article provided the context.

> The murderers of Dr. Chaim Arlosoroff,
> noted young Zionist leader, who was assas-
> sinated in Tel Aviv Friday evening, were
> not Jews, Dr. Arlosoroff believed, accord-
> ing to close friends who were with him
> when he died, two hours after the attack,
> in Hadassah hospital, Tel Aviv. His attack-
> ers were not known to Dr. Arlosoroff per-
> sonally, the Jewish Telegraphic Agency is
> informed, but he was reasonably certain
> that they were not Jews.

Ivor was both astonished and baffled. Why hadn't anyone followed up on this? In all the weeks that he had been in Pales-tine no one had mentioned the dying man's own conviction. And where were the "close friends" who had heard him express it? Apparently, they had disappeared into thin air, or was the Ameri-can newspaper simply running on rumor and gossip, which must have been rampant in the first days after the murder?

Baron was leaving on his trip today; it would be discourteous to bother him now. A day to pull himself together, Ivor thought, and then he would return to Tel Aviv and visit the hospital. Per-haps someone who was there, maybe one of the doctors, would be willing to talk to him.

Ivor walked aimlessly in the city, and inevitably his meander-ing brought him to Tsiona's street and then to her home, where he stood outside in the white air edged with desert gold sunlight and imagined her newly returned, sun beaten from her days on one Greek island or another, opening the door and inviting him in, a witness not to the off-hours of murder suspects but to his new life as a man transformed by love. He looked up at the windows of her flat and thought he saw a curtain move. Real or imagined, it was enough to send him through the garden, into the building, and up the stairs. He knocked on Tsiona's door. There was no answer but when he turned the handle and gently pushed, the door opened.

Inside was a complete mess. Someone had ransacked the place: cupboards emptied, clothes flung on the floor, books removed from their shelves, bed stripped to the mattress and artwork spread all over it. Ivor found Tsiona's sketchbooks where they had been haphazardly chucked on her kitchen table. He sat down, created a space with a sweep of his arm, and methodically began to turn the pages. He remembered that the drawings from the Hasharon café appeared only in the sketchbook with a blue cover. Toward the middle of the book several pages had been ripped out. The sketches of Stavsky and Rosenblatt had gone. He kept turning in the vain hope that he might have misremembered and they would turn up toward the end of the book, but when he came within five pages of the end a different surprise awaited him, for there he was, sleeping, his head on Tsiona's pillow, hair tousled, his shoulders and the top of his chest exposed, a thin creased sheet covering the rest of his body.

He wasn't sure how much time had passed when he decided to leave. He was in a daze, barely aware of where he walked. Outside on the street a man in shabby clothes and a flat cap, his leathery face gaunt and wrinkled by the sun, tried to sell Ivor soap. The peddler carried with him a small scale, held up by string and loaded with heavy green bars. Ivor waved him away and the man squatted down with his back against the wall and waited for more passersby. Ivor turned toward the crowded market, where, pushing his way through among the Jewish shoppers, he spotted the occasional British functionary in a pith helmet unenthusiastically haggling over fruits and vegetables.

He needed to collect his thoughts and found himself drawn

to the Zion Cinema, where at least he could sit alone and undisturbed in the dark. He bought a ticket for *Tell England* without any idea what he was going to see. It turned out to be a film about Gallipoli. The Arabs in the audience booed the English soldiers and cheered the Turks. Did anyone want the British in Palestine? More than likely the British didn't want to be there themselves.

Back in his attic room, supine on his bed, again probing the framed cosmos for help via the narrow skylight, he wondered if he should go to the police and report the break-in at Tsiona's flat. Instead, he thought he would wait for Baron to return and let him know what he had discovered. Later, he decided to do nothing at all.

19

Ivor left early the next morning for Tel Aviv and on his arrival headed straight for the Hadassah hospital on Balfour Street. Unlike in Jerusalem, the air in Tel Aviv was close, with a heat and humidity that felt more like midsummer than autumn. By the end of the afternoon his face dripped sweat and his hair was matted to his head. The hospital, understaffed and overworked, like hospitals everywhere, Ivor thought, was a hive of activity and no one, on either the medical or the administrative staff, had any time for him, especially not when they heard what he was after. He wasn't from the police or the government and everyone he tried to speak to was either suspicious or irritated. Most of them assumed he was a journalist poking about where he wasn't wanted, although he presented his legal credentials with all the confidence he could muster.

As the day progressed and Ivor found himself everywhere rejected, there was a nurse he noticed who began to drift in and out of his orbit as he circled through the offices and visiting areas. On one occasion she seemed about to speak to him but was quickly drawn away on some pressing matter, and Ivor wondered if perhaps he'd noticed her only because of her striking appearance: languid brown eyes, a slight bump in her nose, and a stern fringe visible under her nurse's cap. He was on the point of giving up and had begun to head out of the building when the nurse, approaching down a corridor, touched his arm. Ivor stopped. "Five minutes," she said, "outside."

Ivor found a bench in the shade thrown by two sycamores that stood sentry near the entrance to the hospital. He sat down and lit a cigarette. Shortly, as promised, the nurse emerged through the front doors. She stood on the steps, looked around, spotted Ivor, and lit her own cigarette. Ivor imagined she was either on a break or at the end of her shift. After a moment she came toward him and sat down on the other end of the bench, close enough to be heard but far enough away to avoid any hint of intimacy. When she spoke, in an accent that Ivor thought was probably Russian, she stared straight ahead. He guessed she was about his own age. Her face, in profile, was somewhat severe.

"I would like to be able to trust you," she said.

"You can, you absolutely can. Perhaps you heard, I work for Phineas Baron. We're representing Stavsky and Rosenblatt. Everything you tell me is confidential."

Ivor wiped his arm across his perspiring forehead. If he was lying, he had already managed to convince himself that he wasn't.

The nurse took a drag on her cigarette, then seemed to make up her mind.

"I'm not going to tell you my name, or anything about me."

"No, of course not."

"And you're never going to talk about me to anyone."

"No."

They sat in silence until it seemed the nurse could bear the weight of what she had to say no longer and decided to unburden herself.

"Mr. Arlosoroff did not receive the proper treatment. If he had, his wounds would not have been fatal."

Ivor straightened up.

The nurse paused again as a doctor emerged through the doors and headed off down the exit path.

"A long time passed between the shooting and the surgery to remove the bullet. An earlier blood transfusion would have saved him."

"What happened?"

"When they carried him in out of the ambulance the surgeons had been called for, but they hadn't arrived. The hospital floor was crowded with politicians, they walked around as if they were more important than the doctors. Everyone was in a panic. I was told to attach Mr. Arlosoroff to a saline drip tube, but the tube was leaking so one of the doctors used his handkerchief to stop up the holes in the tubing."

"His handkerchief?"

Now, at last, the nurse turned to Ivor and nodded.

"By the time the chief surgeons arrived it was already too late. I don't know why they had been delayed. They removed the bullet but not in time. . . ."

"And you were there for all of this?"

Again, a nod.

Ivor waited; the gravity of what he had been told demanded that he do so. The nurse tapped the ash off her cigarette. In the distance an orderly pushed a patient in a wheelchair at a snail's pace toward the hospital, victims of the late afternoon torpor that had settled over the grounds.

"I have to go," the nurse said, and stood up.

"Of course. I have only one question. Did Mr. Arloso-roff speak before he died? And if so, did he . . . did he say who shot him?"

It seemed a long time before Ivor got his answer.

"Don't you understand what I'm telling you?" she said. "It doesn't matter who shot Mr. Arlosoroff, doesn't matter if it was Arab or Jew. The hospital killed him. Our hospital."

20

A fortnight passed and Baron was yet to return. The long somnolent hours of hot autumn afternoons were on the wane now,
and so too Ivor's surreptitious activities, although his incursion
into the hospital hardly qualified as clandestine. Some days he
jumped on one of the decrepit buses that plied the route to Jaffa
and walked out as far as he could to where an overwhelming
scent of orange blossom emanated from the groves to the south
and permeated the air: It was intoxicating, or would have been,
if he hadn't been so steadfastly alone.

There remained, he knew (if you read *The Palestine Post,* you
couldn't not know), a seething resentment in the country with
regard to the Arlosoroff murder, bitterness that could turn to
anger and easily erupt into violence, but in his daily life, the
benign routine he had established of strolls around the city,
walks on the beach, and visits to the cinema, he didn't feel it.
Meanwhile, of the letter he had helped to compose for Henry
Green and Georg Oberman he heard nothing.

Day after dry day. In Jerusalem they waited for the rain to

come, in Tel Aviv they knew that it wouldn't, at least not until December. Ivor waited too, more in hope than expectation, for Tsiona to return, preferably uncoupled from Yosef Lombrozo.

One morning, as he returned from a shopping expedition to buy fruit from a local greengrocer, he found Susannah standing outside the doorway of his boardinghouse.

"Your landlady said you'd be back soon," she said, "so I thought I'd wait."

He was happy to see her, as if he had been unaware of the depth of his own loneliness until her reappearance. She'd changed her look; gone were the expensive and high-quality clothes that she had brought with her from America, and in their place, for today anyway, were a generic short-sleeved blue shirt, a pair of dark gray slightly baggy trousers, and work boots. A thin white scar was visible on her forehead above her right eye.

On a street of otherwise cheerless shops, they found a small bakery, a new addition to the neighborhood; bought tea and biscuits; and sat outside.

"Are you ready to be shocked?" Susannah said. "I've decided to stay." Susannah searched Ivor's face for a reaction. "Well," she said, "say something."

"I wouldn't know where to begin. What brought this on?"

"I looked down from the hills to the Sea of Galilee and I had a revelation. I began to feel a mystical tinge."

Ivor wasn't sure how to respond, but then Susannah began to laugh. "You should see your face," she said. "It was nothing like that. We arrived in Tiberias, which, as you may know, is a small, bedraggled, neglected town with maybe twice as many Jews as Muslims, and all intermingling, bound together by hardship and mutual interest, I suppose. We'd gone for the hot springs, but my mother had a contact in the town, cousin of a friend of hers from

Baltimore, a Dr. Morris Samuels, and she became fixated on getting him to remove my stitches. We spent one night in a dreary hotel, then in the morning stopped in on Dr. Samuels. He had a lovely house, nothing grand, but airy and spacious, set at the end of a large, beautifully kept garden."

"That's what did it, the house and garden?"

"Of course not. You really do think I'm a superficial creature, don't you?"

"I'm sorry. Of course not . . . I don't at all."

"His patients were assembled in front of his house, squatting alongside the garden pathway, each one waiting without complaint to enter his office. You don't see that much here, do you? Everyone seemed to be accompanied by at least one relative. They were almost all Arabs. I felt like the rather privileged interloper I undoubtedly was. My mother went to work, of course, tried to get me pushed up to the front of the line, but I refused to let her interfere. Dr. Samuels came out and spoke in Arabic to all the patients. He recommended to Mother and me that we use the day to visit the hot springs and when we returned, we were to stay for dinner, and he would remove my stitches. And I started to think . . ."

Susannah paused and sipped her tea.

"And you started to think . . . what?"

"Well, did you ever read William Blake? I loved him in college, the paintings and the poems."

"I'm shamefully poorly read."

"'He who would do good to another must do it in Minute Particulars. General Good is the plea of the scoundrel, hypocrite, and flatterer.' That's it, I thought. That's how I want to live. I thought, I'll ask Dr. Samuels if I can be of assistance. I mean, obviously not as a nurse, but maybe I could help in some other way, perhaps administratively. Of course, my mother was absolutely livid when I told her."

"But why here? Why not go back to America and do something similar?"

"Well, for a start, there are no Jewish quotas here."

"Oh, but there are, the British impose them!"

"That's different. You know what I mean."

"So, what happened?"

"We took a bus down the side of the lake and got off near these old buildings that the Egyptians built more than a hundred years ago when they occupied the region. My mother was already in a state of high nervousness. Dr. Samuels had told us that the Bedouin women who usually crowded the place wouldn't be there because of a religious festival, but when we arrived the place was packed. My mother wanted to turn right around, and she absolutely refused to go in. I bought a third-class admission ticket. The women were assembled all around the sides of what looked like a small swimming pool. Each of their bodies was tattooed in blue in one area or another; when we got back Dr. Samuels told us it was to ward off the evil eye. For some reason, and I hate to imagine what it was, my own body appeared to be a source of great amusement, everybody started laughing and chatting and I was given a couple of pokes, but then I was alone in the water, soaking up the warmth and minerals, the sky endlessly blue above me, and I don't know why but I suddenly felt utterly at home."

"You baptized yourself."

Susannah laughed. "As it happens," she said, "I kept my head above the water."

Ivor realized, and he wasn't sure if he was relieved or disappointed, that Susannah had lost interest in him, not as a friend but as an aspiration. He was no longer present in the taxonomy of her desires. Her focus of interest had shifted, from person to place. She had found a calling.

"And has your mother come around to your remaining here?"

"Not one bit of it, and she's enlisted my father. They have a problem, of course, always going on about the Jews in Palestine and how we have to help the Jewish state-in-waiting, but they never thought their daughter would actually want to move here! I overheard my mother shouting at him about 'little houses and dreary shops' as if the whole of Tel Aviv could and should be confined to the basement of just one Baltimore department store. I'm the fruit of my father's recent labor in Palestine, but they don't want to taste it."

"Will you go back to Tiberias? How did Dr. Samuels react to your idea?"

"He was torn. He wasn't going to oppose me—how could he? He's an immigrant himself and I share his enthusiasm—but he also tried to placate my mother. He suggested to her that I try things out for a while, stay in Tel Aviv or Jerusalem, get a deeper feel for the place than I've acquired in the King David and the San Remo, find a job, acclimatize myself. He has a friend, Anne Goldsmith, who works at *The Palestine Post*. She's in the advertising department. He offered to put me in contact."

"And did he?"

"Yes, the person you see sitting before you is now responsible for soliciting advertisements from the small shops of Jerusalem, on commission of course, so my time is my own. I know it's not exactly doing good, but it's doing something. You're laughing, but it's not easy. Local retailers haven't yet quite grasped the concept."

"How many advertisements have you secured?"

"One. From Charlotte's, an art shop recently opened by a new immigrant from Czechoslovakia. It's on the same street as the post office, so there should be a lot of foot traffic anyway. And Charlotte herself offered me a job. I'll be working for her in the afternoons. Now tell me about you."

"Nothing much to tell," Ivor said. He thought of the devastation in Tsiona's flat and the desecration of her artwork: the clothes flung across the floor, the stripped bed, the torn pages. Had the agents working against her found what they were looking for in their discovery of the sketches of Stavsky and Rosenblatt? And if so, how had they known that they were there? Had Baron let something slip?

"Well," Susannah said, with a new businesslike authority, "I hope we'll be able to keep in touch."

"Of course," Ivor said, "absolutely."

She kissed him once on each cheek and walked purposefully toward the teahouse door and out, Ivor thought, into her new life. She was going to break her parents' hearts, but not his; his was already broken.

21

For the first time in months Ivor decided to go for a drink at the Casino café but first he wandered farther up the beach to the site of the murder. It was the criminal who was supposed to return to the scene of the crime, not his lawyer, but he was drawn to the spot, as if, as with Baron's notes, he might find something everyone had missed, exculpatory or damning, in the sand beneath the shifting dunes. He stared out over the waves, walked on the wet apron of sand and danced back before the encroaching foam, disentangled himself from a lump of seaweed, picked up a couple of shells, then let them fall.

Once, on a family summer holiday in Broadstairs when Ivor was four, his father had sculpted a boat for him out of sand. Ivor, bucket and spade in hand, had watched as the vessel had emerged, with its impressive prow and a smooth seat. Ivor hadn't known that his father was capable of such productive and beautiful labor: a man who generally appeared in a suit, rose early, and often returned home after Ivor was asleep, and whom he had rarely seen do any kind of manual work. His father put on the finishing touches: seaweed and shell controls, a steering wheel from a piece of driftwood. Ivor had played in the boat all day while his parents sat in deck chairs, his mother taking the sun, his father reading the *News Chronicle*. He had gone to bed happily expecting that the boat would be there all week, but the next two days it rained and when they managed to return to the beach the tide had washed the boat away. Here was a lesson no one wanted to learn.

Ivor entered the café, where somehow the mahogany bar and dark wood décor felt oppressively European, as if Mediterranean life, with its deliriously mingled heat, beauty, and squalor, had crept into his being and rendered him unsuitable for establishments such as this, which evoked an old-world atmosphere and shunted you across time and place to absorb it.

He sat alone at the bar nursing a pilsner. It was early in the evening and the first floor was more or less deserted. After a while a few couples drifted in, and then a larger group talking loudly in English. At its center, his straw-colored hair turned almost white by the sun, was Charles, laughing, gesticulating, and pressing forward toward the bar.

"What's this?" he said when he saw Ivor. "You come here once every three months?"

"Not everyone can be a regular."

"Everybody, this is Ivor Castle, Ivor Castle, everybody."

"Everybody" seemed fairly uninterested in Ivor. Charles shepherded his group to a table and then returned to sit with Ivor at the bar. "New recruits from England for the Anglo-Palestine Company, greenhorns, as our American cousins like to say, and talking of which, I suppose you've heard about Susannah and her stupendous decision."

"You sound as if you disdain it."

"Her parents certainly do, and I can't say I blame them. My

own feeling is that the great Dr. Freud, currently at home in Vienna, but as you know a member of our distinguished board of governors at Hebrew U, might want to pay a visit to the Holy Land and sort everything out."

"What do you mean?"

"Well, it's about Mummy, isn't it? Or maybe Daddy as well. She found a way to upset them both, didn't she? Debutante to do-gooder in the blink of an eye. I'm not sure I can get on board with that. Her respectability and good sense got unhinged by a rise in temperature and the uplifting hardship of waving away a few pesky insects in the malarial north."

"You don't believe that her conviction is genuine, but you're confident that yours is."

Ivor wasn't sure why he felt the need to defend Susannah; he had been somewhat skeptical of her sudden transformation himself, but Charles's self-righteous aggression now had the effect of placing him firmly in Susannah's camp.

"Do you remember that girl at Lady Margaret Hall, Nellie Bamford?" Charles continued. "Went out to join the rebels in Peru—it was Peru, wasn't it? She had nothing whatsoever to do with the place apart from one course studying the Incas. Her father was a Tory lord with an estate in Wiltshire. All she wanted to do was give him the two fingers. In the end she got captured by government forces; took a year and a fortune to bail her out."

"If it was her brother, you'd say he was a freedom fighter with a cause."

Charles smiled, beckoned over the barman, and ordered a beer. "Any sign of your painter with a cause?"

"Why do you care?"

"Perennial interest in your love life ever since I saw you outside the Radcliffe Camera with Mary Buss, who everyone, except you, knew was a true bluestocking lesbian."

"Shouldn't you be getting back to your new friends?"

Charles clinked his beer bottle against Ivor's. "Only teasing," he said. "But one does wonder what your favorite artist has been up to. I hope she's not in danger of any kind."

Ivor caught a faint air of menace in Charles's words.

"Why would she be?"

Charles shrugged. "Company she keeps, I suppose, but I wouldn't worry. I'm sure there's nothing there."

"In that case, when I hear from her, I'll be sure not to let you know."

Charles offered a wry smile. "It's my experience," he said, "that I tend to know about things that matter quite a bit before you do."

"Like Abdul Malik's retraction? I seem to remember that took you by surprise. Perhaps we'll find a check he was sent to encourage him to confess. If so, I hope it doesn't have your signature on it."

"I would say it's far more likely he was paid to retract, which is a shame for you and me both."

One of the Anglo-Palestine crew, a boyish-looking young man stamped with the pale face of the newly arrived, had risen from his chair and was waving at Charles. When he caught his attention, he gestured with a tip of his hand that more drinks were required. Charles turned to the barman and obliged with an order. When the tray arrived stacked with bottles and glasses, Charles lifted it from the counter.

"Everybody's got to serve somebody," he said to Ivor. "The hard thing is to know who you're working for. It's not always who you think it is, is it?" Charles turned away and walked toward his table, pretended to stumble, and drew a laugh from his new colleagues.

Ivor drained his drink and left. He crossed the beach toward the street. Once there he removed his shoes and shook out the sand. Charles loves to insinuate, Ivor thought, to accrue to himself some mystery and exclusive knowledge, to flaunt his power either to reveal or conceal. But his phony concern for Tsiona was disturbing. It was a warning of some kind, and now Ivor wished that he'd pressed him on it. He looked back beyond the Casino, where seagulls bobbed over the waves, roosting for the night, just far enough from land to evade their predators.

22

NOVEMBER

Ivor woke before dawn; he had hardly slept at all. Anticipation of what lay ahead, the first day of the trial, had him insomniac and restless. Baron had recommended that he stay in the Scottish Hospice—"It's cheap, clean, tolerable, and offers a splendid view of the Old City if you get a room facing in the right direction." It was also far enough away from the Jerusalem courthouse to offer a measure of privacy, vital for anyone involved in the case. The entire country, it seemed, was waiting to see what would happen.

In the negligible light thrown by his desk lamp, Ivor polished and brushed his shoes. He'd brought the only suit he owned with him, a white shirt, and his striped college tie. To those who sympathized with Stavsky and Rosenblatt, Baron and, by extension, Ivor, albeit in a minor role, were heroes, so he might as well try to look the part, unless, of course, Baron failed to secure a dismissal for his clients, in which case their status would suffer a speedy decline.

The long, small room was sparsely furnished and damp in a way that Ivor had not experienced since leaving the claustral confines of his Oxford college. It narrowed up to an end filled by a fireplace with kindling and three logs already in place on the grate. The view, however, and as Baron had advertised, more than made up for any discomfort Ivor might experience. His blue-tinted window looked out over the Valley of Hinnom at the point where it cleaved into the Kidron Valley. Ivor could see the flat-roofed dwellings of the Arab village of Silwan emerge through vaporous air as the early November sun burned through.

His plan was to arrive at the courtroom early, well before the crowd that was sure to form outside. He would occupy a seat behind Baron while Harold Cunningham presented the case for the prosecution. Baron had predicted that this would fill the entire day, a short one to be sure, as in their wisdom the powers that be had determined to begin the proceedings on a Friday, and thus Baron himself would not have an opportunity to speak until the court reconvened after the weekend.

Ivor clattered down the stone stairs, poked his head into the dining room, where a handful of early risers were enjoying their breakfast, but he suddenly felt too nervous to eat. A cup of tea was all that he required. He was wondering where he might find a small, inconspicuous café en route to the courthouse when a waiter passed him and deposited two plates of bacon and eggs and an additional plate of toast in front of the occupants of a nearby table. Ivor caught a whiff of the sizzling bacon as it drifted through the air. England, or really Scotland, he supposed, had come to him while he was dressed in his courtroom finery. It was an irresistible way to start a day that would inevitably have an ersatz quality, starting with a brace of undoubtedly eloquent British barristers in powdered wigs.

Ivor hardly had time to butter his toast before two squaddies appeared at his table.

"Ivor Castle? Sorry to interrupt your breakfast, mate, but you're coming with us."

"What are you talking about?"

"You're required at Government House. High commissioner wants a word with you."

"That's absurd. I have to be in court. Don't you know what's happening today? I'm the assistant to Phineas Baron."

"You can finish up your eggs if you want while everyone in 'ere stares at you or you can be a good boy and come with us right now. If you don't want to come with us, we're going to have to march you out, and that's something you might want to avoid, especially from Norbert, he's got a pair of very big hairy 'ands. Isn't that right, Norbert?"

"That's right, Jimmy."

Ivor had yet to let go of his knife.

"What are you planning to do with that," Jimmy asked, "butter me?"

Ivor weakly reiterated that he had to be in court, he didn't know what else to say, but as soon as he spoke Jimmy grabbed his arm and yanked him out of his seat. Ivor tried to shrug off the hold but his movement only compelled Jimmy to tighten his grip and Norbert to circle the table and seize his other arm.

Briefly, Ivor tried to wrestle his way free. The other occupants of the dining room stopped talking, put down their knives and forks, and watched with curiosity and disbelief as Ivor was marched through the dining room. A waiter emerged from the kitchen and stopped in his tracks.

"No point struggling," Jimmy said, "car's right outside the door."

Once outside, they bundled Ivor unceremoniously into the back of a stately, gleaming black Morris Oxford with government plates.

It was a short drive up to the Hill of Evil Counsel. Ivor stared straight ahead, feeling the pressure of Norbert's hand on his arm as the thin stand of pines on the hill's flat top drew closer. He tried to think which of his many indiscretions, witness tampering chief among them, had brought him to this meeting with Wharton. In the end it wouldn't matter, the ignominious fate that he had imagined for himself more than a few times in the last weeks would be the same: shame, dishonor, humiliation, perhaps even incarceration. At the thought of the latter, he broke into a sweat: to be shut up in the same stinking hellhole in Jaffa that currently housed his clients. And for what? At least he knew the answer to that question: for love, his ineluctable crime.

In less than five minutes Ivor could make out the Union Jack on Government House's flagpole; on this windless morning it hung limply, as if it had given up trying to assert itself over the recalcitrant landscape. Jimmy and Norbert had lapsed into a sullen silence.

At the gates to the compound one of the Morris's tires got stuck in a pothole. In his efforts to release it by revving the engine and wrenching the steering wheel, the driver only managed to send a mix of sand, grit, and dried mud into the air. Ivor watched the slow accumulation of dirt on the windshield until it was almost impossible to see through it.

"Fuck this," Jimmy said. "Think you can manage him on your own, Norbert?"

His companion laughed. "I dunno, Jimmy, he looks like a tough bugger. Are you a tough bugger, Mr. Castle?" Ivor didn't answer.

Jimmy got out of the car and began to issue instructions to the driver, but to no avail. The car remained rooted to the spot.

"I think we're going to have to walk you in, Ivor," Norbert said. "Not going to make a dash for it, are you? I wouldn't contemplate anything dramatic. Jimmy's our divisional champion at pursuing escapees."

"I didn't know I was under arrest."

"Oh, you're not, you're not at all. High commissioner just wants a nice cup of tea with you and I'm sure you wouldn't want to disappoint him."

In half an hour the Jerusalem courtroom would open and the trial would begin. Ivor's dereliction of duty would become immediately obvious to everyone.

Norbert marched Ivor up the long avenue until the limestone residence, impressive for a building outside the Old City walls, emerged from the pines and cypresses that both guarded and hid it. The building had an odd octagonal shape: At another time its domes, arches, and crossed vaults might have sparked Ivor's interest, but all he could focus on now was the depth of his own trouble.

Outside the front door a stone fountain threw jets of water into sparkling parabolas that fell in pattering drops to ripple the green water in its pooled basin. Ivor was tempted to run his hand through the water and splash some on his face, but when he stopped for a moment Norbert quickly pushed him in the back to propel him forward.

Sir Douglas Wharton was seated behind a large desk in front of a monumental fireplace surfaced with richly colored tiles that rose at least twelve feet toward the ceiling.

"Armenian pottery," he said, acknowledging Ivor's glance upward. "Impressive, don't you think?"

"Very much so."

"And thank you, Lundin, you may go."

Wharton gestured for Ivor to sit down. His desk held two neat stacks of paper resting in an inbox and an outbox, a blotting pad, two telephones, and a pipe rack. He got straight to the point.

"What in God's name did you think you were doing writing that letter for those incorrigible meddlers?"

"I . . . it was . . . I thought . . ."

"What did you think? That we wouldn't know about it? Trust me, we've had our eyes on you for quite a while."

"There is an ugly persecution under way. It seemed . . . for the Jews in Germany . . . anything I might do to help. It was a small request, editing really, not much more."

"And you believe we're unaware of that? The persecution?"

"No, of course not . . ."

"Well, clearly you knew. You were asking us to endorse—no, much more, make a claim to have engineered a clandestine transfer agreement with Herr Hitler and his gang of Nazi thugs. Do you realize the chaos that such a claim on our parts would inspire in Palestine? You were in Jaffa during the riots, weren't you? Well, something a hundred times worse would have happened and we simply do not have the manpower to put out major conflagrations, and that is why our efforts are concentrated on stopping trouble before it starts. You've been extraordinarily stupid, and should I add 'treacherous'?"

"I'd very much appreciate it if you wouldn't."

Wharton launched into a long lecture–cum–headmaster's scolding, a history lesson with barbs. He referenced various white papers and declarations, outlined the geopolitics of the region and the unique problems related to Palestine. The implication was clear: Ivor was out of his depth, ignorant of the salient issues, the balancing act the British performed on the taut wire stretched between the Arabs and the Jews. Wharton went on, now limning the responsibilities that a great nation owed to those sequestered in its care, then via a circuitous route that took in the defunct Ottoman Empire, the grasping French, and the conniving Americans, he arrived at the Nazi regime in Germany, the need, yes, to oppose it in word and deed, but also the need for caution, diplomacy, foresight, intelligence.

When he had finished talking, Wharton lifted one of his pipes from the rack, opened his desk drawer, reached for a tin of tobacco, and began to stuff the bowl. His light green shirt made his long features look sallow, an extension of his thinning yellowish-gray hair. He fixed his eyes on Ivor (had he browbeaten him enough?), struck a match, and teased the flame over the pipe.

"You're an Oxford man, correct?"

"Yes, sir."

"Which college?"

"Balliol."

A small smile stole across Wharton's face. "Sandie Lindsay's place. Excellent. He'll be the next university chancellor. Mark my words."

Wisps of blue smoke spiraled up from Wharton's pipe as he relaxed back into his chair. The room, despite its vivid ceramics and domed ceiling, felt for a moment as if it had transformed into a cozy Oxford nook, and Ivor realized with an inward burst of satisfaction that Oxford might be about to save him. For once the English side of him was going to trump the Jewish: Ivor the Balliol man was about to rescue him in Wharton's eyes from Ivor the Jewish meddler. One of Sandie Lindsay's chaps couldn't possibly be held responsible for messing around in Zionist politics. Must have all been a dreadful mistake.

"Listen," Wharton said, his voice devoid of anger, "I'm not unsympathetic, you know. We're doing our best, letting in as many as we can. We very much want Palestine to be a principal country of refuge and I've always been prepared to help Jews and the Jewish Agency as much as I can in the admission of refugees. But we can't abide this circumvention. And you can see where it led Mr. Arlosoroff." Wharton pulled on his pipe before continuing. "I liked him very much, you know. In fact, I regarded him as a close friend. I dined with him before he left for Europe; the novelist Zweig was there, one of our new arrivals. Mr. Arlosoroff was a great admirer of English institutions *and* English character. Had binational proclivities, as you know, for the most part quite happy to let us get on with our business. No hatred of the Arabs, although they weren't too pleased with him. I shall miss him greatly; in fact, I already do. Which reminds me, I believe that you have a trial to attend this morning."

"I do, sir."

"And what do you imagine the outcome to be?"

"Vindication for our clients."

Wharton gave a short laugh. "Good man, always stick up for your own team. I think you'll find Justice Corrie to be a fair man, Plunkett too. Can't say I know enough about Ali Hasna and Moise Valero to make a judgment, but it's frequently the case that the Arab and the Jewish members of the court cancel each other out."

Ivor wanted to ask if Wharton had a preference in the outcome. One of the pillars of Baron's defense was his insistence that the government, deeply opposed to militant Revisionists, had stacked the case against Stavsky and Rosenblatt. Yet, if Ivor was sometimes foolish, he wasn't foolish enough to wake Wharton's resentment from its slumber.

Wharton put down his pipe, then stood up from behind his desk and extended his hand.

"You're getting away with a warning," he said, "and do yourself a favor, stay as far away as you can from Messrs. Green and

Oberman. I understand there's a girl involved, but nonetheless, discretion is the better part of valor and so on."

Ivor was left without an escort to make his own way to the courthouse, and nobody offered him a ride. At the foot of the hill a few ragged boys were kicking an old football about on a patch of scrubby land. The goalposts were two crates set a few feet apart. As Ivor approached, one of the kids took a wild shot that landed the ball at Ivor's feet. He couldn't resist; he began a long mazy dribble toward the goal as the kids, yelling with excitement, took him on, stabbing at the ball, kicking out at Ivor's ankles, as he wheeled this way and that. He stroked the ball between the crates, lifted his arms in triumph, and trotted down the road, the cries of the boys—some happy, some derisory—following him until he was out of earshot. He looked down at his shoes, scuffed and covered in gray dust. What did it matter? Nobody here really cared much how you looked anyway.

23

Ivor pushed his way through the raucous crowd, assembled in its hundreds outside the courtroom and overwhelmingly in support of the defendants. All the traffic in the city, every car and cart it seemed, had been held up, a boon for Ivor. The atmosphere was oddly festive for a murder trial, as if the acquittal of the accused were a forgone conclusion. Even the mounted police and the officers stretching the cordon on foot exhibited a genial attitude toward those who filled the jam-packed street. The usual Palestinian Jerusalem mix was on display: heavily bearded Orthodox Jews, women in head scarves, young men on both sides of the political fence, all of them rubbing shoulders with traditionally garbed Arab men and women. They shouted at one another, waved placards, linked arms, and pressed toward the courthouse gates. Near the entrance Ivor found himself squashed in next to a young woman with a fresh shiny manicure and deeply carmine lips. She tried to slip past both Ivor and the guards but as she did so a great roar went up from the crowd and she turned around. The police van carrying the accused had arrived.

To Ivor's astonishment Stavsky and Rosenblatt emerged from the van, cleanly shaven, neatly dressed, and clearly without any anxiety that someone would do to them what they had allegedly done to Arlosoroff. Different elements of the crowd either cheered or jeered, the former group quickly drowning out the latter. Stavsky and Rosenblatt waved to their supporters, and then a woman burst through to them and without hindrance from the police hugged and kissed Rosenblatt. The young woman next to Ivor stood on tiptoes to get a better look.

"It's his mother," she said.

Ivor showed his credentials to the guard at the door and ran up the stairs to the second floor. Only two dozen spectators had been allowed to enter the courtroom, and the last of them, after a lengthy security screening, was taking his seat as Ivor walked in. As he did so Baron swiveled in his seat and glared at Ivor. Ivor would have no opportunity to explain his lateness until the court adjourned for its first recess of the day, but that would not come for hours.

The accused were led into the courtroom, Justice Corrie called the proceedings to order, and soon Attorney General Cunningham was on his feet outlining the case for the prosecution. The four judges sat on their raised dais, the two British members of the panel distinguished by their wigs, a privilege of dress denied by Mandate custom to their Arab and Jewish colleagues on the bench.

Ivor, squeezed into the seat behind Baron that had been reserved for him, heard Cunningham say, "It is very difficult to pin any person down to a precise statement of time when there is nothing to impress it on their memory . . . ," at which Baron scribbled dramatically on the pad of paper on the desk before him. "There is a discrepancy," Cunningham continued, as Ivor tried to settle himself and concentrate, "between the times at which witnesses say that they saw Stavsky and Rosenblatt in Café Hasharon. They put themselves there at some time between half past seven and half past eight. There is a variation as to the exact time. As I say, it is unfair to try and tie down any group of witnesses to a specific time when there is nothing to impress it on their memory. But it is important to the extent that two witnesses for the prosecution will say that they were there between those times and that they did *not* see either Stavsky or Rosenblatt, so that there is a definite conflict between the evidence of the prosecution and the evidence presented by the defense during the preliminary examination conducted by the magistrate when two witnesses affirmed that they *might* have seen Stavsky and Rosenblatt in the café between roughly half past seven and half past eight, but that they could not be sure. When one comes to look into it a little more closely, I believe we will discover that the evidence tendered by the defense on this side is not wholly free from suspicion. . . ."

Ivor tried to focus his mind on Cunningham's opening remarks, but thoughts that had been more or less dormant within him for the last few weeks began to stir, as if Wharton's admonition to stay away from Henry Green, and the relief that Ivor had gotten away with only a warning, had cleared a path for him to focus his mind exclusively on Tsiona, the missing woman.

As Cunningham continued to unwind his carefully constructed sentences—"It is a matter of common knowledge that the time it takes to proceed from Jerusalem to Tel Aviv by motorcar depends no doubt upon the speed of the car, but anyway from an hour to an hour and a quarter, so that putting the case in this way, assuming that Stavsky and Rosenblatt were to be on the beach at about half past nine at night, it would be necessary for them to leave Jerusalem some time before half past eight, I may fairly say eight-fifteen. . . ."—Ivor, staring straight at the attorney general but seeing nothing, conjured Tsiona in his mind's eye, reprising their first breathless night together.

He caught up with Cunningham's remarks only when, with a sudden and urgent emphasis, Cunningham was saying, "If one was able to bring forth a witness who could affirm with absolute certainty, let us say through some kind of written record, the precise times that Stavsky and Rosenblatt arrived at Café Hasharon and, with similar accuracy, the time that they left, and if that written record were to confirm their absence from the Hasharon from eight p.m. onward, then the issue of their ability to make the journey to Tel Aviv in time to murder Haim Arlosoroff on the beach would be settled once and for all. Your Honor will note that with regard to the timing I make no larger claim than this, that a witness who has indeed not pressed time on his or her memory but rather pressed pen to paper would surely be acknowledged as preferential to those witnesses whose evidence before the magistrate contradicted each other.

"It is obvious that the case against the accused who stand before this court must depend to a very large extent upon the view that this court takes of the evidence of Mrs. Arlosoroff. However, a confirmation that the accused can be said with absolute certainty to have had the time at their disposal to make the journey to Tel Aviv implies that any alibi dependent on uncertain sightings by other witnesses must therefore be overridden and the new evidence have an ample and significant bearing on this trial."

Baron's face seemed to cycle through the colors of a kitchen garden, and once more he turned in his seat to scowl at Ivor. Of course, from what Cunningham was saying, it was clear that he had a recording witness as described, but no such person's account had appeared in the boxes of documents that Ivor had sifted through in the last months. Someone new was about to enter the fray. Stavsky and Rosenblatt, who until this point had sat impassively in the dock, taking turns, it appeared, to look down or straight ahead, registered their own surprise, Rosenblatt turning to Stavsky for the first time, while the latter sent a hard look in Baron's direction.

Ivor scanned the courtroom, faces in the public seating area clarifying as if he had wiped a misted bathroom mirror with his hand. His gaze rested on Sima Arlosoroff where she sat in the front row behind the prosecution's desk, her brown hair pulled back into a tight bun, her face a white mask.

The attorney general moved on with his remarks, bemoaning the delay in the trial brought about by the "various unfortunate matters brought into it," which turned out to refer only to the confusion surrounding Abdul Malik's confession and retraction. The judges, who up to this point had exhibited the intricate combination of rapt attention and exquisite torpor that only years of practice on the bench could accomplish, now, to a man, leaned forward, fully focused on Cunningham's words.

"The Abdul Malik episode," Cunningham continued, "is, from whatever point of view one regards it, a somewhat remarkable episode which has done a great deal to complicate the issues in this case and prolong the investigations. The case to be made by the prosecution is quite clear. It is this: that Abdul Malik was invited by these two accused and possibly by other persons on their behalf to take upon himself the responsibility for this crime and that he was told by them exactly what had happened in order that he might be in a position to give the necessary evidence as it were to incriminate himself, and that the opportunity for this arrangement occurred in the lockup at Jaffa where they were all confined at the same time, and it seems that there certainly were opportunities for conversation, and it seems clear that to some extent a conversation took place."

At the mention of Abdul Malik the spectators in the court-room had begun to stir and chatter, and when Cunningham paused in his speech, Judge Ali Hasna, his red tarbush firm on his head like an instrument of the Ottoman penal code, admonished the group to keep silent, otherwise they would be ejected from the courtroom.

"It may be," Cunningham continued, "that the court will feel that although there was a conversation and that although Rosenblatt and Stavsky between them were eager to persuade Abdul Malik to take upon himself the responsibility for this crime, they never, in fact, went as far as to admit to him that they actually committed it, and then, Your Honor, supposing the court comes to that conclusion as being the true view of the facts, it becomes a question in my submission as to whether or not such action on the part of Stavsky and Rosenblatt, owing to the need of corroboration, could be regarded as corroboration. In my submission, it could be so regarded."

Cunningham then embarked on an even lengthier and more serpentine detour into an issue involving material evidence, English law as laid down in Baskerville and its difference from that applied in the case of one Abdul Rachman, as affirmed in the Criminal Court of Appeal No. 30. Of 2927 . . . but Ivor heard no more of what might or might not be construed by the word "material," for at that moment the door to the courtroom opened and on hearing its creak Ivor turned in his seat to see Tsiona enter in the same cinnamon-colored dress that she had worn on the day he met her. He watched as she made her way to the back row of the public seating area.

Ivor knew he had to turn back to face the judges, but he was transfixed. Tsiona saw him, she couldn't do otherwise, but her features remained implacable, and so he turned slowly away from her, then quickly, a minute later, looked back once more, as if she might have disappeared as mysteriously as she had arrived.

Cunningham's phrases slid past him and left no mark on his consciousness . . . "a breadth of interpretation as to what is meant by 'material,'" "*C. F. King v. Christie,* an English authority to the contrary," "if he has sought to cause a witness to give untrue evidence." Only after a further forty minutes had passed did his receptors pick up the words that he had been waiting to hear: "I do not think it is necessary for me to add anything further."

Cunningham sat down, Justice Corrie with a thump of his gavel declared the court adjourned until Monday, and Ivor rose from his chair only to find his passage to the back of the courtroom blocked by a melee of individuals making their way to the exit.

As he pushed through, forcefully edging aside slow-moving individuals in his way, Ivor heard Baron calling after him, "Castle! Now, wait a minute there." Ivor ignored the injunction and, once through the door, rattled down the stairs, almost tripping on the polished stone. Outside in the blanched November sunlight, his line of vision obscured by the pack of warring demonstrators and mounted policemen keeping them in check, his path was obstructed in all directions, until, shoving and dodging, he managed to break through and cross the street. And then he saw her.

She was standing a hundred yards away next to a small black car, its passenger door open and its engine running. It was parked between a bus emitting black smoke from its exhaust, a vapor whose foul smell enveloped Ivor as he approached, and a donkey tethered to a cart busy unleashing a torrent of piss.

Tsiona was alone, but then, before Ivor could reach her, she wasn't. A young man whom Ivor immediately recognized as one of Cunningham's assistants, Jeremy Kaiserman, Ivor's equivalent on the prosecution side, had approached and was engaging her in animated conversation. Ivor thought he saw Tsiona nod in agreement, but perhaps he was mistaken. After a few moments, Kaiserman walked away, lost in thought, staring down at the sandy path that passed for pavement next to the road, and Ivor was able to skirt around him without being seen. Tsiona watched Ivor walk toward her, her face impassive, as it had been in the courtroom.

"Get in," she said as he drew close. "You drive."

She took the passenger seat and slammed the door.

"Quickly," she said.

"Where are we going?"

"North."

Ivor experienced a wave of joy. For however long it might last, he felt, at this moment, that he had all that he wanted: He was free of accusation, free of the trial, and the possibility of a weekend, two shining days with Tsiona, stretched before him like a sunlit path. He was about to speak, but she turned to him and put her finger to her lips.

24

It was almost nightfall when they reached Safed. A pale moon, as if it had risen too early, lay weak and transparent against the sky waiting for the sun to sink behind the hills. Tsiona had stayed silent most of the way and Ivor, after a few attempts to engage her toward the end of their journey, understood that she was not yet ready to reveal anything to him.

For the most part on their descent through the terraced hills outside Jerusalem she stared straight ahead or out of the window. The ribbon of road unwound past sparse thickets of pine or cypress, then straight across a slowly greening valley. Somewhere close to Rishon LeZion a chill crept into the air. Tsiona shivered and rolled up her window.

The cool late autumn air penetrated the car, growing colder the farther north they drove. At one point, Ivor pulled off the road and handed his suit jacket to Tsiona, who slipped it over her shoulders. He forgot everything except the fact that she, the focus of his muddled adoration, was sitting beside him, and against all the contraindications of circumstance he was deliriously happy.

They left the car at the foot of the hill and walked up together toward the hut. Halfway along the path darkness fell, as it always did in Palestine, like the sudden drop of a heavy curtain. Tsiona had climbed this path a hundred times and it was Ivor who stumbled, his shoes ill suited to their scramble up the rock-strewn trail.

A cold wind ruffled Tsiona's dress as she fumbled with her key. She unlocked the door and pushed it open. Ivor stood to the side so as not to block the thin sliver of moonlight that spilled into the room. Tsiona struck a match and lit an oil lamp; the contours of the objects in the room came into view. Ivor breathed deep, as if recovering from the climb, but she must have known what he was thinking. There it was in a corner of the room, the bed, a double bed, the only bed.

There was no reason to be surprised. Charles Gross had told him months ago that Tsiona had a lover, and he had seen him himself: at her door in Jerusalem, once outside this very hut, and again on the gangplank in Jaffa. He knew and he knew, and yet she had denied the relationship and against all the evidence he had wanted to believe her.

Tsiona knelt to light a small kerosene heater, then stood as the blue flame took.

"Come here," she said, "warm me up."

Ivor looked around the hut as if by doing so he might buy enough time to collect himself. Aside from the bed the room's furniture consisted of a large wooden table, a single bookshelf supported by bricks, two chairs, a small sink with a single tap, and a two-ring camper's kerosene burner that supported a beaten copper coffeepot with a long handle. Two folded easels filled one corner, and canvases of various sizes leaned against all four walls wherever there was space for them. From its cluttered surface it was clear that one half of the table functioned as a storage space for paints, brushes, and bottles of turpentine while the other was a repository for cups, saucers, cutlery, and dinner plates.

Tsiona waited for him by the bed. She began to unbutton her dress. Ivor stood for a moment and watched her shadow flicker on the wall.

"We'll talk in the morning," she said, "come here."

Thin envelopes of light carrying the sun's first messages of the day slid under the door and between the wooden shutters on the window.

When Ivor awoke, Tsiona, still wearing the white slip that she had slept in, was sitting in one of the chairs sipping coffee from a small eggshell-blue cup. Ivor sat up in bed and leaned his back against the stone wall. He remembered the touch of her hand on him and his near delirium of the night before, his face buried in her hair, the slip pushed halfway up her back.

Tsiona put down her coffee, rose from her chair, and opened the shutters. White light fell in a long shaft across the room. Ivor shielded his eyes.

"Don't you think you should leave the shutters closed?"

"No one can see us, and no one knows we're here."

Ivor got out of bed. "Where's the . . . ?"

"Outside, at the back, there's a lean-to . . . make sure you empty the bucket."

He pulled on his shirt and trousers and stepped outside. High above him a lone hawk circled, its wings spread wide as it rode currents of warm air that took it higher and higher above the brown hills.

When he came back in Ivor washed his hands from the cold-water tap and splashed his face. Reaching for toothpaste from the table, he almost picked up a tube of paint by mistake, and for the first time since he had seen her in the courtroom Tsiona laughed.

She poured coffee into a cup whose handle was thick with paint and handed it to him. Ivor drank a little and grimaced.

"It's bitter," he said.

"We ran out of sugar."

He tried to ignore that "we," but he couldn't—it meant that he was only a substitute, at best a stopgap lover, auxiliary, and undoubtedly soon to be made redundant again.

He chose to return to the mattress and prop himself against the wall rather than sit next to her at the table. "You're a witness for the prosecution, aren't you?"

Tsiona didn't respond. On their drive north they had stopped to buy pita bread and tomatoes from a roadside stall and now she made a small sandwich, cut it in two, and offered half to Ivor.

He shook his head. "First tell me," he said.

"I don't have a choice."

"You'll have to explain that."

"I'm not sure that I want to."

"You owe me at least that."

"Do I? I always hoped to avoid owing people anything."

"Please, just tell me what's going on."

Tsiona took a sip of her coffee. "They came to us in Cyprus. We had a room in Paphos above a shoemaker's, Mr. Solomos. I don't know how they found us."

"Who came?"

"Someone, two men . . ."

"From the prosecution?"

Tsiona offered a noncommittal shrug.

"From the government?"

Tsiona looked hard at Ivor. Her left eye, always slightly off-center, looked tired and had turned farther inward. "They're almost the same thing, aren't they? But these men weren't British, they were Jews. Of course, they didn't say who they represented but given their offer, I suppose . . ."

"What offer?"

"For Yosef."

Tsiona lit a cigarette, then threw one to Ivor followed by a box of matches.

"Go on," he said, striking the match.

"I'm not on the witness stand."

"But you will be."

Tsiona's face tightened. "Don't be a child," she said.

There was a moment when Ivor thought that she might stop talking altogether but she seemed to make a decision to ignore his petulance, whatever it might cost her to do so.

"Yosef was with Haim Arlosoroff in Berlin. I think you know that. Yosef has been Haim's economics advisor for a while, and he was with him when the transfer agreement was set up. He was useful to Haim in many ways, but there was one in particular that set him apart. Haim had asked him to contact a woman who'd been Yosef's close friend at school in Berlin, Magda Ritschel. Haim thought she could now play an important role. You see, she is married to Joseph Goebbels."

"A Jewish girl? That's impossible."

"Her stepfather was Jewish."

"And did he, your Yosef, did he contact her?"

"Perhaps, perhaps not."

"Well didn't you ask him?"

"It doesn't matter what he did. He was there to help Jews get out. He played his part, gave advice, met German bureaucrats, and he did what Haim told him to do, talked with them about foreign currency, raw materials, economic recovery . . . oh, I don't know. And what happened? They killed Haim when he came home, and they would kill Yosef too if they could."

"Who is this 'they'?"

"Who is it? You work for them!"

Tsiona's face reddened with anger. Ivor put his hands to his face.

"You don't know that," he said. "You can't know it for sure. There are other explanations. There's a confession."

"A withdrawn confession. And anyway, it doesn't matter. If it wasn't Stavsky and Rosenblatt it was two others just like them. There are hundreds of Stavskys and Rosenblatts, any pair of them willing to take Yosef's life: in league with Goebbels's wife! Can you imagine the hatred that has unleashed?"

"So, you decided to save him."

"Was that wrong?"

"What did they offer you?"

"They offered me nothing. They promised Yosef free passage to France, a new life there, a new name."

"And in exchange?"

Tsiona hesitated. Outside, farther down the hill, the bleating of goats merged with the tinkling of their bells. "They had my sketches with them, ripped from my notebooks. All my drawings of Stavsky and Rosenblatt. They wanted me to put a time and date on them. Testify that the last sketch I made was shortly before they left the restaurant, that Stavsky and Rosenblatt had plenty of time to get to Tel Aviv that night. They were on our side, they said, and from our side, people who only wanted justice and the best for the country. They would pass my sketches on to the prosecution. I'd be in court for a short time and then I'd be gone. Everyone knew Stavsky and Rosenblatt were guilty, didn't we want to make sure they didn't get away with it? Yosef didn't want me to do it. They already had a passport for him."

Ivor stared at Tsiona. Everything in the room was vivid: dust motes spinning in their cylinder of light, tomato seeds on the edge of the knife, the red glow of her cigarette, every crease in Tsiona's skin, every pore on her face.

"It isn't as if my evidence can convict them," she continued, "it only allows for the possibility. And perhaps it's true? I told you from the first, I wasn't paying attention to the time."

"There was nothing to impress it on your memory," Ivor said softly, echoing the words that Cunningham had twice repeated in his opening remarks.

"That's right."

"They could be hanged."

"If they are, it will be because Sima Arlosoroff identified them, not because I signed, dated, and noted the time of a drawing."

"You can tell yourself that if you want, but it isn't true. You're making an enormous contribution to the prosecution's case. You mustn't do it. It's perjury, interference with the administration of justice . . . and in a murder case!"

Tsiona smiled wanly. "Sometimes I forget you are a lawyer," she said.

"You didn't forget when we met, did you?" The rage and fear that he had managed to contain or divert into love and passion through almost all his hours with Tsiona rose to the surface. "It was all a lie," he said, "from the beginning. I was a complete fool. You didn't mean any of it. You, you and Yosef, you needed to know, didn't you, about the case? And I fell into your lap. Everything has been a lie, even last night."

"It wasn't all a lie. Only a very small part of it. It isn't a lie now."

Tsiona stubbed out her cigarette, skirted the table, and stood before him. She took Ivor's head in her hands and ran her fingers through his hair; then she let fall the straps of her slip, pressed his face between her breasts, and held him there.

When Ivor lifted his face and pulled back, he saw for the first time since he had met her that she had tears in her eyes, but what the tears were for—herself, the man who was on his way to Paris, or the terrible situation she presently found herself in—he couldn't tell.

"Are you going to rush off now and tell Baron?" she said.

"I should, shouldn't I?"

"And have him humiliate me in court? Have me arrested?"

Ivor kissed her eyes, tasted her salt tears on his lips, kissed her mouth, her neck, her breasts, he couldn't help himself.

The cries of the muezzin calling the faithful to morning prayers penetrated the room. When the voice fell silent, they could hear the sound of the goats' bells draw closer. For a moment Ivor pulled away from Tsiona.

"Perhaps I should be like you," he said, "cut a deal. I mean, what do I get if I keep quiet?"

"You get me," Tsiona said, and then repeated quietly, as if she had surprised herself, "you get me."

25

In his dream it was early morning. Ivor stood in Port Meadow surrounded by a murmuring sea of green grass dotted with white cowslips. The thin strip of the river divided it from a gray mist out of which rose the spires, towers, and domes of the city. He was late for an appointment with his tutor, and worse, he was unprepared. He walked to the riverbank and removed his shoes and socks to dangle his feet in the cool water. Slowly, the rising sun burned off the mist, and when it did so he saw that he wasn't alone. Tsiona (was it Tsiona?) was standing on the opposite bank. He could cross over, although it seemed that he shouldn't. If he did, he would never make it into Oxford on time, and he would surely fail. To stay put was the right thing to do, even though the woman had recognized him and begun to beckon in his direction, and yet somehow, he knew that if he didn't cross, his decision not to do so would haunt him for the rest of his life.

The sun blazed as it rarely did in England, erasing everything in the radius of its white glare. Ivor put his hand up to shield his eyes, squinted, but now he was awake, looking across an expanse of white pillow at the red highlights dancing in Tsiona's hair. She was turned away from him, the sheet gathered around her, but she must have felt him stir as she stretched an arm behind her to touch him. Half-asleep, she whispered his name.

They had spent the previous day in happy truancy. Tsiona had dispatched Ivor into town to buy food and coffee, and with most places closed for the Sabbath he had struggled to find the necessary provisions. By the time he returned to the hut she had already set up her easel and had begun to paint. Ivor knew that he couldn't disturb her, and so he plucked a book from her shelf and settled down on the bed. He had no choice in what to read, as there was only one book available in English: George Orwell's *Down and Out in Paris and London*. He couldn't think why she should own this, but there it was. A desperate Parisian couple operated a scam. They passed off wrapped postcards as pornographic when, in fact, the images were of benign landscapes. The buyers, too embarrassed to check their purchases on the street, were also too ashamed ever to return the faulty merchandise.

Without discussion, it seemed, they had decided to establish a moratorium on any discussion of the trial, the parts that they were yet to play in it, and the terrible bargain struck between them.

Eventually Tsiona broke from painting, but only to take up her pencil and sketchbook. "I'm going to draw you," she said, and Ivor sat for what felt to him like an eternity as she admonished him to keep still or to lift his head or turn it to the side.

"Hold the book as though you're reading it."

"I am reading it."

He told her about the couple with the pornographic postcards.

"I'd have been happy with the landscapes," she said.

Now the sketches she had made of Ivor lay across the table.

She piled them up and set them aside. He watched her from the bed as she soaped and washed her face and the upper half of her body. Was this how days would begin from now on? His rapt attention to her body, the sun seeking her out through the windows of her Jerusalem studio, Ivor in a kind of trance, enchanted, content.

They walked down the hill toward the car. The trial would not reconvene until Monday and they were not in a rush. Somewhere near Tabgha on the shores of the Galilee they stopped to look out over the lake. Church bells pealed from an unseen chapel, the sounds resonating over the water.

For a long time, they didn't see another vehicle on the road. Ivor picked up a map from the back seat and began to study the route.

"You don't need that," Tsiona said.

In the distance Ivor could make out a group of white cupolas. On his left the lake was festooned with little headlands covered with rose laurels; a few cows grazed nearby. A single boat with mother-of-pearl sails pushed out from the shore. Closer to the road a cloud of dragonflies enveloped a thick ribbon of rushes.

A motorcycle appeared in Tsiona's rearview mirror. It approached at some speed and then slowed when the road narrowed as if waiting to overtake. Ivor, his window rolled down, watched as a pair of steel-blue birds, swallows he thought, dove toward the water where it blotched with straw sunshine. She mustn't do it, Ivor thought. More than anything he wanted to keep Tsiona in his life, but not like this. The risk was too great. She would have to tell Baron the truth; you couldn't lie in a murder trial. He hoped against hope that she would stay with him anyway: London in the rain, the flame of her hair against the gray sky as they stepped out of the station.

He turned to speak to her but at that moment the motorcycle drew level with their car. At the last second Tsiona saw the pillion rider, black goggles, arm outstretched; he pointed his gun directly at her, she ducked and wrenched the steering wheel. The car careened off the road, skidded through a scree of loose pebbles, hit a tree, and came to rest under its swaying branches in a muddy patch of high damp grass. Ivor slumped forward. The motorcycle sped on. Tsiona, thrown back in her seat, took Ivor's head in her hands as blood flowed from his left eye and down his cheek.

26

The doctors in the small mission hospital in Tiberias couldn't save Ivor's eye, but they saved him. The bullet hadn't entered his skull, only glanced off his eye socket, but he bled so profusely in the car before help arrived that they weren't sure he would make it. In the end, after the surgery, he slept for days, oscillating between terrible pain and the soft blue twilight of sleep. There was an open realm somewhere, a place Ivor apprehended in the distance, a clean mowed field, mist risen. He could smell the fresh hay. He thought he could get there if only he had the strength.

His left leg was broken, badly mangled, but they had stitched it up and put it in a cast. Soon they would allow him to get out of bed—eventually, they promised, he would be able to walk. He didn't remember when his parents had arrived from England, but they were there now. Ivor, when they thought he was asleep, had overheard Baron telling a nurse that they were on their way: "Imperial Airways to Cairo and then the train, must have cost them an arm and a leg . . . sorry . . . bad choice . . ." Baron's voice had trailed away before he'd coughed and continued, "I mean unless you're a Rothschild or a sheikh, those fares can bankrupt you. Good they'll be here though."

They came each day during afternoon visiting hours, sat in silence mostly, or talked about getting Ivor home after he had recuperated, after he had *adjusted*. Sometimes, on the edge of sleep, he could hear his mother crying.

Slowly, Dr. Torrance weaned him off morphine, and the undulating waves of his dream life stopped lapping into his daytime conversations, brief as they were. Of course, he had asked about Tsiona, repeatedly, or so he imagined. They had let him know that, bloodied and bruised, she had waved down a passing vehicle, but it was Ivor's blood on her dress, not her own. Through some miracle she had emerged unscathed. Beyond that, nobody seemed to know very much, or what they knew they didn't want to reveal.

One afternoon his parents arrived with a portfolio. Baron had given it to them on their arrival, a gift for Ivor from the young woman he was always asking about, something to pass on when Ivor was ready. His mother untied the blue ribbon that held the covers in place and then began to hold Tsiona's drawings up, one by one, so Ivor could see them. There was Ivor, sitting in a chair, naked to the waist, his handsome face outlined in a few deft, economical charcoal strokes, so too the slope of his shoulders and his broad chest. And here he was standing on a balcony, swollen blooms in window boxes and a fruit tree behind him. His mother traced the contours of the sketches with her finger as if she were touching her son's face, his face as it had been before he was shot and one of his soft brown eyes replaced with glass.

It was left to Baron to break the news. He waited weeks to do so. Tsiona, he was reliably informed, had left for Paris a few days after the shooting, at a time when Ivor was still barely conscious.

"Did she bring me here?"

"She did, along with a lorry load of chickens. Got you in the front seat with the help of the driver and held you there, ripped her dress, tried to staunch the bleeding."

"And did she visit after that?"

"I know she wanted to," Baron said. "Perhaps it wasn't safe. It was her, wasn't it, that they were trying to kill? It's possible she was here. A nurse said a woman came one night." Baron paused. "Whoever it was, they told her you had come through."

"Have I?" Ivor said.

"The sad thing, the *tragic* thing, is that it wouldn't have made any difference if she *had* testified for the other side. Luckily for us the prosecution was absolutely hobbled by that ridiculous local law that I managed to dig up. I must admit I'd forgotten all about it. Why on earth, all other evidence landing on the persuasive side (not that it was), *two* corroborating eyewitnesses should be required, I shall never understand. But I'm hardly going to complain about the presence of this particular Ottoman contribution to the legal system: Madame Arlosoroff's shilly-shallying deserved no better. Insufficient evidence!"

"Then it's over."

"Yes, in the end they got off scot-free, both of them. Absolutely raucous ending. Here, I brought you this. You can read all about it. You can read, can't you?"

"I'm getting used to it."

Baron pulled up a chair, then dropped a month-old copy of *The Palestine Post* on Ivor's bed. Ivor picked it up. The presiding judge's declaration, interrupted apparently by groans and cheers, was quoted in full: "The court, by majority, does not find the other material evidence required by Section Five of the Law of Evidence Amendment Ordinance, 1924, to corroborate their identification by Mrs. Arlosoroff. The accused are therefore acquitted of the offense of which they stand charged."

Baron had stood outside the courthouse to express his satisfaction with the verdict. He'd declined to speak further but the reporter from the *Post* had found someone in the crowd to talk to: "It would have been an outrage if these two men had been found guilty, that simply could not be allowed to happen." The bystander was identified as Charles Gross, an employee of the Anglo-Palestine Company.

"Yes," Baron said, "friend of yours, I believe."

Ivor lowered the paper. "When did she give you the portfolio?"

Baron had clearly been wondering when Ivor would ask. He knew he had to answer very carefully. "The day after the trial had ended, at her flat in Jerusalem."

"You were there?"

"Yes. Not for very long. Miss Kerem wanted to hand over the gift. That was all. The place was in disarray."

"I suppose she was packing."

"Yes, she was."

"What did you talk about?"

"Oh, this and that. Your health, of course, then I left."

Ivor imagined Baron lingering inside Tsiona's walled garden, tugging a few weeds from an overgrown pot, but then he was there himself, continuing down the cobblestone path toward the wooden door that opened onto the street. He turned to look up at Tsiona's red balcony, watched her grab a corner of her mattress and drag it inside.

"Well, I should take my leave." Baron stood up from his chair.

"That's it," Ivor said, "she only asked about my health."

"Well obviously that's what was concerning her most."

Ivor told his parents he wasn't ready to return to London and they didn't have to stay any longer. He knew his father had work to do. They should take the long way home, by boat this time, stop in Greece, Christmas in Athens, stop in Italy, New Year's Eve in Rome. When was the last time they'd taken a holiday together? He was going to be fine. He just wasn't ready for London life, needed a little more time. They had to stop worrying about him—that's what would speed his recovery. In the end this was the argument that worked best on them, that and assurances from Dr. Torrance that it wouldn't be long before Ivor was able to travel.

"In fact," Dr. Torrance told Ivor while his parents sat by the bed, "soon we're going to move you." He was a small, neat Scotsman with limpid gray eyes and a wry smile. His father had founded the mission forty years ago, "a place for patients of all races and religions."

"I seem to be increasingly in the kind hands of the Scots," Ivor replied. "I was staying at the hospice in Jerusalem before I came here."

"Well now we're giving you over to someone else's kind hands: a surgery not far from here with a delightful garden. It's been arranged." Dr. Torrance turned toward Ivor's parents. "Trust me, he'll be well looked after by Dr. Samuels. He's a good man and a fine doctor. And then you'll have him home in no time."

It wasn't until far into the night when he was on the verge of sleep that Ivor remembered Dr. Samuels and his relationship to Susannah.

27

1934

Susannah came to see him every weekend. She was happy, she said, to be living in Jerusalem, even if only temporarily, happy too to be working at Charlotte's selling Roman glass pendants, Armenian ceramics, amulets, rings with an ancient coin instead of a stone, amber necklaces, all manner of artifacts—some genuine antiques, most simply pretty. She told Ivor about the sellers, some who came with small beautifully engraved copper bowls from the Old City, and others with shards of ancient pottery that they claimed King David had used to store his oil. Charlotte, the young owner, assessed every piece; she had a fine eye, matchless taste, and, it seemed, a deep knowledge of the city's historical layers. Her only blind spot, Susannah said, was she thought she was taller than Susannah. "Believe me, Ivor, I tower over her. She told me, 'If only you were as tall as me, you'd be very pretty.'" Then there were the buyers, suspicious, circumspect, always ready to bargain. Often, far too often, they were more knowledgeable than Susannah about their chosen piece and would lecture her on its origin and proper value. Of course, everyone thought that Charlotte inflated her prices.

Her stories—Ivor called them "tales of a young Jewish shopgirl"—were all distraction, of course, attempts to forestall the black depressions that rolled over him. For the most part, while she was there, Susannah succeeded in lifting his spirits, although Ivor was embarrassed by her kindness. He felt that he didn't deserve it. She never asked once about Tsiona, and nothing of the shooting or the crash. They sat in Dr. Samuels's garden; even in December there were still warm days to savor, and Ivor tried his best not to be morose. Once, Susannah brought up the trial. She'd read that after it was over the chief justice had declared that if the case had been heard in England the defendants would undoubtedly have been convicted. This was in keeping with what Baron had said: Here, the absence of corroborative evidence to support that of a single witness had sunk the case. Now, in the aftermath of the judge's remark, the Left and the Right were at each other's throats again. "I had no idea when I came here," Susannah said, "the depth of the hostility, the bitterness. I suppose I heard it in a minor key in the arguments between my father and Charles, but it didn't really register. What about you?"

"I know," Ivor said, "we were innocents abroad and now we're scarred for life."

They watched the ubiquitous hoopoe birds cross from tree to tree, marking the sky in quick black and white strokes. Meanwhile, two crows, in their Middle Eastern attire of black and gray morning coats, settled on the eaves of the house. Ivor had noticed that Dr. Samuels's patients didn't like them very much. Sometimes the boys aimed small pebbles in their direction.

He knew he didn't ask her enough about herself. The best he could manage was to say, "You've changed."

"I have changed," she said. "I don't know quite how or why. Last week I was in the Hotel Eden trying to secure an advertisement. The lobby was crowded with American tourists, women from the Hadassah organization. I couldn't have felt more distant from them if they had been visitors from another planet. At night I went back to Pension Friedman, where I'm staying; there was an electricity failure. Mrs. Friedman had given me a candle; I lit it and took it with me into the bathroom. The tub was full of invitingly warm water. I knew someone must have recently gotten out and forgotten to pull the plug, and I knew there would be no more hot water for hours. I locked the door, undressed, and got in. I didn't care that it was someone else's water. I immersed myself anyway."

Ivor didn't know how to thank her. He couldn't go and buy her something, couldn't even pluck a few flowers for her from the garden. All he could do was tell her repeatedly how grateful he was for the attention she'd paid him, how he knew he couldn't have gotten through his ordeal without her, and he was still getting through it, and she was still there every weekend. Dr. Samuels was a pleasant enough companion, but he was a busy man; on Saturday and Sunday he mostly slept. Susannah waved away Ivor's gratitude, begged him to stop thanking her and to stop apologizing for the moods that came over him when sometimes he would sit for hours without saying a word, while Susannah read or took a bike ride. Sometimes his glass eye bothered him, and he wore a patch instead. Slowly, he adjusted to his loss of depth perception. "I'll be an ace at darts," he told Susannah, "if I ever get back down to a pub again." He didn't know who was paying for his upkeep and care at Dr. Samuels's. He assumed his parents had taken care of everything before they left, but he also had a suspicion that Henry Green might have gotten involved at the behest of his daughter. One day he asked her, "Do I have something else to thank you for? Is your family covering my rehabilitation?" He knew she wouldn't tell him, even if it was true, and as expected she simply said, "Don't be ridiculous."

When the long winter came to an end and with it Ivor's season of self-pity, he began to make amends, or so he hoped, for what he had dumped on others, by helping around the surgery. He moved supplies, brought food to the kitchen (aubergines were high on the menu), and, most often, helped with the laundry. Sometimes, after the rain, the pathways around Dr. Samuels's house turned muddy, and when darkness fell, lit only by kerosene lamps that threw ghostlike shadows, they became hard for Ivor to negotiate. Still, whatever the difficulties, he was happy to be alive.

One morning, at Dr. Samuels's urging, he visited the hot springs at el-Hammam. If he was hoping for a revelation such as Susannah had experienced, it wasn't to be. Ivor happened to arrive at the same time as a small group of off-duty British soldiers. They were soon immersed in the sulfurous water, cheeks turning red in the thick steam.

"Come on then," one of them yelled at Ivor, "what are you waiting for? Get in. Good for the rheumatism." Suddenly a heightened self-consciousness about his eye overwhelmed him. Would they think he'd been injured in some violent skirmish with the locals? Treat him as a courageous comrade, differently and better than he deserved? He stayed on the side, staring up at the rock face that hung over the baths, where two buildings with white cupolas had been cut into the side of the hill, a synagogue and a yeshiva. "Also works for paralysis," the soldier shouted, and everyone laughed. Ivor forced a smile, waved, turned away, and headed back to the sanctuary of the surgery. He told Dr. Samuels that his dip had done him a world of good; he'd had an inkling it would finally rid him of his lingering headaches.

On May Day, Susannah showed up unexpectedly. She was in a light spring dress, blue and dotted with red flowers, like the anemones that were beginning to spread in the doctor's garden. She seemed to have found a middle path between the high fashion of the wealthy debutante and the rough garments of the pioneer. Was she a chameleon, Ivor wondered, or simply a searcher? He thought now that it had to be the latter. Either way she was kindness itself to him, and immensely tolerant of the all-too-often-empty shell that was his own character. One night, not long after his transfer from the mission, he had broken down and sobbed in his bed and she had held his hand, then climbed on the bed and let him rest his head on her shoulder while he wept. They never talked about it. He wondered if she had someone else whom she saw during the week, or perhaps she had many suitors. She was pretty and ever so clever, and fun to be with. Why she devoted her weekends to him, a miserable invalid, was a mystery. She owed him nothing and she knew he'd been a fool.

Susannah was free because Charlotte had closed her business for the day. May Day in Jerusalem wasn't what it was in Tel Aviv, Susannah said, where everything shut down and huge parades took place with red flags, green branches, posters of Karl Marx and Stalin, rousing speeches and robust singing of "The Internationale," but still it was something, and there were even gatherings where Arabs and Jews mingled together, joined in the spirit of socialism. Susannah hadn't come to drag Ivor off to a workers' rally in Tiberias, however. She had something else in mind.

At first, he didn't want to head back north, the memories were too fresh, the wounds too deep, but in the end, with encouragement from Dr. Samuels, she prevailed. The next day

Susannah borrowed the doctor's car and they headed for Upper Galilee, where the Lag b'Omer celebration took place every year at Meron, a little way from Safed.

"I don't even know what it is," Ivor said.

"Nor did I. Charlotte told me about it. It's the end of the time of mourning for the destruction of the Temple. You wake up on the thirty-third day of counting the Omer, whatever that might be, and all of a sudden you can get married when you couldn't before, if you want to, that is; the whole day is a carnival."

They drove along the lake. For a while the only noise came from the car's engine, which sputtered as soon as they hit an incline.

Safed was overflowing with visitors, all of them, it seemed, trying to crowd onto the same few buses that were available to shuttle them to Meron. Susannah and Ivor parked their car, then smuggled their way onto the last bus out and sat together as, gears grinding, it slowly made its way up the Galilee hills.

In the shadow of snowcapped Mount Hermon, a great gathering of families—Eastern Jews, Moroccans, Persians, and Bukharians—were busy settling down with the household goods they had brought with them—cooking utensils, colorful blankets, as well as live chickens and sheep. Nearby, the Ashkenazi Orthodox in long black coats and fur-trimmed hats made their camp. Wine was distributed far and wide. The huge crowd shouted, argued, sang, danced, and wended its way toward the tomb of a rabbi martyred almost two thousand years ago.

When darkness fell the revelers lit bonfires and tossed into the flames all kinds of articles of clothing, scarves, shawls, and cloaks, while women stood in groups clapping and singing. And then the dancing began, wild, uninhibited, ecstatic. Susannah was quickly drawn into a circle. Ivor watched as she gave herself over to a world of utter abandonment. When two young men tried to grab him into the dance, he pointed at his leg and sent them away.

"No sign of Karl Marx," Ivor said when, dropping her partners' hands, Susannah stopped to draw breath.

"No," she said, "only mystics and miracles."

They drove back to Tiberias with Susannah at the wheel.

"Would you want to?" Ivor said.

"Would I want to what?"

"Get married now if you couldn't before."

Susannah smiled. "Oh no, the opposite. I might have wanted to before but now I don't."

They were silent while the headlamps picked out dark trees that flanked the dusty road before them.

"What about you?" Susannah asked.

"Oh, I think I'll wait here awhile," he said, "see what happens. I've learned to be patient."

28

JUNE

Ivor walked down the street behind the post office, stopped, and waited for her outside Charlotte's little shop. A British armored car was parked at the foot of the otherwise deserted street. He hadn't told Susannah he was coming. He planned to surprise her, enter as a customer, watch her face when she looked up after hearing the bell. But now he had grown nervous. Perhaps she wouldn't be there. He looked in at the window display, blue glass from Hebron, Uzbek pottery, all manner of embroidery, Armenian tiles, just as she had described. He could see someone moving around inside the shop.

He went to push open the door, but she was there before him. For a moment they simply looked at each other.

"Did you come from Jaffa Road?" Susannah said. "They took down the swastika flag from the Hotel Fast. Did you notice? Someone made them."

"Union Jack's still there though, isn't it?"

"Yes."

"So, all's well with the world."

Susannah laughed. "What are you? An Englishman or a Jew?"

"I'm an English Jew, it's an oxymoron."

"I have another question for you," she said, "but it can wait."

"I can give you the answer now," he said. "It's you I think about, all the time."

"That's not what I was going to ask you."

"Well," Ivor said, "ask me anyway."

Susannah stepped out into the street and lifted her hand to shield her eyes against the sun.

"Perhaps I will," she said.

Acknowledgments

Like any novelist trying to plumb the depths of a gone world, I found certain books by other writers to be of inestimable value. I am particularly indebted to Edwin Black's *The Transfer Agreement;* A. J. Sherman's *Mandate Days: British Lives in Palestine, 1918–1948;* Norman and Helen Bentwich's *Mandate Memories: 1918–1948;* Sylva M. Gelber's *No Balm in Gilead: A Personal Retrospective of Mandate Days in Palestine,* and the catalog *Sionah Tagger: Retrospective,* edited by Carmela Rubin to accompany the artist's retrospective at the Tel Aviv Museum in 2003–2004.

It took me a while to write this novel, and, as the years rolled by and Covid rolled in, I accumulated a good number of people to thank along the way. First among them must be Deborah Garrison, who has edited my writing so deftly and elegantly on and off for more than twenty-five years, first at *The New Yorker* and then at Pantheon/Schocken. She saw this novel through numerous incarnations and one major reincarnation. Her aim, as reader, editor, and friend, is always true. Also at Schocken, I want to thank publisher Lisa Lucas for bringing this novel into the daylight, Zuleima Ugalde for all manner of helpful assistance, and Aja Pollock for her meticulous copyedit.

Charles Dellheim, extraordinarily generous with his time considering that he was writing his own book, talked through the novel with me over many lunches, while he and Laura Gross both offered warm friendship and great advice. Gabriel Levin and Adina Hoffman helped me tackle the mysteries of certain Jerusalem streets and their shifting names during the 1930s. Help and much-appreciated advice also came from Ziv Lewis, Elizabeth Riley, Marian Thurm, and Joseph Olshan. My long-time agent, Gail Hochman, offered unwavering support and encouragement.

I feel a special debt of gratitude to Jaime Clarke and Mary Cotton, owners of my delightful local independent bookstore, Newtonville Books. A home away from home for me before Covid, Jaime and Mary's store sustained and augmented my reading life during the worst of the pandemic with roadside pickup and allowed the store to continue as my favorite destination, even when you couldn't go in.

I spent two productive weeks working on my novel in the idyllic environment of the Hermitage Artist Retreat in Englewood, Florida. I'm grateful to everyone who facilitated my stay there.

Here's where I really lucked out: my family. Each member helped in his or her own way, and increasingly as the pandemic ramped up. My wife, Sharon Kaitz, read the novel as it progressed, and, as always, had shrewd comments and suggestions. Meanwhile, unable to go to her studio during Covid, she stayed home and painted, her work, as always, a source of deep inspiration for me. The exigencies of Covid brought my sons, their wives, and children to stay in our house, sometimes for months at a time. Adam, Sarah, Julian, and Raphael; Gabe, Julie, and Louis, without their uplifting presence and continued support this novel might still be stuck in the sand dunes north of Jaffa.

A NOTE ABOUT THE AUTHOR

Jonathan Wilson is the author of eight previous books, including the novels *The Hiding Room*, runner-up for the Jewish Quarterly–Wingate Prize, and *A Palestine Affair,* a *New York Times* Notable Book, Barnes & Noble Discover finalist, and a 2004 National Jewish Book Award finalist; two collections of short stories, *Schoom* and *An Ambulance Is on the Way: Stories of Men in Trouble;* a biography, *Marc Chagall,* finalist for a 2007 National Jewish Book Award; and the soccer memoir *Kick and Run.* His fiction, essays, and reviews have appeared in *The New Yorker, ARTnews, Esquire, The New York Times Magazine, The New York Times Book Review, The Paris Review Daily*, the *Los Angeles Review of Books, Tablet, The Times Literary Supplement,* and *The Best American Short Stories,* among other publications. Wilson has been the recipient of a Guggenheim Fellowship, and his work has been translated into many languages, including Dutch, German, Hebrew, Hungarian, Italian, Polish, Portuguese, Russian, and Chinese. He lives in Newton, Massachusetts.

A NOTE ON THE TYPE

This book was set in Hoefler Text, a family of fonts designed by Jonathan Hoefler, who was born in 1970. First designed in 1991, Hoefler Text was intended as an advancement on existing desktop computer typography, including as it does an exponentially larger number of glyphs than previous fonts. In form, Hoefler Text looks to the old-style fonts of the seventeenth century, but it is wholly of its time, employing a precision and sophistication only available to the late twentieth century.

Typeset by Scribe, Inc.,
Philadelphia, Pennsylvania

Printed and bound by Berryville Graphics,
Berryville, Virginia